TRAITOR
OF THE
TIDES

Published by Renegade Publishing

Cover art by Wizzylee

Typography by Covers by Combs

Map by Karina

Editing: Leslie Copeland

Proofreading: Red Ink Ninja & Maddie

ASIN: B0CW1G1FT9

Paperback: 979-8-9911912-8-9

Hardcover: 979-8-99111912-7-2

✻ Formatted with Vellum

To those in their female rage era.

Synopsis

A banished sirenidae princess sold to her sworn enemy.

Mer has one goal: avenge her fallen love. But getting close to the cold Methian king isn't so easy. She'll have to infiltrate his court, marry him, and *break* his heart. But charming her gruff husband is harder than she anticipates, and Mer finds herself either wanting to kill him or fall for him.

A ruthless king who will do anything to save his empire.

A deadly plague grows in Methi, King Raziel's only hope to save his people is a marriage alliance. He wasn't prepared for his new bride to try to kill him on sight, nor the blinding attraction he feels for her. His court calls for her death, but Raz can't afford to endanger the treaty. Instead, he must do something far more dangerous: make his wife fall in love with him.

A battle of wits and hearts.

When their marriage becomes a game of wills, deception, and secret societies, Mer and Raziel are pitted against each other in a millennia-old war as they play for the throne, each other's secrets, and love.

May the coldest heart win.

The Hunt

The Rook

The Heir

The Beast

The Hood

The Wolf

THE AERMIAN FEUDS UNIVERSE

The Aermian Feuds Series

(Dark Epic Fantasy)

Rebel's Blade

Crown's Shield

Siren's Lure

Enemy's Queen

King's Warrior

Warlord's Shadow

Spy's Mask

Court's Fool

Prince's Poison

The Aermian Feuds Collection

Kingdom of Rebels & Thorns

Queen of Monsters & Madness

Reign of Blood & Poison

DOMINION OF ASH

(Post Apocalyptic Fantasy)

A Spire of Lies

A Kiss of Shadow

A Touch of Mayhem

NEVER MISS A BOOK RELEASE.

Get exclusive giveaways, bookish news, review copies, and a free gift upon sign up by subscribing to Frost Kay's newsletter:

https://www.frostkay.net/book-loot

THE WASTING CORALS
CAVES
THE L
SKIGARA
SUNKEN AMPHITHEATER
THE BORDER PASS
RAVEN KEEP
MANXT MERCHANT HARBOR

DEVIL'S CAGE
SAELEN
DEN OF WRAITHS
LAOS
LAOS FLEET HARBOR
THE FOREST OF FIRE
MERVOS
TRENCH OF CORVAIUS
WHIELPOOL

Trigger Warning

Dear reader,

Thank you so much for reading Traitor of the Tides!

This story is set in the Aermian Feuds world. While this series is considered New Adult, I would give it a PG-13 rating. There is nothing explicit.

That being said, this world deals with difficult hard hitting subjects. I want everyone to have a safe and enjoyable time reading this romantic fantasy, but it might not be for everyone. Please mind the TWs and take care of yourself.

Trigger warnings as follows:

- Loss of spouse
- Survivor's guilt

- Mental illness
- Brief mention of suicidal ideation
- Trafficking
- Underage marriage
- Underage pregnancy
- Drowning
- Fear of heights
- Death of a child
- SA (not explicit)

The Rift

A Millennium Ago

"The humans grow more and more dangerous each day. We cannot continue on as we have. We must decide. This council has dallied too long," Duke Odyum thundered.

King Alon glanced at his irate twin and waved a tired hand at him, seawater swirling lazily around his abalone throne. "This is not an easy decision, Odyum."

His brother glared back, his fuchsia eyes sparking. "It is a matter of survival. It is kill or be killed, *my lord*."

Some of the council shifted uncomfortably in their whalebone seats at the sneer in Odyum's tone.

Alon bit back a sigh.

Two and a half minutes.

That was all it took to place enmity between Alon and

his twin. That was the difference between being the heir and the second born to the Sirenidae throne.

Two and a half minutes.

And Odyum hated him for it.

Alon kept his mask firmly in place and studied the council. Personally, he wanted to withdraw to the sea and leave the surface dwellers to their own devices. Odyum wanted to wage war and conquer them. Only half were on Alon's side; the other favored his brother's ill-advised ideas.

"Our place is in the sea. This is our home, our way of life. The surface holds no future for us. I will not risk our people for an unnecessary war," Alon declared, finality ringing in his voice.

Odyum rose from his seat, his silvery hair floating around his reddening face. Alon held his breath and prayed his twin would reel in his anger. The Sirenidae always encouraged lively discourse, but word had reached his ears that his brother had been up to something far more insidious.

Sedition.

He prayed to the depths that it wasn't true. But Alon had seen the signs, and it could not continue. Their people came first.

"You are a coward," his twin spat, a mad glint in his eye. "Completely unequipped to do what is necessary for the vindication of our people—but not I. Today, you are through." Odyum nodded, and Alon's heart fell as half his council launched themselves in his direction.

A true coup.

Even though it hurt, he wasn't unprepared. He'd always been shrewd. He'd had his own men hidden inside the room, waiting for this exact possibility. Alon's fingers tightened on his trident as two-thirds of the traitors were cut down in minutes. His stomach clenched at the sightless eyes and gaping silent mouths drifting through the room. Silvery swirls of blood clouded the water, and he forced himself to swallow down the bile that flooded his mouth.

So much death over greed.

Disgust filled him as he stood from his throne, triton in hand. His webbed toes dug into the pale sand as he glided toward his brother. He took no pleasure in seeing his twin bleeding and forced to kneel in the sand.

Alon stared down at Odyum and held back his flinch when his brother smiled up at him with bloody teeth.

"Finally ready to kill me, brother?"

Alon shook his head as sorrow, hurt, and a touch of guilt swirled in his chest. "How could I take the life of one who shared the womb with me? No, you and your ilk shall have a different fate." Odyum wouldn't die this day by Alon's hand. Alon knelt on one knee, meeting his twin's angry eyes. "You've always presumed yourself to be the smartest person in the sea, Odyum. In your pride and arrogance, you assumed that I've been ignorant to your scheming. I have not been."

His brother arched a brow and snapped his teeth at one of the soldiers holding him down. "So, it's to the trenches for me? Slave labor? A life with the humans?"

Alon scoffed, letting his anger bleed through his pain. "Where you can continue to recruit and spread rebellion in my kingdom? I think not. Since you desire to rule, I will let you." He paused, watching a hungry look cross his twin's face. "You and your sycophants are to leave. You are banished to the Northern Sea. There, you can make your own life."

The color drained out of Odyum's face. He jerked against the soldiers' hold. "You wouldn't be so cruel? Leaving our waters is certain death. No Sirenidae has ever survived outside our kingdom. The temperatures alone will kill us, not to mention the creatures . . ."

"Since you presume yourself a king, make it happen," Alon murmured and then stood, floating in the water. He turned his back on his twin, finding no joy and only grief at losing his last living kin.

"I will kill you."

The king glanced over his shoulder at Odyum, heart heavy. "Good luck, brother."

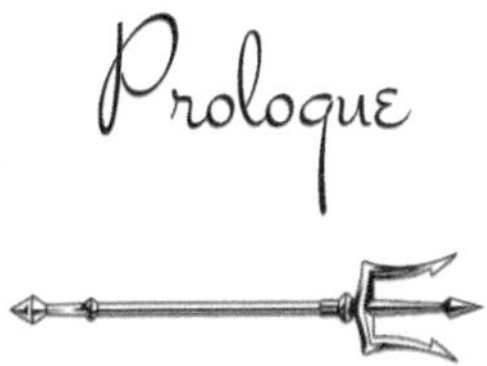

Prologue

MER

Sirenidae weren't supposed to drown.

Mer kicked toward the surface of the ocean, cannon fire lighting the water above in splashes of orange and gold paint. She gagged as blood, oil, and the scent of death filtered through her gills. Shards of wood bit at her skin, stinging like jellyfish.

Only a little bit farther.

With a sharp burst of movement, Mer broke the surface. The silence of the depths below shattered as a cannon impacted an Aermian warship. The explosion rocked the ship, the waves tossing Mer sideways. She swiped the water from her eyes and blinked hard into the stormy night.

Lightning streaked across the dark sky, followed by

bone-shaking thunder and the screams of cannons. She gritted her teeth as the change overtook her body. Her lungs seized, forcing the water out through her gills before they sealed, and she took her first full breath.

Fatigue rode her hard as waves battered her, trying to force Mer below. As much as she wanted to sink into the cool embrace of the sea, the battle raging around her demanded she fight. She swam toward the Aermian ship that was hanging on by a limb. Its sides were pockmarked and riddled with burns, but it still held. Thick rope ladders hung from the deck down to the waves, a welcoming gesture for the siren allies.

She dodged a body and tried not to look too closely at the pale face, her heart pounding. Now was no time to balk. This was war and that meant casualties. Mer seized the dark wet ladder that dangled in the water. She hooked her right arm through the rope and sagged, her legs limp. Just one little break and then she'd join the soldiers above.

As Mer caught her breath, she observed the madness of the battle around them.

Black powder scented the air. Broken ships bobbed in the harsh stormy waters. The clash of steel against steel cut through the air.

Their mortal enemy would not relent.

No matter how many Scythians the Aermians and their allies cut down, there were always more berserker monsters to replace them.

Lightning zigzagged through the night once again, highlighting the shapes of *fiilee* and their riders bravely attacking from the angry-looking sky. Her breath caught, and the scales along her arms lifted slightly as one of the flying felines was hit with a bolt and fell from the sky.

Her gaze latched onto the largest feline that tucked its wings and dove, its rider practically lying on its back. She shivered as they plunged toward their fallen comrade. The rider on the dead *fiilee* yanked frantically at their harness. Mer gasped when the rider launched off the back of their mount into the air. The large *fiilee* swooped below him and caught him before they hit the water, the dead mount crashing into the waves with a mighty splash before the ocean hungrily claimed her prize.

Mer mourned for the feline. The Methian aerial riders bonded with their mounts for life.

It was another dead to lay at the Scythians' feet.

Her heart slowed, and her breathing evened out. She wanted to crawl into a hole and sleep to regain her strength, but every moment she dallied was another life lost. Mer prepared to throw herself back into the water when the large *fiilee* dove from the sky. The massive feline landed on the nearest Aermian ship, both riders sliding from its wet back in one smooth movement.

A flash of lightning illuminated the riders.

She'd know his wine-colored hair anywhere. Her lips parted.

The Methian prince, Raziel.

She'd heard of the handsome Methian prince and had even caught glimpses of him in the last several weeks as he launched aerial attacks on the Scythian fleet, but she'd never been this close to him. Her gaze narrowed when the *fiilee* flared its leathery wings and knocked two Scythian warriors from the ship. Raziel launched an attack and she cursed, noting that the ship wasn't just fighting the storm but an influx of Scythian warriors. How had the scoundrels boarded it in this weather? She'd barely managed it.

We cannot lose that ship.

Lightning lit up the night sky in consecutive bursts as if the storm wanted Mer to have a better look at the hulking Prince Raziel. His clothing was soaking wet, clinging to his body, and the sharp lines of his face twisted with effort as he fought with a dark figure. They turned, and she gasped when she recognized his adversary.

A familiar shock of silver hair caught her gaze.

Ream, her husband.

Her brain scrambled to understand why allies would be fighting each other.

Wrong, wrong, wrong.

Her husband slipped beneath the prince's guard and stabbed him in the back.

"No!" she shouted. What was Ream thinking?

The prince tossed his head back in pain a moment before he flipped his sword and stabbed backward.

Time seemed to stand still, and Mer clung to the rope, not believing her eyes.

The sword protruded just to the left of Ream's spine.

Her husband stumbled toward the edge of the deck. The prince spun and brutally yanked his sword from Ream before kicking him in the chest.

A scream tore from Mer as her husband toppled over the railing and into the choppy waters.

No, no, no, no, no.

This wasn't happening.

Mer released the ladder and dove into the water. Debris from damaged ships and bodies littered the waves as she propelled forward as fast as she could. A sharp pain bit into her side, pulling her from her panic. Someone had tried to shoot her with a harpoon.

She popped her head just above the surface, her eyes scanning the area.

A Scythian soldier, with his eerily perfect face, grinned at her from a nearby ship. She narrowed her eyes and pointed a nail at him. She wouldn't forget his face. He'd pay for every drop of blood he spilled later.

Mer dove deep, frantically scanning the area for Ream.

Their enemies had wised up to their underwater attacks and now hunted the Sirenidae. Their bright silver hair made them easy targets, especially at night.

Ream, where are you? Please be okay.

As if her prayer had been answered, Mer spotted her husband in the murky water.

He sank slowly, silvery blood leaking from his chest in winding tendrils.

He was losing too much blood. She needed to get him somewhere safe immediately.

Mer dug deep, adrenaline surging through her body as she sped ahead and caught him under his arms. Her stomach sank as she saw the extent of his wounds. She needed healing herbs from the trench *now*.

She hauled him away from the warship toward the coral beds. A sandy cover with a circular wall of blood coral would do well to protect them while Ream was so vulnerable. No beast nor Scythian could reach them there. While the striped leviathans were normally friends, that could easily be washed away in the frenzy of blood and battle.

Her knees hit the white sand as she laid Ream down. He groaned and pressed his hands against the wound, his handsome face creased in pain. She brushed hair away from his paling cheeks before moving around to his side. Sand swirled through the water as Mer fluttered her fingers over his wound.

It was huge.

"A broadsword?" she growled, glaring at the raw edges of the cut. "How can I help you? Tell me what to do."

Ream was the healer, not her.

He shook his head.

Mer frowned at him before squeezing his hand. The damage was too severe to do anything of use. "I'm going for help. Hang on. I'll be back soon."

She released his hand and began climbing to her feet when Ream caught her fingers in his own.

"Don't go."

"I have to."

He shook his head again. "There's not much time."

Her pulse began to race. "Don't say such things. You're going to be fine." She gave him a stern look.

"We must speak. This is important."

Her mind screamed at her to find help, but her legs folded beneath her, and she pressed her own hands to his wound, trying to stem the blood. "Very well. You'll have to deal with me as your nursemaid until you get better."

Ream grimaced, his face a mask of pain.

"I'm sorry it hurts, but I have to put pressure on it." She glared as silvery blood still leaked from beneath her fingers. She glanced around the cove. There weren't any sort of healing plants nearby, although there was some wide seaweed. Mer placed Ream's hand on the wound before yanking the seaweed from the sand. She knotted the strands together quickly and then painstakingly wrapped them around her husband until they sealed the wound.

"There we go. That's better," she croaked, then cleared her throat. It wasn't enough. She could already see blood pooling beneath the leaves of the seaweed.

He was going to die.

No.

They'd only been married for three years, and yet it felt like she'd lived a lifetime with him. He was her person. Mer couldn't lose him.

"I need to get help. This is far beyond my knowledge."

Once again, he shook his head and gave her a soft yet sad smile. He reached for her hand, squeezing gently. "This is of my own doing, my love."

"Don't be ridiculous."

"It's true."

She swallowed hard and frowned, trying to come up with a reason why he would say such a thing.

Why did he attack the prince? Our ally?

As if he could read her thoughts, he replied, "I had no choice. They have my daughter."

Mer flinched.

His daughter had died alongside his previous wife in a terrible accident at least seven years before they married. She leaned closer and examined his pupils. Was he hallucinating?

She smoothed the hair back from his brow. "I don't know what you're talking about, but there's time to figure this out later. We need to get you healthy, my love." His loose grip suddenly tightened on her hand, almost to the point of pain. "You're hurting me."

"I need you to listen to me right now." His bright lucid gaze held onto hers. "The Pernicious are coming.

They are clever and know all. You must find my daughter before it's too late. Trust no one. Find Lysa for me."

She blinked hard, trying to make sense of his words. "What are you talking about? Who are the Pernicious? And Ream, your daughter is gone," she said softly, as if that would make the reminding blow any less painful.

"The Scythians gave me proof. They have a likeness of her."

Scythians.

Mer froze, staring down at her husband.

He'd been in contact with their enemy?

She frowned as she ran over the events of the evening. Ream was a healer, not a warrior. He shouldn't have been on that warship in the first place. He'd attacked the prince, and the Methian royal had only defended himself.

Mer began to shake. "What have you done?" she whispered.

"What I had to." Ream pleaded with her with his gaze. "It's my daughter."

Dread clogged her throat. "Was it you?" she questioned. No one knew how the enemy had obtained knowledge on how to hunt the Sirenidae. "Did you betray us? *Me*?"

Ream reached up and cupped her cheek, his fingers so cold. "You will understand when you have your own child. There are no lines you won't cross to protect them."

That was a yes.

Her heart broke.

Her eyes burned, and tears slipped free, sparkling lavender drops mixing with the seawater. "I don't understand."

"I'm sorry for it, but I don't regret it." Blood gathered at the corners of his lips and drifted away like smoke vapor.

She wasn't a healer, but she knew the signs of internal bleeding.

His grip on her face slackened, and she pressed it harder against her cheek. "Don't do it. Stay with me!"

"Forgive me."

Mer shook harder when he gave her one more sad smile. She couldn't get her lips to work, could only release soul-crushing sobs.

"Find my daughter," he whispered.

Then the life drained from his eyes.

Chapter One

MER

Six Months Later

"Tell me what you know!" Mer growled at the Scythian warrior.

The bulky man clenched his perfect jawline and continued to glare up at her with utter hatred. Silent as the grave even when his life was at stake. In her peripheral vision, the tip of a fin sliced through the water. It would be so easy to feed him to the leviathans. But he had information she desperately needed.

Mer tempered her emotions as a drop of blood ran down his cheek. Soon enough, he'd pay for his crimes. Her gaze dropped to the coral knuckle cover on her right hand.

It was a beautiful weapon—smooth on the inside so it didn't damage her own hand, and sharp on the outside. The cream coral held scarlet stains that tugged at her conscience .

What are you becoming?

Mer brushed away the unwanted thought and stood from her crouch, the algae on the wet rock squishing between her toes. The warrior pulled at the chains that tethered him to the large stone, muscles straining. The iron seemed to groan, but it held. Even if he did manage to escape them, there was nowhere for the fiend to go. The tide was rising, and the leviathans were hungry.

Even now, their hunting song grew in excitement.

Time for a different tactic.

Mer caught the warrior's eye. "Your Warlord is gone. Scythia has retreated. What are you fighting for?"

A spark lit in his dark eyes. "Our lord will never die."

Now she was getting somewhere.

She smirked. "He looked pretty dead to me when my friend slayed him." The man bared his bloody teeth at her, and Mer leaned closer to run the tip of her coral brace along the warrior's cheek. "It turns out your leader was nothing more than a *common* man. A dead man who will be forgotten."

"Our Warlord will live on, you abomination." His chest heaved with the declaration. "Your seas will fill with blood until you choke on it, but before your last breath Ceto will find you and destroy everything you hold dear."

Ceto. That was the second time she'd heard that name whispered.

A flurry of excitement danced in her chest. Maybe this was the lead she'd been looking for. "I'm not worried about dear old Ceto." Mer leaned into the warrior's space. "I have nothing left to lose."

The Scythian smiled through chapped lips, and it sent a chill down her spine. A tendril of fear wound around her chest as he tipped his chin up to her until they shared the same breath. Her fingers clenched the coral, and she fought not to take a step back.

You hold the power here. Not him.

"Ceto is creative." A manic grin warped his features. "Your fear is delicious. Run, little siren. The depths are coming for you." He snapped his mouth closed so hard that something cracked. The warrior's body began to convulse, his chains rattling so violently that the leviathans began thrashing in the water.

Mer screamed, grabbing his face with both hands to pry his teeth apart. A black liquid slipped from the corner of his mouth. "You cannot die!" she hissed. "You will tell me the truth. Where are they? Where are the women? Where is Lysa?"

The Scythian's eyes rolled back into his head, and all at once, his body went slack, feet slipping off the narrow ledge until he hung limply over the water. Mer's hands shook as she placed her fingers at the warrior's pulse point.

Nothing. He was dead.

Mer screamed again, the expanse of the empty ocean eating up her pain and frustration.

She cursed and pulled her hands away from his clammy skin. Mer turned her back to the body, staring sightlessly out at the calm sea but for a dark fin slicing through the water before disappearing beneath the surface. Of course, he'd been equipped with poison. How could she have been so stupid? She yelled wordlessly, the frustration making her throat ache. Mer tossed her hands in the air before sinking them into her silvery wet hair.

This wasn't working.

She couldn't keep abducting Scythian criminals and interrogating them. Someone was bound to notice. Especially since their bodies were never found. She nudged a clam clinging to the black rock with her big toe as tears blinded her eyes. While Mer hadn't killed them herself, she'd let the ocean decide, and the ocean was a cruel mistress.

Just how much further are you willing to go?

The answer scared her.

Angrily, Mer wiped the tears from her cheeks, hating how sticky they felt. The monster didn't deserve her tears. She lifted the key to the manacles from the long chain around her neck and knelt to unclip the chains around the dead man's ankles first. Next, she reached across his chest to unlock his left hand, holding her breath when her face neared his own. No one knew what the Scythians did in their laboratories, and she was taking no chances.

The warrior's heavy body sagged toward her, hanging by one arm. She quickly undid the last manacle, and the Scythian dropped into the water. Mer swallowed hard as his body sank beneath the surface, his black hair floating around his face.

The leviathans' haunting song rose into a crescendo a moment before a dark shadow slammed into the warrior.

The feeding frenzy had begun.

Mer backed away and moved to the other side. She got to her hands and knees, thankful that the moon was out. While her sight was better than most humans, the depths always proved tricky in the dark. She dipped her face into the water and opened her eyes. A large female leviathan to her left noticed the movement and swam Mer's way. Mer dove into the water, the moonlight causing streams of light to ripple like dancing ribbons. Mer's gills flared, forcing the air out and the water in. It burned as her body adjusted to the seawater. She reached out a gentle hand to the beastie's snout and redirected the leviathan. Her fingers drifted along the scaled side of the massive predator, making sure that it didn't decide to investigate Mer again.

She glanced above, noting how high the moon was.

Blast it. She was late.

Mer spared the frenzy behind her one more look before darting forward.

She was going to miss her meeting with Sin.

That couldn't happen.

Too much counted on what he was smuggling.

Chapter Two

RAZIEL

"W E   N E E D   T O   S P E A K ."

Ever since the queen had passed the crown down to him, he'd been buried in paperwork. Raziel glanced over the top of the latest trade proposals from the new Aermian king, Tehl, and locked eyes with his mother.

She'd always been dramatic when entering a room. Her taffeta dress rustled as she stomped through his personal study and library before placing her hands on the top of his mahogany desk.

He inwardly groaned and set the trade agreement down. Just what had set her off? "When have I ever denied you, Mum?"

She narrowed her silvery eyes—the same ones he'd inherited from her. Well, the gray, at least. Surviving the

Mirror Plague had given them both a metallic sheen to their gaze. The dowager queen clicked her long red nails against his desk. "Don't you 'Mum' me. You constantly defy me."

"Isn't that what you want in a king?" he teased with a smile.

"What I want is for you to stop shooting down every eligible woman who comes your way."

So that's what this was about.

Raz leaned back in his chair and crossed his arms over his chest, feeling prickly. This was a constant sore subject for them. She wanted heirs for the throne and a cure for the plague, and he wanted to make Methi more secure by trade agreements.

They were at an impasse.

"Evanthe was not for me." The thought alone made him queasy.

"She would have made a lovely queen."

Raz gritted his teeth. A ruthless queen, to be sure, but he couldn't imagine living with the woman. They'd grown up around each other, and it would be like marrying his sister. An irritating, fierce sister.

His mother tossed her hands in the air and flopped back into one of his leather chairs in a very unqueenly way. Her steely eyes pinned him to the spot as she laced her fingers over her stomach. "What do you want, Raziel? Ever since Mira denied you, you've changed. You're drifting with no true anchor."

He hated the little twinge of pain that pricked him at the mention of Mira—the woman he'd loved and had hoped to make his wife. But she'd not been for him. Mira had been happily married for a few months to a good man, although one who didn't deserve her.

As if you were worthy of Mira.

He sighed and glanced to the right at the fire in the hearth—away from the knowing glint in his mother's gaze. Raziel had never been able to hide anything from her. She had an uncanny way of pulling his secrets from him.

"I loved her," he whispered softly. A painful truth. One he did not regret.

"And because of this unrequited love, you refuse to take a wife?"

"No." While there was a special place in his heart for Mira, he wasn't still pining. "My illusions of finding a love match like yours and father's are well and truly over. I have moved on and will only marry for the betterment of Methi."

His mum arched a brow. "Is that so? And Evanthe?"

He cleared his throat. "I've found no woman that fulfills those terms, including Evanthe."

His mum snorted. "Terms. How unromantic."

She slowly sat up and climbed out of the chair. His mother rounded his desk and laid her hand over his shoulder. He peered up at the woman who'd lost the love of her life too early, raised four children on her own, mourned two, and made a kingdom prosper despite the sickness. With her graying hair and wrinkles kissing the corners of her eyes and mouth, she was beautiful.

"Have you really decided not to look for a love match?" she asked softly.

"I've made my mind up," he replied gruffly. "There are too many things our kingdom needs. I cannot be so selfish as to marry for love. It will be by necessity."

"So be it." She squeezed his shoulder with a sigh. "Then I have a proposition for you."

"Oh?" he questioned, arching a brow.

"I've found what you seek. A trade agreement for Methi and a bride that comes with it."

He pursed his lips and narrowed his eyes at his mum. There were Aermian duchesses, but none who could offer his kingdom what they needed. Blaise, the new Scythian Queen, was currently settling her kingdom after deposing the Warlord. They wouldn't be offering a political marriage. Plus, his brother seemed quite enamored with the woman. He'd heard rumors of Nagalian princesses, but they were trying to rebuild their deserted kingdom. Just who had his mother secured?

The queen mother gave him a sly smile. "You don't know, do you?"

He cocked his head. "Who is it?" A sinking feeling settled in his gut.

"A Sirenidae princess."

Blast it.

A blessing and a curse.

"You cannot be serious," he snapped. "They are demons in disguise. They collect bones for treasures. They're not natural."

"Be that as it may, they also have healers and access to the best herbs in our known world. We need both desperately. If we don't stop the newest wave of the blight, we won't have any people left to govern."

Raz pushed out of his chair, running his hands through his hair. He spun and faced the three arched windows of his study. The capital city of Skigara sprawled around the castle that was carved into the side of the Hollow Mountains. Dark green pine trees kissed the edge of the city and spread out like a large blanket, only broken up by farms and smaller villages. It was beautiful, but its beauty hid the truth.

His people were dying.

You must do something.

Bile burned the back of his throat as he thought of taking a Sirenidae princess as his bride. Would her skin be cold and clammy? Would she try to control his mind using the Lure? Would she steal his soul and feast on it?

"Do you truly have a contract from the Sirenidae king?" he forced himself to ask.

"I do."

"Why now?" He turned and met his mother's gaze. "We've been at odds with those creatures for years. What could they possibly want from us? What are they not telling us?"

"It's my understanding that Sirenidae live a very long life. If a daughter of Thalassa was married to a king," she blew out a breath, "then once you die, the kingdom would belong to your heir . . . and she would be regent."

Anger heated his chest. "So, they seek to steal our kingdom."

His mother rolled her eyes. "Every country seeks to expand their borders and improve their land—Sirenidae are no different. We just need to have a plan put into place."

He picked a *fiilee* hair from his black velvet vest and stared at it before tossing it out the window. "We gain healers for the Mirror Plague."

"And herbs from the trenches."

His gaze sharpened. "Are you quite sure?" The life-lengthening herbs were impossible to get their hands on, even if they were royal. The Sirenidae guarded the plants fiercely.

"We've been granted an allotment along with treasures from the sea."

Raziel smirked. "You mean treasures they've pilfered from sunken ships that were probably ours to begin with."

His mum huffed. "I see you're determined to be negative, so I shall take my leave."

He reached out and caught the dowager queen's hand

before she could leave. "I will think on this. Please have the contract brought to me. I will consider it."

"That's all I ask." She squeezed his fingers and then bustled out of the room as quickly as she'd come in.

Scrubbing a hand over his face, he sat in his chair and stared blankly at the desk. The existence of the Mirror Plague was a fiercely guarded secret. Methi's borders had been closed until the Warlord's War. Even then, only loyal warriors who'd survived the plague were permitted to leave. Not one foreign person had set foot on Methian soil in over thirty years. If the plague ever spread, their kingdom would be blamed.

They needed a remedy now.

It seemed a dangerous cold bride could be just the cure.

MER

"THAT'S THE LAST OF IT," SIN SAID, BRUSHING his palms together.

Mer nodded, tucking the stolen Sirenidae herbs carefully inside her cloak. They would save so many human lives. "You have my thanks." She pulled the leather pouch full of gold from her leather belt and held it out to her brother-in-law.

Well . . . former brother-in-law.

The thought pierced Mer, and she inhaled sharply.

Sin shook his head, the shells in his silvery locs clinking softly at the motion. "I won't take payment for something that is my duty. It's not right to keep the bounty of the trenches to ourselves. We should share it with others."

"My sentiments exactly." Mer stepped closer, took his hand in her own, and placed the pouch in his large palm. "You never know when you'll need it. Please take the coin."

The tall Sirenidae studied her with familiar light magenta eyes. "How are you holding up?"

She closed his fingers around the coins and stepped away. "I'm fine." A simple word for complicated feelings.

"Lies," he murmured as he tucked the gold into the back of his ill-fitting leather breeches. Aermian clothing never fit their race quite right. Always too big around the waist and too short. "It doesn't look like you're taking care of yourself."

Mer glanced around the dock and at the nearby brothels. There were quite a few people about, but no one was paying them any attention. The sailors and merchants were either too drunk, or otherwise occupied. She turned her attention back to her former brother-in-law.

"I'm doing the best I can." *A lie and a truth.*

He shuffled on his bare feet and pushed the hair out of his square face, a face which was so similar to her husband's that it hurt Mer to look at him for too long. He was a painful reminder of her failures.

Don't go there.

"Don't think I don't know what you're doing, but I can see you want a subject change." He pursed his lips. "Let's talk about your upcoming judgment. I don't understand why your grandfather postponed it again," he muttered, crossing his arms, the moonlight catching on the lilac scales scattered along his forearms.

Mer gritted her teeth. She'd hurt the king's pride and his heart by going behind his back and helping the humans. He couldn't let her disobedience go unpunished, and coupled with Ream's betrayal . . . there was a price to be paid. But the old man didn't know what to do with her. She didn't know what to do with herself. Her royal blood made her too valuable.

"It wasn't right of you to protect us," Sin said quietly. "We should be standing beside you. It's cowardly to stay silent about the part we played in helping the humans and let you take the brunt of what occurred. We chose to fight and support the surface kingdoms in their time of need. You should not have to face the old king's wrath on your own. It's wrong."

"I took the lead in disobeying him. I shoulder the blame alone." She tipped her chin up. "The goal was to help our allies, not tear our kingdom apart." Her actions weren't meant to start a revolution. Only help those in need. They couldn't hide beneath the waves anymore, or the enemy would soon come to them.

"We would rally for you. You are the heir. You are *our* queen."

She glared at him, eyes narrowed. "Keep your voice down," she hissed, scanning the dock once again and then the water. One could never be too careful. "Men have been killed as traitors for less in our court." She huffed out a breath. "And you will not do such a thing. There's been enough death as it is." It was a command.

"No, we will not," he replied grudgingly, bowing his head in deference. "No one wants civil war. We're already too divided as it is."

"And that is why you need to keep silent," Mer reminded him. "My grandfather will not listen to me. I disobeyed him, but I didn't betray him to our enemies. I may have gone behind his back to help the surface, but there are those among the Sirenidae who are not loyal and who are infinitely more dangerous. Our enemies have been supplied with herbs from the trenches, and our people have been disappearing for years. I need you and your people free to discover who was working with the Scythians—to find our people."

Sin nodded curtly and glanced at the black waves lapping gently against the dock. "Or who is still working with the Scythians."

Goosebumps rose on her arms. Who indeed?

"Any luck on the Pernicious?"

"Nothing," she grunted. "Everyone I've spoken to has never heard of this group, if they even exist."

Her lips thinned. It could have been the rantings of her dying husband, but he seemed so certain when he spoke about them. Even with all the digging she'd done, nothing had been revealed. Even the Spymaster of Aermia had come up empty-handed. That worried Mer more than anything.

She had nightmares about the bloodthirsty monsters of Scythia. While Aermia and Scythia had signed a treaty of peace and Blaise, the new queen, was now in control of the throne, the Scythian kingdom was one strike away from disaster. Far too many of the Warlord's bloodthirsty men still held positions among the court.

"The war is not over," she said softly.

"It has changed into something far more dangerous."

"Subterfuge."

He nodded once.

She'd thought her time playing cloak-and-dagger had come to a close, but it seemed she was only getting started. Mer rubbed at her forehead and sighed, suddenly exhausted. All she wanted to do was curl up and sleep. But even sleep offered no peace, for all that awaited her were nightmares.

"You know we still love you, right?" Sin asked.

"What?" She blinked up at him tiredly.

Sin cocked his head. "Just because Ream is gone doesn't mean that you're not family. You are still my sister. No matter what the king decides, you will always be my family."

He held his arms out, and Mer didn't hesitate to walk into them. Sin hugged her tightly, and she blinked back tears as she inhaled his familiar scent of salt and sand. He smelled like home.

Do you even have a home anymore?

Not since her husband had died. Not since she'd failed utterly.

What Sin didn't know was that she'd saved the life of the man who'd murdered his brother. It was her greatest shame. A mistake she would not make twice.

"You need to eat more," he mumbled into her hair. "My brother would be beside himself if he saw the state of you."

Her tears did fall this time, stinging her cheeks. No one spoke of Ream except for Sin, like his betrayal negated his entire life.

"I miss him," she whispered brokenly.

"I do too," Sin replied.

"Do you know what the worst part is? If he'd survived, I don't know that I could have lived with the knowledge that he helped the Scythians hurt our people. I think in my heart, I wouldn't have forgiven him. But, despite that, I still mourn the future we'd planned." Mer pulled away and wiped at her face, hating the tears that caused her cheeks to itch. She never had this issue in the sea. "I wanted a family, and all of that is gone now." She inhaled roughly. "Am I selfish?"

"Let yourself mourn. It's natural." Sin cupped her cheek, his long fingers tangling with her hair. "Your future is not gone. Changed, yes, but not gone. You can still have a family."

Mer hiccupped and gave a watery laugh. "I am a traitor to the crown by supporting the people of the surface. No good Sirenidae man would have me, and even if he did, my actions would always bring shame upon our family and our children. I couldn't bear it."

"You are not alone. You will get through this."

She nodded and pulled his hand away, giving it one squeeze before using her shirtsleeve to scrub her face. "I'm sorry for the self-pity."

"You never have to be sorry for your grief. You've suffered much, and your trials are not yet finished."

That sobered her. "Have you heard anything about my judgment? Any indication what the king plans to do?"

Sin frowned and crossed his arms. "Nothing."

"It's been postponed twice." She stared out at the darkened outline of the nearest ship bobbing in the bay, a sliver of moonlight gleaming off the waves. "What is he waiting for?" Other than to torture her.

"You're a favorite of your grandfather's. I'm not sure he knows what to do with you."

"He has a vindictive streak. Make no mistake. He isn't delaying because he's unsure. He's delaying because he wants it to hurt me as much as I hurt him." She snorted. "And because he knows how much I hate waiting."

"Patience is not your virtue," Sin agreed, a twinkle in his pale magenta eyes.

"Ha ha," she huffed.

Her brother-in-law gave her a half smile before glancing over his shoulder back at the sea. "I need to return before someone notices my absence."

"Be safe," she said, swallowing the lump in her throat. While he wasn't blood, he was her brother through and through.

"You as well. I'll see you next week."

Mer nodded and spun on her heel, refusing to say goodbye or watch him leave. She'd already said goodbye too many times to people she loved.

Chapter Four

MER

HER GAZE LANDED ON HER AUNT'S OLD BUT well-kept vessel, the *Sirenidae*, skipping over the shouting merchants nearby. The ship had been painted pale green in contrast to the dark wood of its hull and deck. It had a few more scars than it did before, but the ship was still majestic.

Mer ignored the sailor's bawdy stories as she strode down the dock and across the ramp to the ship, gripping the rope rails. When her feet met the deck, Mer peered around curiously. The ship was clean, its wooden deck well oiled and practically gleaming in the soft lantern light. Large white sails billowed in the breeze, a stark contrast to the clear black night sky dotted with stars.

She hovered on the edge of the lantern's light. All seemed right, but it was too quiet.

"You're right to be leery, *ma fille*," a smoky voice called softly from the stern.

Mer sighed. Nothing got past Lilja.

"Lurking in the dark?" Mer called, moving toward the stern. She jogged up the stairs and arched an eyebrow at her aunt who leaned casually against the far railing, a pipe dangling between her fingers. "What is that?"

Her aunt smiled. "I won it in a card game. I'm deciding if I want to keep it or toss it into the waves below for a wee one to find."

"Toss it," Mer said, slinging her left hip against the staircase handrail. "Discovering treasure is exciting."

Lilja tossed the pipe over her shoulder and into the sea. She brushed her palms against her leather trousers and sauntered forward. Mer kept her expression blank, even as she began to sweat. Her aunt was up to something. Lilja paused at the top step and studied Mer.

"Are you going to tell me what you've been up to, or do you plan to lie to me some more?" her aunt asked softly.

Mer pursed her lips. The best strategy was to keep silent. She'd learned from a young age that Lilja could even coax secrets from the stones.

"You know I love you, right?" Lilja said.

That was not what she expected to hear. "I love you too."

"Do you trust me?"

"I do," Mer said slowly.

"Then listen to me closely. You are in over your head."

Her hackles rose. "Excuse me?"

Lilja stared down at her, her expression grave. "I'm not ignorant of the herbs from the trenches you're distributing, nor am I unaware of your association with the Spymaster of Aermia. I am worried for you."

"I can handle it."

"You are beyond capable, but if your actions are reported to the Sirenidae king, you will not come back from this. He is a bitter old man with too much pride and time on his hands."

"Do you expect me to do nothing?" Mer replied calmly. "People are suffering, and I have the means to help them."

"No, but I don't want you to be banished from your home permanently."

"You've done just fine."

"I've carved out a life for myself, but that's not to say it hasn't been excruciatingly painful at times. I would not wish the tragedies I've suffered upon anyone." Lilja arched a brow. "Why didn't you come to me? I would have helped you with your crusade."

"When exactly? Between the times Hayjen's not dragging you somewhere private?" Mer's stomach lurched, and she glanced away from her aunt's piercing gaze that always seemed to see too much. She was truly thankful that her aunt had survived the Warlord's attack, but it was excruciating to be around Lilja and Hayjen when they were so wrapped up in each other. Every look that passed between them was like a dagger to Mer's heart, reminding her of what she'd lost.

Of what she'd never have again.

"I'm so sorry about Ream."

"Are you?" Mer asked woodenly, staring out at the dark waves. "He was a traitor."

"You loved him, and you're hurting. Your pain is my pain," Lilja said, placing a hand on Mer's shoulder.

She shook the hand off and turned her back on her aunt, descending the stairs. "You have no idea about the kind of pain I'm dealing with. Every time I think of him —" Her breath caught. "Every time, it's as if I can't breathe. When I close my eyes, I relive him dying in my arms, begging for his daughter, pleading for forgiveness. His choices led to the deaths of innocents. Ream isn't here to atone, but I am. I have to set things right."

"You are not to blame for his actions."

"Am I not?" Mer bowed her head. "I was so wrapped up in the affairs of the world, the enemy got to him. I could have protected him from that if I'd paid attention. I won't fail to protect others. I don't care if it gets me banished from the sea. I will never stop fighting those demons. I will fight until every last one pays for their sins and draws their last breath."

"Revenge won't bring him back. It will eat at your soul," Lilja murmured.

Mer laughed sharply. "What soul? Mine died in the Thalassan Sea with my first love."

Chapter Five

RAZIEL

THE SCENT OF DYING FLESH MADE KING RAZIEL'S
eyes water.

He breathed shallowly through his mouth as he
moved through the plague camp, the stones of the
pathway crunching beneath his boots and those of his
inner circle. Raz hated coming here. Tents lined the road
like silent sentinels awaiting the gallows. The wind whistled through the tall pine trees above as if it were
mourning for the sick.

Raziel tugged at the red scarf wrapped around his nose
and mouth, the fabric dampening with each breath.
Healers scurried between tents carrying soiled bandages
and pots of honey. A young-looking healer caught his eye
and bowed before hurrying away. This was not the place

to linger in conversation. Even the healers seemed like they wanted to run away from the plague camp screaming.

Raz reached the nearest canvas tent and lifted the flap without hesitation. The scent of putrefied flesh and disease nearly knocked him on his arse. He swallowed hard against the bile that flooded his mouth. His people deserved more than him, more than a king who wanted to flee from their disease.

He forced one foot in front of the other, his men trailing behind him as his eyes adjusted to the dim tent. Rudimentary single beds lined the walls, each hosting a shriveled pockmarked person. Some had their hands and legs secured to the wooden frames. In the later stage of the disease, when it feasted upon the brain, the person sometimes became violent. It killed Raz that in the final days of their lives, they had to be strapped down—without any freedom.

He scanned the large tent, and his throat bobbed as he spotted a small shivering body in the middle on his left.

A child.

It hurt the most when a young one became ill. The disease wasn't prejudiced. It attacked men, women, and children alike.

He swallowed hard and then strode over the dirt-packed floor to the foot of the wee one's bed. He stared down at the little girl who gazed back, her thin cracked lips pressed into an unforgiving line. Most tried to sit up or bow when they recognized the royal insignia on his tunic—not that it was necessary—but the little girl didn't even move. In fact, her metallic blue eyes narrowed on him.

A trait of the Mirror Plague. Once someone was truly infected, their irises gained a reflective quality.

"What do you want?" she rasped harshly, a wheeze rattling in her lungs.

Crossing his arms, he pasted a bright smile on his face, not that she could see it behind his scarf. "I came for a visit."

The little girl snorted. "A visit? How very lucky for you that you can visit this hell and then leave."

Raz cocked his head, wine-colored hair falling over his forehead. The little one had fire. She'd need it to survive the plague. "What's your name and how old are you?"

She harrumphed. "It doesn't matter. I'm going to die here anyway."

That was enough of that talk. He'd come here with the goal of being uplifting, and he'd do it if it took every trick in his book.

Rounding the mattress, he pulled a stool from beneath her bed and sat. The wood groaned under his bulk.

The girl scowled at him, her brown hair drenched in sweat at the temples. "What are you doing?"

"Sitting with you."

"I don't need you."

"Be that as it may, I bear a gift." He reached into his

chest pocket and pulled out a tiny figurine of his feline companion Skye and held it out to her. The girl couldn't have been more than nine. Her blue eyes rounded, but she shuddered, her expression almost bored. "This is my *fiilee*. She's a protector. Any time you're afraid, just hold Skye in your hands, and she'll help you through your trial."

The girl blinked at him and warily took the wooden figurine from his fingers. She traced her shaking fingertips over the arched bat-like wings of the *fiilee*. After a moment, she held it out to him, shaking her head slowly.

"I can't take gifts from strangers. My mama said so."

"Where is your mama?"

"Dead." Her voice was flat.

"And your father?" he asked, already knowing the answer.

"Dead."

King Raziel stared at the young girl and reached for his scarf, pulling down the fabric beneath his chin. He could give her this, could make the little one feel less alone.

"My lord," a deep voice chastised, but Raz waved off Valen—his commander and one of his best friends.

He held his hand out to the little girl. "My name is Raz."

She blinked slowly at his bare face and then his outstretched hand. "No one but the healers can touch me."

"You can see my eyes, no?" She nodded. "I once had the plague. My eyes are permanently silver now. I beat this sickness, and so can you. And now we're not strangers." He held his breath, waiting for her reply.

The little one studied him and reluctantly slipped her bony hand into his own. A lump rose in his throat at how delicate her hand was—as if any pressure could break her.

"My name's Maple." She yanked her hand from his and began fiddling with the figurine.

"It's nice to meet you." He stared at her for a bit and then held his right hand out to Valen hovering behind him. A worn leather book was placed in his palm. Maple eyed the book.

"What's that?" she asked.

"A book of stories I stole from the royal library. Would you like to hear one?"

A glimmer of excitement entered Maple's eyes although she tried to hide it. "Sure."

Raz hid his smile, cracked open the well-loved book, and began reading.

He'd spent the day reading to Maple. At one point, she fought her heavy eyelids, but they inevitably won. Even then, Raziel kept reading. Only when the sun began to set did Valen place a hand on his right shoulder.

"We should return, my lord."

King Raziel nodded and held the book out to Valen. His oldest friend took the book as Raz stood from the stool. His back pinched and his arse ached, but it had been worth it. He gently tucked in Maple's arms before pulling the blanket up to her chin. Her little chest labored for breath, her inhale much wetter than he would have liked.

Leaning down, he whispered into her left ear. "Don't give in, Maple. You can fight this, little one."

She didn't stir when he stood to his full height and shoved the stool back beneath her bed. The air still stank, but it had lessened. Valen took his place next to Raziel's right, and the other two warriors brought up the flank as they exited the tent. Raz waved to the other patients, touching their feet as they left.

Exiting the tent didn't bring much relief as the scent of ash and burned flesh permeated the air.

"You should cover your face, my lord," Valen said softly.

A hollow laugh escaped Raz. "What can it possibly do for me? I've already been sick."

"The plague is changing. You risk yourself unnecessarily."

King Raziel grunted but lifted the red scarf over his nose and mouth before striding through the camp once again, drawing closer to the large fire that burned in the distance.

They paused on the outskirts of the massive bonfire, and Raz dipped his head in respect for the dead they were burning. His eyes watered, and the world swirled around him. This couldn't be the fate of his kingdom, to die a slow painful death. They had to figure out something.

He had to figure out something.

Or soon, there would be no one left to save.

You have a choice.

His lip curled. There was only one choice.

The Sirenidae bride.

"Is my mother at the castle?" he barked.

"Yes," Valen replied. "She was training some new *fiilee* mounts when we left."

"Send for her. We have a contract to sign."

Chapter Six

MER

"I HAVE NEWS," SIN ANNOUNCED AS HE WADED out of the moonlit sea.

Mer's heart sputtered, and she pushed away from the tree she was leaning against, her skin prickling slightly at the cool night breeze. She stared at her brother-in-law, her sharp gaze taking in his grim expression despite the darkness. His thin lips firmly pressed together did not bode well. Sin's visit wasn't a happy one.

"Get on with it," she barked, her toes curling in the wet sand. The suspense was killing her.

"The king has made a decision, and your punishment shall be enforced within the next fortnight."

Only fourteen more days. Her shoulders sagged, and she focused on the frothy waves lapping gently at Sin's ankles. Most people would dread what was coming, but Mer welcomed it. She'd been in limbo for too long. Knowing that her punishment was coming eased some of her anxiety. The unknown was the worst.

She looked back up at Sin. "Do you know what my punishment will be?"

"The king has kept everything very close to his breast." Sin's expression turned sad, his familiar magenta eyes holding pain. "Whatever it is, it will not be pleasant. I suspect that part of it will be banishment."

Mer's heart sank. It was what she deserved, but the thought of being exiled from her family for the rest of her life cut deeply. She fiddled with the end of her long braid. It was less than she deserved. Banishment wouldn't be the only consequence for her actions.

Sin pulled a sealskin pouch from his hip and held it out to her. She took a step forward into the water and took it from his fingers before tying it to her belt.

"That is the last of the herbs for a while," Sin said softly, nodding to the seaweed. "The cultivators are keeping careful watch over their crops. That was all I could collect without getting caught."

"It's more than enough." Mer hugged him, seawater seeping into her clothing. "I appreciate what you've done."

Her brother-in-law hugged her back before releasing her and running a hand down his face. "The Sirenidae have been too stingy with the healing herbs for far too long."

"You've gone above and beyond what anyone else has done, Sin. You have saved many with the risks you've taken to obtain these herbs."

"This is just a little thing. I wish I could do more." He kicked at the surf. "Whoever has been stealing from the fields has made a real mess of things."

Mer's brows furrowed. "One of our people?"

He shook his head. "No. The cultivators have the crops locked down securely. The thieves were very sloppy."

That was bad news.

She walked around Sin until she reached a large rock and leaned against it, kicking at the water as her mind started running over his words. Who would steal from the fields? It had to be someone apart from her people since the herbs were made available for all of them. "Do you have any idea who did this?"

Her brother-in-law shook his head. "They were sloppy in their execution but extremely careful to cover their scents and tracks."

"Odd," she murmured. If they could hide their scents, surely they were able to steal the seaweed without leaving a trace? Unless it was on purpose. Maybe they were just trying to make trouble.

"That's what I thought. I know your aunt has her

own things going, but she wouldn't have left a trace in the first place. No one ever knows Lilja has stolen from them."

Mer snorted. "That's a fair assessment." Her aunt was like a wraith in the wind. "Speaking of Lilja, have you discovered what she's been up to?"

Sin smirked. "They're trained well, but I've been able to discover a few spies. They've been digging deeper about the missing girls you brought to her attention."

That was news to Mer. Her aunt hadn't said a bloody thing.

Her jaw clenched, and she kicked at the water. Mer had been searching for information on Ream's daughter for months. She hadn't found anything on Lysa, but she'd discovered the disappearances of over twenty young Sirenidae girls in the last six months. They'd disappeared all over the sea kingdom, so no one had connected the dots.

Until Mer.

"What has she found?" she asked.

"There's no sign of them anywhere—not even in Scythia."

"Scythia is a mess right now. They could be hidden."

Sin nodded. "True, but you know how thorough Lilja is. It's as if the girls have just vanished. What worries me is that I've heard rumors that it's not only Sirenidae girls that have disappeared but also young women from Scythia and Aermia."

She frowned at her brother-in-law. "Scythians have been stealing women for years. That's nothing new."

"True, but that was *women*. We are speaking about children, Mer." He crossed his long arms. "Whoever has taken the girls leaves no trace of their activities. You're poking into their operation. Tread carefully."

"I'll be fine," she replied. No one was coming for her, and if they did . . . well, she wasn't sure she cared all that much. "Keep your eyes and ears open. I'll see you soon."

Mer pushed away from the rock and prowled toward the tree line.

"You'll always be my queen," Sin called. "No matter what happens."

Mer glanced over her shoulder and gave him a dark smile. "I'm no queen. I'm the traitor of the tides."

Chapter Seven

MER

MER HELD HER HEAD HIGH AS SHE GLIDED
through the underwater assembly toward her grandfather.
He sat on a huge throne carved from abalone, his long
silver hair floating around him, the pale whalebone
columns rising behind him in the amphitheater.

The stares of her people pricked her skin like a thousand needles—some angry, some sad, some betrayed.

Today she'd receive her punishment.

Finally. Waiting was torture.

Somewhere in the crowd were Lilja and Sin. Her aunt
and brother-in-law wanted to accompany her but she
turned them down. Mer needed to accept the consequences of her actions alone.

Plus, she didn't want to appear weak.

She stopped before the dais, her feet settling gently in the sand. Her pulse rushed in her veins as she gazed up at her grandfather impassively. Shame threatened to rise up at the whispers, but Mer shoved it down. Her actions hadn't been shameful when she'd helped their allies. The only thing she regretted was hurting her grandfather. Even now, she could see pain lurking in the king's pale magenta gaze.

He stood, trident in hand, and she knelt in respect. Sand billowed in a cloud around her knees.

"Mer Thalassan, royal daughter of the tides, you have been convicted of traitorous crimes against our people. You disobeyed the king, conscripted your own army, assisted the surface kingdoms, and conspired against the crown. Are you ready to accept your fate?" her grandfather said, his deep voice cutting through the depths of the ocean.

"I am," she responded, her voice ringing clear and strong.

"For your crimes, you are to be cut off from your people indefinitely."

She swallowed thickly and tried not to cry. Mer had already suspected she'd be banished, but hearing it cut her to the soul. The Sirenidae were her home.

Her grandfather continued. "You will be marked as a traitor so all will know you for what you are."

Mer bit the inside of her cheek. She was to be branded

and her hair cut. No Sirenidae would ever again acknowledge her.

"And finally," he said.

She bowed her head, bracing herself for the final blow. Was her punishment not enough? No Sirenidae had been punished this harshly in five hundred years.

"The council and I have taken into account your royal blood as well as your good deeds in the past for our people. Even though you will not be welcomed here, we will not toss you out into the world without protection. We've found a solution suited for your royal status."

Mer lifted her head and tried to calm her breathing as she locked eyes with her grandfather. The king's expression held no sympathy and no condemnation.

"You are no longer a widow." Shock radiated through her. "You have been married by proxy to a king who we deemed suitable for you."

Her mouth gaped open, and it felt like she was drowning. Marriage? "To whom?" she rasped as the ocean tilted around her. Mer dug her fingers into the sand to ground herself.

"You are wed to King Raziel of Methi. Prepare yourself. You will depart for your new home and husband immediately after your marking."

The world dipped out of focus, and her hands shook.

"Do you accept your punishment?" her grandfather asked.

Don't let them see you falter.

Mer released the sand as she slowly stood, her long hair rippling around her. It was on the tip of her tongue to refuse and accept the death sentence. She'd *never* accept the man who murdered the love of her life.

The loss of Ream threatened to choke her, the shame of saving his murderer almost too much to bear, but she pushed it down.

Think through the pain.

She nodded once, words caught in the back of her throat. Maybe this torture was a blessing in disguise. Killing the Methian king had been on her list since Ream's death. This gave her the perfect chance to get close to him and make the monster suffer.

"Do you accept your punishment?" the king asked again.

Mer lifted her head and smiled serenely at her grandfather, despite the rage and pain boiling inside her chest.

"I accept."

HER EYES FELT HOT AS SHE SWAM THROUGH THE airy palace—the bleached coral walls gleamed softly in the light, but it had lost all its beauty. Now it just looked like a sad prison.

The warriors stationed at the oval abalone doors

stepped aside without making eye contact. They knew better than to stop a princess, even a banished one.

Mer slammed through the doors that led to the throne room, leaving them to slowly drift closed behind her. Why even bother with doors under the water? Whether the sea king wanted to admit it or not, he admired things from the surface.

Smooth agate stepping stones caressed the bottoms of her feet as she walked into the throne room, her newly shorn hair floating about her face. It was too light—the comforting weight of her hair gone—just like her honor.

Get it together.

Her grandfather sat on his carved throne set inside the gaping jaws of a leviathan skull. As a child, it scared her, but now she knew it was just another intimidation tactic.

He didn't look surprised to see her. His lips turned down slightly, but that was the only indication he gave that he felt anything at the sight of her.

She forced herself not to march up to him, and leaned her head back to meet his familiar pale magenta eyes that used to look at her with fondness, not apathy.

Silence stretched between them.

Mer felt herself tongue-tied. Her grandfather had always had this effect on her. His stone-faced mask had frightened her as a child, but he would let it melt away and always had a smile for her.

Those days were finished.

That man was gone, and in his place sat a king.

One she'd betrayed. *You broke his heart.*

Pain and guilt pricked her. She'd gone behind his back and helped the Aermians after he'd explicitly told her no.

She brushed a strand of her newly shorn hair from her face, feeling like it didn't belong to her. Sirenidae prided themselves on their lustrous long hair. Short hair was a dishonor, one she deserved.

Her jaw clenched as the silence stretched on between them. Her grandfather always liked to play mind games, to gain the upper hand. Normally, she held out, but today, there wasn't time.

"How could you?" she demanded, her voice wavering slightly.

"How could I?" His deep voice sliced through the room, an undercurrent of disgust hitting her fully in the chest.

It hurt.

Hold on to your anger.

"Marry me to him." The Methian prince turned king. The murderer.

Her grandfather arched a white brow. "Your marriage was always mine to arrange. I allowed you to choose Ream because I thought the older widowed healer would ground you. Look how well that turned out." Her stomach dropped to the floor, and her fingers curled into fists at her sides. "That traitorous wretch put ideas into your head. He poisoned you against me. It's good that he's dead."

It felt like he'd slapped her.

True, Ream had made a bad decision, but he hadn't poisoned her. She'd made her own choices. Decisions that had left her husband isolated and prey to the enemy. Guilt surged, and it was on the tip of her tongue to defend Ream, but she swallowed the arguments down. Her grandfather wouldn't hear them. He'd already made up his mind about her former husband.

"Sirenidae royalty have always been able to choose their mates," she stated firmly.

"Only for the last five hundred years. Before, the king arranged all his children's marriages."

"You mean you changed it when you became king so you could take grandmother as your bride?"

His gills flared along his neck. "You dare to speak of her?"

"She wouldn't want this, and you know it."

He rose from his throne, the shafts of light from above reflecting off the large scales covering his shoulders. "You know nothing but your own silly wants. You've been married to the king. You will leave immediately after your branding."

"I will not." She lifted her chin and held her head high, despite how her heart raced. "I will not remarry. I agreed in front of the assembly only to spare you embarrassment." There was nothing worse in her grandfather's eyes than a public disagreement.

"Stupid selfish girl!" he spat. He darted forward and towered over her, his hair fanning out like angry snakes.

"Do you really think you have any control here?" His eyes sparked with intensity. "That I don't know about what you've been up to?"

She kept her expression blank. "What do you mean?"

Her grandfather scanned her placid mask and scoffed. "You forget that I know you, Granddaughter—that I helped raise you. I taught you all your tricks. Did you really think I wouldn't discover the theft from the trenches?"

Don't react.

He couldn't trace it back to her.

The sea king smirked. "I can see the thoughts flitting through your eyes. I'm not unaware of the fealty you've gained, nor of those who wish to rise against me in your name."

"I would never usurp you," she breathed. And Mer meant it.

"And yet that's exactly what you did when you rallied soldiers behind my back. You made me look weak."

His pride was hurt.

"That was not my intention, Grandfather. I only sought to help those who needed it. Isn't that what you taught me? You raised me to stand up for those who could not protect themselves."

"*Our* people," he snarled. "Not the humans."

"All creatures of the world have value."

His expression hardened. "Since you love them so

much, you shall spend your life with them. With the King of Methi."

Mer began shaking. "I will not."

"You will." He leaned into her space. "Or I will slaughter the rest of Ream's family as they deserve."

She blinked slowly at him. "You wouldn't." But Mer wasn't sure. Her grandfather was ruthless at times.

"Betrayal runs deep, Granddaughter. I must make sure to root it all out."

Her pulse picked up. Ream had sisters, nieces, and nephews. *Sin.* "The children?" she whispered.

The sea king locked his eyes on hers. "The *entire* line. Vengeance is in our blood. If I was to leave one child, they would eventually rise. The poison needs to be purged from our community." He paused, the silence strategic. "Or you can take your punishment and save an entire family."

"I marry or they die?" She swallowed. "That's how it's to be?"

Her grandfather smiled, but it wasn't nice. "You're already married, but your compliance protects their lives."

He spoke true. The sea king had committed many wrongs, but he'd never lied to her.

Bile burned the back of her throat as she thought of sharing a home with her husband's killer. "I want your word."

"You have it. Ream's line will be safe if you go quietly."

She could never risk their lives for her own happiness. "When do I leave?" she rasped.

"After your branding. Your things have been packed along with the dowry. A Methian ship awaits you in the harbor." He captured her chin. "There will be no time for goodbyes."

That was even crueler. "You would deny me that?"

"You denied me my heir. The survival of Ream's line is the only concession I will give you."

She stepped back from him, staring at her grandfather like she didn't know him. Mer shook her head, staring him down as another part of her heart broke, pathetic thing that it was. "I've defended you for years. The cold cruelty. The pragmatism. But I now see you for what you are."

She gave him a mocking bow and turned her back to him, pushing off the floor of the throne room toward the doors.

"And one more thing," the sea king called. Mer glanced over her shoulder. "You may have let me down as my heir, but I still expect you to act like a princess. If the king dies, I'll hold you responsible. Ream's line will be cut off."

Translation: *if you kill the king, our deal is off.*

She squared her shoulders and smirked at him. "As you wish."

Mer might not be able to kill him, but she could make his life miserable.

Some fates were worse than death.

Chapter Eight

RAZIEL

"THEY FOUND THE *ZEPHYR*."

Raziel's attention snapped to Valen's metallic teak eyes. "Where?" The fishing vessel had been missing for two weeks.

"To the north of the Wasting Corals," his commander replied, his dark brown lips pressed into a firm line.

Raz slowly lowered the quill and stood, already knowing the answer to his next question. "Any survivors?"

"None."

He placed his hands on his desk and hung his head. The documents by his fingers blurred as his mind spun. There were children aboard. "What happened?"

"We don't know. I'm on my way to inspect the ship myself."

The king straightened and rounded the table. "Then I shall go with you."

He passed Valen, who was just a touch shorter than he was. Valen huffed and adjusted his leather belt before falling in line. Their boots rustled against the thick deep-red carpets as they made their way down the corridor. The arched black-stone ceilings were simple in their design but effective. With a palace built into the side of the mountain, it wasn't easy to make the place feel open.

Lush tapestries hung along the walls—both beautiful and practical in nature. The stone didn't keep heat, but the fabric deterred much of the chill.

They reached the wide spiral staircase at the end of the hallway and jogged downward, their boots clicking with each step. As a child, Raz hated the stairs. It took too long to get anywhere, and they made his legs hurt. Now, as an adult, he still didn't care for them. He'd rather meet Skye on one of the landing balconies every residence had for their own *fiilee* and fly wherever he needed to go.

"You're quiet," Valen commented as they exited the stairs toward the nesting grounds and the face of the mountain.

Raz grunted. "Not sure what to say after your announcement."

"I've known you since we were children. It's more than that."

"It seems trivial now." Raziel glanced at his friend from the corner of his eye. Valen brushed one of his brown braids from his shoulder and arched a brow. The king knew that look. His friend wouldn't let it drop until he spoke the truth. "I was married today."

Valen's brows rose high. "I didn't know you'd made a decision."

"It must be done."

"But a Sirenidae?" Valen shuddered. "They're monsters."

He agreed but just shrugged. "Our people need healers and solutions. The devils of the deep have the answers." He hoped.

The corridor widened slightly, and the scent of animals, straw, and warm stone reached him. The king paused at the end of the corridor where it opened into a massive cavern. *Fiilee* nested in all corners. Some felines watched them with curiosity, others with boredom or wariness. *Fiilee* only bonded with a rider and possibly their mate, but it wasn't always guaranteed.

Valen whistled, and a female *fiilee* striped black-and-orange dove from a nest high above. She circled several times before landing with almost no sound in front of Valen. She took a swipe at his commander who dodged it easily. If Sunset had wanted to hurt him, she would have. Sunset was just as playful as Valen could be, which was why they made such an excellent pair.

Raz whistled his own tune, watching as Valen pulled a treat from his pocket and held it out to his *fiilee*. She snuffled his flat palm before gently taking the gift and swallowing it whole. Sunset released a deep purr before pressing her head under his arm.

A familiar roar pulled the king's attention to his own *fiilee*. Skye circled high above, his coat almost blending in with the cavern ceiling. The showoff spun and looped a few more times before closing his massive bat-like wings and diving. Raziel held his position. It was a game he and Skye liked to play to see who'd flinch first. His heart raced as the gigantic feline sped toward him. At the very last moment, Skye flared his wings, blasting a gust of air and dirt over Raz, blowing his hair back.

Skye dropped to the floor, his light blue eyes looking all too smug.

"You cheated. I had to blink because of the dirt you stirred up," Raziel growled, eyeing his preening beast.

His bonded chuffed and sauntered closer until they were eye to eye. Even after all these years, Skye still amazed him. The *fiilee* dropped his head and butted him in the chest. At one time, the greeting would have knocked the king off his feet but no longer.

Sinking his fingers into Skye's soft fur, he hugged his feline, and Skye released a contented chirrup. There was nothing quite like the companionship of a *fiilee*. Even though the animal could not speak to him in words, they understood each other in a way he didn't understand most people.

"We must go," he murmured, combing his fingers through Skye's thick fur that was more black spots than faint white undercoat. "Our people need us." He released Skye and walked to the cavern wall. Harnesses, saddles, and a variety of riding gear hung in all sizes. "Saddle?"

Skye's light blue eyes seemed to narrow.

Raziel sighed. It had been worth a shot. While he didn't need a saddle and preferred to be without one, when they traveled over the sea, the king liked to have the extra assurance that he was secure. He could swim, but there was something about the ocean that unnerved him. It was unpredictable and dangerous.

Just like your new wife will be.

He brushed the thought away and yanked the harness from the wall harder than he meant to. He held it out to Skye. "Shall we?"

THERE WAS NOTHING MORE BEAUTIFUL THAN flying above Methi. Between the sharp peaks of the Hollow Mountain range, to the jeweled forests of Laos, to the rolling waves of the Emerald Coast. They passed over the hot springs and then all too soon, the Wasting Corals rose in the distance. The lime-green coral protruded from the sea like witch's fingers—sickly and misshapen.

His stomach dipped as they began their travels over the sea.

Water closing over his head, silence, and panic...

Raziel pushed away the older memory and focused on Skye. The beast would not let him fall into the sea. And even if they did, Raz knew how to swim. He just needed to battle the fear.

His *fiilee* chirruped and the king patted his bonded. "I'm alright."

They flew around the eastern perimeter of the corals. It was forbidden to fly over them. The corals were poisonous. All it took was just one touch or scrape for your life to be over. And it wasn't quick. The poison took its time, making you so sick, you couldn't eat or drink until your body wasted away or gave up.

Raziel frowned as he spotted new corals growing beneath the water. It was spreading more rapidly than it had in years past.

Why? That was the question.

Still, they soared on until they reached the northernmost edge of the Wasting Corals.

A Methi ship bobbed a safe distance away from the poisonous corals, but the *Zephyr* was aground them. Large spears had pierced the hull, and the mast was snapped in two. Parts of the deck were still in good condition, and his stomach dropped as he spotted bodies strewn about.

He and Skye landed on the warship.

The king slid from Skye's back and landed on the deck in a crouch. He stood and the crew bowed. Even after years of being royal, the practice still made him uncomfortable. Raziel was there to serve, not the other way around. He nodded to them, and Captain Eliah limped her way to the front of the crowd, short brown ruffled hair falling into her metallic green eyes.

"My liege," Eliah said, before getting down to business. "How would you like us to proceed?"

"Why haven't the bodies been recovered?" he asked.

"The laws forbid us from approaching the Wasting Corals, my lord. And as you can see, the corals have expanded. The ship is well beyond our reach." She gestured to the lime-green smudges underneath the water. "We have no aerial support, and even if we did, the ship is unstable. It's too much of a risk to endanger the *fiilee* and it's against the law." The captain rubbed her leg, a permanent repercussion from the Warlord's War.

Despite the seriousness of the situation, Raziel grinned. There was no one more devoted to the law than Eliah. "I agree with you. I would not risk the *fiilee*, but we need to recover the bodies. They should be returned to their families. Do you have a dinghy?"

"We do, my lord."

"Then we shall make use of it." The thought of traveling over the Wasting Corals in a tiny boat made him feel sick, but it needed to be done. Raziel steeled himself. "Only those who are experienced swimmers will travel with us. We need four men in addition to me and Valen."

Eliah blinked at him. "We work on a ship, my lord. We are all excellent swimners."

Raz smirked, balancing on the balls of his feet as the ship rocked. "How right you are."

Valen stepped closer to his side. "I don't think it's wise for you to go."

"I must see this through."

Skye's tail flicked from left to right as he turned to his bonded. "You cannot come with me this time." The feline huffed, biting at his shirt. "I know you don't like it, but there's no other choice."

"All ready, my lord," Eliah called.

The king strode across the starboard side of the ship. He slung a leg over the railing and nimbly descended the rope ladder. Once his feet touched the bottom of the dinghy, he quickly sat and picked up an oar. Three other people joined him in the boat: an older man with a long salt-and-pepper beard, a boy who was as gangly as a sapling, and a young woman with her hair shoved into a faded knit hat. He frowned as she kept her gaze averted from his as if looking at him was painful.

Valen plopped down next to him, and Eliah shoved away from the ship. Raziel's stomach flipped, and he gritted his teeth as the little boat bobbed and Eliah positioned herself at the rudder.

Raz could do this. The ocean wouldn't be the death of him. He'd survived its claws before.

Sweat dampened his brow as they began to row

toward the *Zephyr*. Water splashed over the edge and onto his hand. He barely kept from flinching.

A mouth full of water. Too much pressure . . .

"Steady all," Eliah called. The little dinghy passed over the Wasting Corals border. "Keep your paddling shallow, ya?"

It was eerily silent as they made their way to the *Zephyr*. The chartreuse coral rose from the depths below, at first peeking out of the water and then rising like deformed sculptures.

"How did they get this far?" Raz murmured. The ship must have plowed over several hundred feet of coral before crashing. "Was there a storm?"

"Not the stormy season," Eliah muttered, redirecting the boat around a large chunk of broken coral that looked as if it was oozing water.

"Then what happened?"

"We don't know. No one in their right mind would come near the corals, especially a fishing vessel."

That was his thought as well. He exchanged an uneasy glance with Valen as they neared the *Zephyr*.

"Coven, scale the ship and toss down a rope," Eliah commanded.

"Aye, Captain," the young woman replied. She gathered up a lasso of rope and tossed it over her shoulder as the captain navigated the boat next to the ship.

"Be careful."

The young woman nodded, her eyes still averted from

Raz. His heart leapt when she jumped from the dinghy, rocking the small vessel onto the side of the *Zephyr* and slamming her blade into the ship. His jaw dropped as she scurried up the side in record time. She disappeared over the railing and began tying off the rope.

"Impressive, isn't it?" Eliah commented.

"She has skills," he admitted. Someone with reflexes like that should be a rider.

Coven tossed the thick rope down, and Raz stood.

Valen held a hand out. "Let me go first, my lord."

The king allowed his commander to shimmy up the rope and over the edge before he hauled himself up. Raz's breath heaved in and out as he reached the deck. Not because the climb was strenuous but because he kept imagining falling back into the water.

He scanned the deck, counting the bodies.

Fifteen total.

The stench hit him, and he swallowed hard before sucking in a short breath. The older sailor with the long beard moved past him and knelt next to the nearest body. "There's a hole." His voice held shock.

Raziel strode to his side and tried to make sense of what he was seeing.

The man was missing his heart.

"Her heart was torn out," Valen whispered.

The king glanced at his commander on the port side of the ship, the hair along his arms rising. "What did you just say?"

Valen's blue eyes met Raziel's and held. "Her heart was yanked from her chest."

"This one as well," Eliah said, her voice ragged.

Raziel wiped his hand over his face. "Check them all."

Every person bore marks from the sun, scavengers, and decay, but they were all missing their hearts.

"What would do such a thing?" Coven whispered, covering her mouth, her eyes haunted. "What would kill just for the heart?"

A chill ran down his spine.

Sirenidae.

"We need to leave now." Valen's tone held no room for argument. "This is too dangerous."

"I agree, my lord," Eliah added. "We can come back for the bodies."

"No," Raziel growled. He scanned the bodies along with the dried blood that led to the edges of the deck. "We get them now."

"What's wrong?" Cove asked.

"Sirens," the older man growled. "Clearly, this is the demons' work."

The king's throat bobbed as he spotted a smaller body on the deck holding a stuffed animal. Raziel tuned the crew out and tugged the shirt off his body, kneeling. He tried not to look too closely at the wee one as he wrapped them up. Tears dripped down his cheeks as he tucked the ragged toy into their hands.

This was wrong.

It should never have happened.

He pulled the small body into his arms, woodenly moving toward the railing. Rage, pain, and hatred boiled in his chest. The Sirenidae would pay for what they'd done.

"I will avenge you," he vowed.

They'd declared war, and Raziel would answer tenfold.

Chapter Nine

MER

It was all Mer could do to not get into the water.

It had been almost three weeks since she'd been in the ocean. She didn't fear disobeying her grandfather, as they'd long since left the warmer waters of her kingdom. Sirenidae couldn't survive the cold waters of the north, so no one would be following them to report back.

Yet Mer still stayed on the deck of the ship despite how the healers took a short dip now and then. Just long enough to be refreshed even though they returned with blue lips and shaking limbs.

She'd done a lot of things she wasn't proud of, but her honor wouldn't let her break her word on this. She was a banished one. The sea would spit the likes of her right back out or swallow her whole.

Misery clung to her as she strained her eyes south, as if she could still see her home if she squinted hard enough, but the turquoise waters of Thalassa were gone. Along with part of her heart.

A raspy laugh escaped her at the thought, and she squeezed the smooth railing.

Mer didn't have a heart left.

It had been torn from her chest when Ream died and then again when her grandfather had shackled her to her husband's murderer. Only three things kept her going when despair threatened to drown her.

First, that she'd protected Sin and the rest of their kin.

Second, she finally had a lead on Ceto thanks to Sin. He'd managed to smuggle himself onto the Methian ship. A merchant had seen two of the missing girls on a ship bound for Methi. It wasn't a lot to go on, but it was something. Two missing Sirenidae girls from different cities on the same ship? It wasn't a coincidence. It wasn't proof of anything, but at least it was a direction to go in. Mer didn't know what she would find in the forest kingdom, but hopefully soon, she would have some answers.

And third, she kept imagining the Methian king's demise. He'd pay for what he'd done.

Just like you have?

Her gaze dropped down to her hands, and she ran her thumb over the pads of her fingers. They seemed slick, as if covered in blood. There were things she'd done that would haunt Mer for the rest of her life, but she couldn't go back and change the past. Only move forward.

Determination filled her. Mer would do anything to fulfill her husband's last wish.

Even if he was a traitor. Even if he had lied to her. *Even if* he had done horrible things.

It was her secret shame.

She still loved the man who'd betrayed her and their people.

He didn't deserve her kindness, but she would do this one last thing.

Especially if it helped others.

It would put his memory to rest, and she could find some peace if such a thing existed.

A vibration went through the ship, and she frowned as the water rippled unnaturally across the waves.

What the devil?

Sailors began cursing around her. Mer tore her attention away from the odd ripples and glanced over her shoulder to see the crew fly into a flurry of movement.

Captain Velicu barked orders as she dropped down onto the deck, her sleeveless long coat flapping in the wind. Her reflective brown eyes met Mer's.

"What's wrong?" she demanded.

The stern female captain frowned, her golden face a mask of bad news. "Danger, my lady. You must get below."

"Danger from what?" Mer asked, fully facing Velicu.

"Kraken."

"A kraken?" Mer's brows rose. They were the stuff of myths—old fish tales told to scare little tadpoles into going to bed early and to never wander too far. "You cannot be serious?"

"Deadly," Captain Velicu deadpanned. "Let's pray it's not hungry."

Her first mate, Jelei, joined the group, his attention on the captain. "There should be none this far south. We're not even in their territory."

"I know," the captain bit out.

"What can I do to help?" Mer felt panic in the air. Even the Sirenidae healers looked terrified, huddling near the mast.

Velicu pushed the gray-and-brown braids from her face, lips thin. "Call on whatever God you worship that we make it out alive." The vibration came again, almost rattling Mer's teeth. "Man the harpoons!" the captain roared.

Another harsh tremor, along with a hum that came from beneath Mer's feet.

The ship lurched to the right, and Mer launched for the railing.

"Fire!" Captain Velicu shouted.

The hum paused for a moment before a massive tentacle shot from the sea and slammed onto the deck. Mer gaped at the milky limb covered in bright blue-and-gold circular markings. A sailor stabbed at it with his sword. The tentacle slammed into him, grabbed the screaming man by the foot, and yanked him into the sea.

Mer yanked the dagger from the sheath at her thigh and peeked over the edge of the railing. The screams slowly faded as her heartbeat took up cadence in her ears. Three more tentacles as thick as the mast were crawling up the port side of the ship.

How was any creature that large? Just what kind of monsters did they raise in Methi?

Mouth dry, she watched the tentacles explore, their translucent suckers the size of dinner plates kissing the side of the ship as if looking for any weakness.

"My lady!"

Mer tore her gaze from the horror below as the captain strode through the chaos on high-heeled boots like she battled monsters every day.

The captain glared at Mer and pointed toward the mast. "Get away from the railing. We're abandoning ship."

Mer shook her head as if she didn't understand her words. She caught sight of two dinghies the men were trying to get into the water. "We can't."

"We must, princess. The kraken has chosen this ship as its own. It will sink. No one will survive. We need to leave now while the beast is busy. This ship belongs to Ceto now."

Mer startled. "Ceto?"

"Sea."

She'd have to revisit this conversation later. Mer eyed the two small boats again, then the crew and the healers. One thing was abundantly clear.

There wasn't enough room for everyone.

"You plan to get everyone off this ship?" Mer shouted over the chaos.

Velicu grimaced. "We will do what we must, and you are my priority, tasked to me by the queen."

That wasn't good enough. Mer's palms grew sweaty as she glanced down at the creeping tentacles nearing the deck. No one should have to die because they were transporting a traitorous princess.

She swung over the railing just as the captain lunged for Mer. Velicu held her wrist in an iron-tight grip.

"Get back over here," the captain growled.

"I am saving us all." Mer met the woman's steely gaze. "Tell your men to stop shooting. I'm going to draw it away."

Captain Velicu studied her for a moment and then released her. "If you die, I'll bring you back and kill you myself."

"Deal." Mer grinned at the captain and then turned her back to the railing. She tightened her fingers around the hilt of her dagger. The seeking tentacles had almost reached her bare feet. She took a deep breath and then dove.

Air whistled through her ears a second before she sliced through the water. Mer gasped as her gills immediately flared open. The shock of the cold water bit into her tender flesh and caused the scales along her arms to slightly shiver. Mer put space between herself and the ship and blinked her eyes hard to clear her vision.

The water felt . . . denser, as if it sought to put her down.

She spun around and gaped.

The kraken was larger than the merchant ship. Larger than most homes.

The giant beastie clung to the bottom of the ship like it was trying to devour it. Sharp ivory teeth hovered right in the center of its tentacles, like it was ready to pierce the bottom of the ship. The kraken hummed again.

Mer palmed her dagger, her fingers aching because of the cold. Killing the creature wasn't impossible, but it wasn't easy. The kraken clicked, and the translucent fringe around its head began to flutter. It reminded her of the squid of Thalassa. Was it trying to communicate?

Try singing.

It couldn't hurt.

She licked her lips and began to hum. Mer didn't know the language of this creature, but it couldn't be that different from the squid and octopi of the south. They were highly intelligent creatures. Surely it would understand she was trying to communicate.

Unless it thinks you are prey.

Every inhale she took burned, but she kept singing. The dark eye of the kraken latched onto her, and Mer could tell she had its attention. Its tentacles began to writhe angrily, thrashing harder.

That wasn't the right tone.

Mer grimaced, treading water and adjusting her tune, trying to match the kraken's hums and vibrations. Her heart raced as its tentacles slowed their jerky movements. It was listening to her song.

That's it. Be calm.

Her stomach dropped when the kraken started to release the ship and drifted away. It was too good to be true. It didn't swim away or sink into the glittering emerald water down to the dark trench below that gaped like a giant mouth. Instead, it faced her, looming so large, it was almost like a mountain. She held steady as it gracefully glided toward her.

Mer held her hand out, her fingers screaming at how tightly she gripped the dagger. The beast paused, just listening as she continued to sing. A thread of panic tightened around her chest as one massive tentacle reached toward her.

Don't run.

Ever so gently, it explored her hand and the blade, the tentacle wrapped around her forearm. It would be so easy for the beastie to kill her, and yet . . . the kraken was infinitely gentle in its exploration. Her breath caught as the kraken hummed and light illuminated the circular markings on its body and the fringe outlining the crown of its head.

She'd never seen something so beautiful.

A faint trill reached her ears.

The beast released her and drifted away.

Mer watched it move toward the trench. She squinted as a creature darted into the dark. Mer swam a few paces forward, but it was gone. The kraken gave one more vibrating hum before stuffing itself into the trench and disappearing as if it had not been there at all.

She stared after the beast until her feet touched the sea floor.

Startled, she glanced toward the surface and back to the trench.

Mer had just interacted with a myth. A living legend.

Her heart raced with fear and a bit of excitement.

Shivers started to rock her body, and each movement seemed a little bit slower than the next.

Pushing off the rocky bottom, Mer swam for the surface, the cold water sucking all her energy. It was like swimming through syrup, each movement stiff and diffi-cult. Mer gritted her teeth as her head swam. This was how Sirenidae died in the north.

They froze to death.

With all her remaining strength, Mer struggled back to the ship. She popped up beside the ship, shivering as her gills purged the water and sealed shut. Her first breath felt like inhaled needles, sharp and painful.

Shouts from above cut through the air, and soon a rope was dropped down. Mer slipped her arms through the loop and hung as the crew pulled her up and over the railing.

Captain Velicu glared at Mer as she shivered on the deck. "That was one of the most foolish things I have seen in my life," the captain chastised, tossing her long coat around Mer's hunched shoulders. "But we owe you our lives."

"It was nothing," Mer chattered, feeling like her eyelids were too heavy.

The captain rubbed her hands up and down Mer's arms. "Your lips are blue, and I'm assured that is not a natural state for Sirenidae. It seems you maybe have hypothermia. Best be off to bed before you catch your death."

"What could a little cold do when I tamed a kraken?" Mer chattered, her teeth clacking together.

Velicu rolled her eyes. "There will be no living with you now. The next two weeks are going to be miserable, aren't they?"

"Perhaps."

A Sirenidae healer took her arm. "Let's get you settled, my lady."

Mer let herself be led away, but she overheard Jelei saying, "Just wait until the king hears about this. With a queen who can control the kraken by his side, Methi will be unstoppable."

Disgust filled her along with a healthy dose of dread at

the thought of seeing the Methian king. It was quickly followed with the rage she kept kindled especially for him.

She wouldn't let him make use of her in any way. The time was coming for retribution. Mer glanced out at the horizon.

He'd pay for what he'd done, and she'd take everything important to him.

And maybe, just maybe, she'd use an army of krakens to do it.

Chapter Ten

RAZIEL

THE SMOKE FROM THE PYRES CLUNG TO RAZIEL.

The taste of ash coated the roof of his mouth. It was as if ash coated every inch of him.

They'd laid to rest the fishermen from the *Zephyr* and with that, heralded the arrival of his bride.

His horse pranced beneath him, feeding off his dark energy. Each step closer to the coast, his anger ratcheted up a notch. He hadn't asked many questions about Mer Thalassa when his mother offered him the marriage contract. Raz vaguely knew of her from the Warlord's War. She was the sea king's granddaughter and the one responsible for all the attacks on enemy warships. He was unconscious at the time, but apparently, she'd saved him from drowning. By all accounts, she was a masterful tactician with a compassionate heart.

That's how the stories went.

Raziel didn't know if he believed a single one. The Sirenidae hadn't interfered in the politics of the surface in eons, and yet they did now.

Why? That was the question.

What agenda did they have to join the war? Or to marry one of their princesses off, for that matter?

None of it made sense.

It doesn't have to. You got what you wanted.

King Raziel had secured a bride with powerful healers and drugs. Surely, they'd end the Mirror Plague, and his people could prosper.

As long as sirens weren't ripping their hearts out.

He cursed underneath his breath, anger igniting in his belly once again. While no one had seen the Sirenidae attack the *Zephyr*, there was undeniable proof.

The missing hearts.

The Sirenidae were elusive, and the only proof of their existence was the carnage of ships and bodies left in their wake. Every once in a while, a sailor or fisherman would claim to have seen one, but their descriptions were all different. Haunting songs were supposed to drive a crew to madness. No one had truly come face to face with the siren and lived to tell the tale.

Including children.

His fingers tightened on the reins, and he squeezed his eyes shut, trying to block out the stuffed children's toy from the ship. Nightmares about the *Zephyr* had plagued him for two weeks without letting up.

Enough. Focus.

He blew out a breath and opened his eyes.

Soon he would have one in his hands: a Sirenidae who would answer for what her people had done.

He'd get the answers he sought.

Even if it meant he ended up a widower.

WAITING ON THE DOCKS WAS EXCRUCIATING.

Not because of the needle-like ocean spray or the winds that howled but because he'd meet his new bride soon.

Or new enemy.

He squinted at the sails of the Methian flagship in the distance.

Soon enough, he'd meet her.

"Don't worry, my son. She's your perfect match," his mother said softly.

He nodded but said nothing.

What a perfect match looked like, Raz didn't know.

All that mattered was that he needed a queen, a cure, and answers about the latest attack, not a friend or wife.

Someone to fill the position and bring prosperity to Methi.

Liar.

Raz brushed the thought away. All he needed to do was focus on her dowry. The Sirenidae king had been generous with the sum. The dowry would keep Methi running for several lifetimes even if the whole kingdom did nothing but lay around and drink.

It was everything he wanted.

Then why did he feel so hollow? So bitter?

Because you're alone.

A grunt escaped him.

His mother arched a brow. "Something on your mind?"

"It's nothing."

"Mm-hmm." The dowager queen pulled her cloak tighter around her figure. "I'll let that lie go."

Raziel shot a smile at his mum. She'd always known him best.

The ship drew closer and with it, the ire of the storm.

The dark skies broke open, and water rushed from the heavens, drenching their party in seconds. He wiped the rain from his eyes, and his breath seized when he spotted a lone figure standing at the bow of the ship. Her unusually short silver hair just touched her pale bare shoulders. He could almost feel her magenta gaze running over him, appraising.

She was tall for a woman. Willowy but strong as she held the railing while the rain, spray, and wind tore at her. She didn't move, almost as if she couldn't look away from him.

"Are you ready?" his mother asked.

"I was ready the moment I signed the marriage certificate." He'd made his choice weeks ago and hadn't wavered. This was the right decision. For his people. For the future.

The dowager queen snorted. "Marriage written on a scroll is something completely different than marriage in and of itself." She scanned his face and frowned. "Stars above, son, paste a smile on your face. You look like you're attending a funeral."

Raz arched a brow. "I just left a funeral." He ignored the grief that creased her face at the reminder, and his attention moved back to the Sirenidae who'd be his queen, but the bow was empty. "It's better she sees me like this than for her to hope for something that will never happen."

The blue-green waves crashed against the dock and battered against sharp black rocks jutting from the sea around them as if they wanted to lay claim to the land too. Rain slicked the wood beneath his boots as he shifted. The flight home would be rough.

The ship entered the harbor.

Goosebumps rose along his arms as a haunting tune cut through the air and seemed to vibrate from the sea. His attention snapped to the murky water.

Leviathan.

A huge black fin sliced through the water before disappearing beside the dock as if it had never been there.

"It seems the princess has brought monstrous protectors with her," Valen commented behind Raz.

His mother tsked. "The Sirenidae's entourage proceeds her."

And what an entourage it was. This area wasn't known for leviathan. It wasn't good hunting grounds, and yet they swarmed the area.

They were the wolves of the sea.

The dowager queen took one step closer to his left side and away from the dock edge.

"Do you really think Sirenidae can control them?" he asked his mum.

"I've seen a great many things over my life, and they can communicate through song and whistles with the beasties. I don't know if they control them, but they can influence the leviathan," she answered, eyeing one who rolled onto its side as if to study them.

Uncanny and yet . . . useful for Methi if the queen had such powers.

The ship groaned as the crew weighed anchor.

He frowned.

The ship looked rough, like it had been through battle.

What the blazes happened on the journey here?

They lowered a dinghy, and Raz stared hard as the crew parted, standing on either side of a swinging rope ladder. Raziel watched as his queen strode to the edge of the ship and stared at the little boat.

She lifted her head, the wind tugging at her silky dress that melded to her body in the rain and wind.

Time stilled as they stared at each other.

There was something hauntingly beautiful about her and yet also . . . off-putting.

The princess smirked at him and glanced at the water, breaking the spell.

A yell caught in his throat when she ignored the ladder and instead dove over the dinghy and right off the side of the ship, plunging into the churning water. The songs of the leviathan rose in pitch, and he clenched his jaw, taking one step closer to the edge of the dock.

Why the theatrics?

He scanned the water for any sign of his bride.

It wouldn't do if she was eaten in his bay before they'd even properly met.

Delicate hands surged from the water and seized the edge of the jetty. The Sirenidae princess hauled herself from the freezing water, magenta eyes pinned on him. He flinched as her gills spurted water along her neck and then sealed closed. She flashed him a smile, her incisors sharper than his own.

More fish than human.

Disgust rolled in his gut, but he schooled his expression.

He held his ground and refused to back down as she cocked a hip and sashayed his way, too much skin on display—her dress nearly transparent. Raziel gritted his teeth and yanked at the clasp of his cloak, ready to toss it over her shoulders. While she didn't care for her modesty, it seemed he would have to.

His fingers spasmed, and he gasped as the most intoxicating scent reached him. He inhaled deeply and lurched forward. Raz found himself striding toward her, the cloak slipping from his grip and dropping onto the deck in a damp puddle. Heat flushed through his body, and he reached a hand toward the Sirenidae. All he wanted was to just touch her skin. One single touch would be enough to douse the raging inferno inside him.

She smiled, batting his hand away, and stepped into his space as if to embrace Raziel. His eyes closed, unable to stifle the groan that escaped him when her fingers traced his chest.

Yes, this was exactly what he wanted, no, what he needed—

Lightning quick, she shoved and knocked his legs out from underneath him. Raz slammed onto his back, air leaving his lungs. Cold magenta eyes glared down at him as his bride straddled him. He smiled at her, barely registering the prick of pain at his throat when his hands rested on her bare thighs. Fog settled over his mind, and all he could think of was the beauty hovering above him. Distantly, he registered shouts, but Raz couldn't care less. This was exactly where he was meant to be.

He shifted restlessly, wanting to press against her body, but couldn't find it in himself to move. It was as if he was drunk.

She snapped something at him in a lilting language, pulling his attention to her soft pink lips, the shade of the inside of a shell. He wanted to taste them. No, *needed* to taste them.

Another whisper of pain registered fleetingly as he leaned up into her space, desperate to sample her lips. To assuage some of the desperate longing.

Her breath caressed his own. "I hope you suffer as much as I am," she hissed.

In the back of his mind, warning bells rang, but he couldn't focus on them.

Deep pain registered a moment before the princess was torn from his grasp.

Raz bellowed and rolled to his feet, blades in each hand. His arms shook as he stared at the two warriors restraining the queen. How dare they put their hands on his wife?

"Release her," he growled, taking a step toward the princess.

He paused when his mother placed a firm hand on his chest. Raz stared down at her hard dark eyes. "What?"

"Come back to me, my boy. Take a step back." She slipped her handkerchief to his neck. "Move away."

"I want," he rumbled, not able to take his eyes from the beautiful woman as his mum gently pushed him away. "She needs me. I need . . ."

"No, my love. Take a deep breath and come back to me."

Raz frowned, trying to understand her words.

He hadn't gone anywhere, had he? All he wanted was . . . Raziel shook his head, trying to clear the fog and lust clouding his mind.

Sharp pain shot up his neck to his jaw, and he flinched.

He blinked repeatedly at his mother, who still had not released him. All the while, his female guards dragged the fighting queen down the dock toward the beach. Slowly, he touched the handkerchief just beneath his ear. Pulling back, he saw that his fingertips were bloody. That didn't make any sense.

"Take another breath," his mum whispered, stepping close to tie the scarf tightly around his neck.

"What just happened?" he asked gravely, feeling like the world had turned on its side. Everything was foggy.

His gaze was pulled toward the fighting princess, his new queen.

His mum cupped his cheek and turned his attention

back to her. She bared her teeth, and her expression was full of anger. "Your new wife attacked you."

Raziel blinked slowly.

That was a first.

No one had ever wanted to kill him before they even knew him.

Chapter Eleven

MER

SHE WAS GOING TO DIE, BUT IT WAS WORTH IT.

A wild laugh bubbled from her lips as the king of Methi glared at her with blood running down his neck. She'd almost slit his throat. Only a few more seconds beneath her shell blade, and he would have been dead.

As dead as Ream—the husband he'd stolen from her.

She licked her lips and continued to fight the warriors that held her. The dowager queen stepped away from her son, her lip curled in distaste. The queen mother had been smart, siccing female warriors on Mer. The Lure didn't work quite as well with them. She glanced at the two women, noting they were mirrors of each other. Same long curly brown hair, same metallic bronze eyes, a sprinkle of freckles across their noses, and warm umber skin.

Twins. How quaint.

Mer dismissed them and locked gazes with the dowager queen. She bared her teeth at the queen mother in a victorious smile. His dear mother didn't like that.

Mer had planned to ruin the king's life, but when she saw him on the dock, something snapped inside her that she couldn't control. The look of horror on his face when he shook off the Lure was enough to satisfy the fire of hate that raged inside her.

Just a little bit.

Mer licked the saltwater off her lips and shuddered. It tasted nothing like home, less salty and more like algae. Goosebumps ran up and down her arms as shivers wracked her body. Swimming in the ocean one last time, even if it wasn't home, had been worth it. She'd sung the hunt song with the leviathans, glimpsed the kelp forests with their waving scarlet fronds, and experienced the serenity of the water.

It was the perfect goodbye to this world.

The rain pelted them as the wind and waves battered the dock. The storm was worsening.

Her body wanted to hunch over to conserve heat, but Mer held her head up high. She wouldn't cower in her last moments. The warrior to the right clipped a set of manacles too tightly around her left wrist, breaking the skin before they clasped her right. The pain was momentary.

Plus, they'd made a mistake. They'd cuffed her hands in front of her. The warriors had given her a weapon with which to strangle the king.

He had recovered, his expression turning from infatuated to frosty.

She smiled at him and winked, watching his expression harden further.

Good. She wanted him as angry as she was.

He pulled a black kerchief from his pocket and wrapped it around his nose and mouth. The king had learned his lesson, it seemed. Raziel stalked down the dock. There wasn't another word for the way he moved. It was predatory, and it called to the darkest part of Mer.

The warrior to her right kicked Mer's legs out from beneath her, and her knees hit the wet, rough wooden deck. Pain ricocheted up her thighs, but she ignored it.

"You will kneel before your king."

"He is not my king," she snapped, staring down Raziel, the Methian King.

Death was prowling her way, and she didn't want to miss a minute of it.

He paused before her, and she had to tip her head back to meet his glare from over the edge of the kerchief. Mer blinked the rain out of her eyes. His dark red hair hung around his face in ropes, looking like rivulets of rich Aermian wine. His eyes were like the fine edge of a blade as he stared down at her. Sharp and piercing. Deadly.

Was this how he looked before he cut Ream down?

A wave of grief, rage, and hate crashed over her.

Mer lunged for him, managing to get to her feet. He caught her by the throat, his calloused palm abrading her sensitive gills. She snapped her teeth in his face and sank her nails into his forearm.

Two could play that game.

He lifted until her toes scrambled for purchase on the slick wooden deck. Time slowed as she stared up into the fierce eyes of the one person who'd taken her world from her. A deranged laugh gurgled in the back of her throat as she fought to breathe.

"Do it," she challenged.

King Raziel cocked his head. "What?"

"Kill me." It was a dare and a plea. She was so bloody tired of the nightmares, of the sleepless nights, of the world and its pain.

He pulled her a little closer until their noses almost touched. "No, I need you, unfortunately, you bloodthirsty little thing."

Then she'd make him do it. Mer lurched forward to bite his throat, intending to tear it out with her teeth if necessary.

His gaze flattened, and he slammed his head against her temple.

Stars and pain burst across her vision, and she managed to slur out, "You'll never survive me."

THE METHIANS DID NOT TAKE KINDLY TO assassination attempts.

Mer discreetly tugged at the manacles that were tightly clasped around her wrists. She'd awoken to the gentle sway of a horse, a pounding headache, and the scent of wet horseflesh in her nose. They'd tossed her over the mount like common goods.

So, they hadn't killed her. Interesting.

Keeping her eyes closed and breathing shallowly through the nausea, she pulled on the cuffs again. Nothing.

"Stop wiggling," a sharp female voice commanded. "Or you'll fall off the horse."

The game was up.

Mer stopped pretending to be asleep and lifted her pounding head.

The dowager queen rode beside them. The regal older woman arched a cool eyebrow but said nothing else. As if she was daring Mer to argue with her.

Not in this position. While she hated the king, the older woman Mer could have some respect for.

Each step the four-legged animal took jarred Mer, the shoulders of the horse digging into her ribs. She'd be bruised for sure. Blood rushed to her head, and she swayed. That wasn't good. A firm but warm hand pressed between her shoulder blades as if comforting her.

Mer's brows furrowed. That was unexpected.

"Deep breaths and steady yourself," one of the female warrior's demanded.

Mer squinted, turned her sore neck, and peered up at the woman who rode behind her. "What's your name?" she croaked.

The woman's eyes narrowed, but she answered grudgingly. "Mazie."

"What a pretty name."

Mazie scowled, tossing her head, long curls bouncing with the movement.

"You have gorgeous hair." And Mer meant it. Although, it seemed impractical not to have bound such hair as a warrior. Gauging from the polished leather uniform, they weren't planning on an actual attack.

Fools.

Mazie frowned, her deep coral eyes turning downward.

Flattery wasn't going to get Mer anywhere with that one.

She hummed and scanned the convoy. Ten riders total including herself, the dowager queen, and the king. Very little protection for three royals. It wouldn't be too hard to . . .

"You're not going anywhere, so get that out of your head," Mazie warned.

"What makes you think I was planning an escape?" Mer replied with a lazy air.

"You just assessed each of the riders."

Point to Mazie. The woman was sharp.

Mer wasn't trying to escape. She was measuring what she was up against. The king hadn't killed her, so that told her either he was extremely tolerant or a deviant who planned to torture her. A sigh slipped past her lips. There was only one person she could blame for her predicament and that was herself.

She'd lost her temper, and it had cost her.

All the careful planning of the last few weeks went right out the door when she'd locked eyes with the king. His smug-looking face coupled with the ache of losing Ream had overwhelmed Mer until all she could think of was revenge.

It was as if the last six months had not passed. The guilt and loss and rage had all rushed back in a fierce cocktail of pain. One she couldn't break out of.

Ream's betrayal hadn't mattered in the moment when she'd dove off the ship, or when she'd hunted the king from the sea, or when she'd pulled her shell blade and slit his throat.

All she could see was the light leaving Ream's eyes and the heaviness of his still form in her arms.

A shiver wracked her body as the bloody rain began again. It dripped down her cheeks but not down her back. She glanced over her shoulder, noticing a black cloak thrown over her. It held the scent of pine, smoke, and something spicy. Who'd given their cloak to her?

Her lips thinned as she observed the group. The king only wore a soaking wet linen shirt and a leather harness on top with various weapons strapped to it. Immediately, she wanted the cloak off. Childish, yes, but necessary. Mer managed to unclip the cloak, her manacles clinking together. She smiled with satisfaction when it slipped from her back and onto the muddy ground.

Mazie sighed, slowing the horse. "You are troublesome."

"You have no idea." She shrugged. "If you try to put that cloak back on me, I will only remove it again."

"Leave it then," the dowager queen snapped at the female warrior. "If she wants to suffer in the cold, so be it."

"Yes, my lady," Mazie replied.

The commotion had caught the king's attention, and he'd slowed directly across from Mer but not close enough for anything dangerous to occur. She felt his gaze on her, but she refused to give him any attention. Instead, she studied the horses and humans alike, even as her skin crawled due to his staring.

Methians were large.

In general, the nation boasted tall, strong humans. Even the women.

Over the course of the Warlord's War, Mer had observed that Methians had a wide variety of skin tones varying from tan to bronze. The assembly around her was no different. It was an enjoyable change to the sea kingdom where her people had a collection of silver, lavender, pale peach, and seafoam skin tones.

The mud squelched beneath the hooves of the horses, and the prickling at the back of her neck intensified. She gritted her teeth.

Enough. Just look at him.

Another chill ran down her spine as it continued to rain. Her hair hung in her eyes as she glanced across the short span, locking cool gazes with the Methian king. The longer she stared into his cold eyes, the more likely it seemed that they glowed like smelted silver. Her new husband now loathed her.

The feeling is mutual.

Mer forced the sneering expression on her face into a placid one. "Do you like what you see, my lord?"

He didn't answer but continued to stare over the edge of his black kerchief.

She was here for the long game. The lives of Ream's family depended on it. She'd had a moment of weakness, but now that the shock had worn off, she needed to be strategic. Gaining the king's trust would be difficult now but not impossible. All men had their faults, and this one, well he was proud. She could see it in every line and angle of his body. He thought himself better than she was.

A dark chuckle sounded in her chest, and she smiled

at him, baring her teeth. "I think you do. I think you like the fact that I'm a little vicious. Just like you."

Her smile dropped when he stroked her shell knife that he'd stolen. The king had boldly placed it in the sheath at his chest.

Don't let him rile you. He's just testing the waters.

If she were a betting woman, Mer would hazard a guess that he didn't like to be challenged.

What fun it would be to toy with him.

"Keep it," she murmured, batting her lashes. "As a loving keepsake from your new queen."

His fingers spasmed against her blade, and she swallowed down her glee. She'd ruffled him, even if he was trying to hide it from her.

How delicious.

Mazie clicked her tongue, and the horse began moving faster. Mer hid a wince as the mount jostled her. The ground sped by, and Mer found herself knotting her fingers in the horse's wet mane, praying she did not fall from the mount to be trampled underneath its massive shaggy hooves.

Nausea rose up, and Mer tried to focus on the tall dark-green pine trees that crowded along the road like stoic sentinels. The muddy lane abruptly ended in a large grassy meadow dotted with deep red flowers that looked as if they had tiny little faces.

Her eyes widened as a pair of light blue feline eyes

appeared underneath the darkened boughs of the trees, and a shiver went down her spine.

Fiilee.

Mazie slowed the horse and swung down from the saddle. She wrapped her hands around Mer's bruised ribcage and helped her slide from the tall horse. Mer wobbled and locked her legs, refusing to look any weaker than she already did. Wet grass tickled the bottoms of her bare feet.

Mer swiped the water from her eyes, not moving as she watched five winged felines saunter out from beneath the pines. Her breath caught.

The *fiilee* were a sight to behold.

Her gaze latched onto the largest feline. It was covered in so many dark spots that it appeared to be black, but on close inspection, the creature had a thick white undercoat. It stretched its massive bat-like wings and shook the water off before folding them against its strong lithe body.

She'd never been this close to one of the beasties before. During the war, she had seen them in the skies, but this was something altogether different. Mer took one step toward the *fiilee,* mud and grass squishing between her toes. The feline eyed her and laid its ears back.

A warning not to come any closer.

Mer listened and redirected, keeping her eyes on the feline who watched her with glittering eyes. Mazie silently trailed her, her hand resting near the sword on her hip.

"I know," she whispered. "I'm not invading your territory. I'm just escaping the rain. You stay there, and I'll stay here."

Her legs tingled uncomfortably as Mer tried to work feeling back into them, the worst of the rain blotted out by the thick pine boughs. Just how long had she been unconscious? Her legs were numb from thigh to toe. In the water, she was light and weightless, but not here. It was always disconcerting how heavy her body felt on land.

"What are we doing here?" Mer asked Mazie.

The warrior woman said nothing, just stared at her.

The dowager queen urged her horse closer, haughtily staring down at Mer from beneath the hood of her cloak. "Whatever our king wishes."

Lovely. A spoiled king with an overprotective mother.

What did you expect?

Mer smiled at the woman and turned her back, purposely dismissing the queen. She edged farther underneath the bough of pines, her breath fogging the air.

Mazie followed behind, the gait of her steps differing.

"How'd you wound your leg?" Mer asked rubbing at her arms.

Trenches bite. She hated the cold. It was enough to make anyone grumpy.

"I was born this way."

Mer's brows rose. "And yet you're an elite warrior in the king's guard. You must be very, very good with that sword."

"I am." Not false modesty, just raw truth.

Note to self: don't anger Mazie.

She surveyed the convoy from beneath her lashes. It was telling that they hadn't brought along the Sirenidae healers and handmaidens, nor any of her things. Either it wasn't safe to travel with those, or they had wanted to get her back to the palace immediately.

It seemed none of her people were to be trusted.

Especially after you tried to kill the king.

It wasn't her best choice, but Mer couldn't find it in herself to regret her actions. Every time she saw the blood-soaked scarf around his neck, she gained a little thrill of vindictive pleasure.

Mer rubbed at her abused wrists, noting how her left still bled. They'd trussed her up like a common criminal.

Isn't that what you've become?

Scythian bodies flashed through her mind.

She shoved the thought down and gently probed at her temple. Her fingers came away bloody. The king was hardheaded, it seemed. If the headache and nausea were anything to go by, he may have given her a concussion.

Depths below, she hated him.

Goosebumps prickled across her arms, raising both the fine hair and small iridescent scales that ran along her skin in patches. Mer hated the cold, and while she had never minded being wet before, right now all she wanted was to be warm and dry.

She held her arms closer to her body to conserve heat.

No one offered her another cloak. Not that she would have taken it.

Don't show weakness.

Mer forced herself to straighten and sauntered toward the nearest tree. She leaned against the rough bark, watching the king's entourage confer with each other. She studied the man standing to the right of the Methian king, his strong jaw tight, but his fingers were gently combing through the orange-and-black fur of his *fiilee* hovering right behind him.

He was tender with the animal despite his outward anger.

A man who harbored strength and tenderness. A dangerous combination. She'd have to watch out for him, or perhaps she could use it to her advantage. Only time would tell.

The group broke apart, and the king finally faced her, seeming to swell in size. Her nose wrinkled. Sirenidae men were strong but svelte. The Methian king was built like a mountain—huge, sharp, and brutally beautiful.

She scowled at the thought. There wasn't anything beautiful about the beastly man.

He sneered right at her, and then his gaze shifted.

Mer followed his line of sight and stiffened, her scowl sliding right off her face.

The largest *fiilee* had crept up on her, its sharp eyes assessing. A hum formed in the back of her throat, but she swallowed it quickly. This was no sea creature she could soothe with her song.

"I won't taste good," she murmured, holding the predator's eyes. Its ears perked at her words and crept another soundless step closer. If Mer reached out, she would have been able to touch the feline's whiskers. "Begone, beastie. I don't concern you."

The *fiilee* ignored her and took another step, shoving its pink nose against her side. Mer's heart galloped as she stared down at the top of the *fiilee's* head. It was huge. If the beast wanted, it could rip out her whole side with one bite.

"Easy," she whispered. "If you bite me, my scales will cut up your gums."

The *fiilee* snuffed her, unconcerned, huffing warm air against the wet silk of her dress.

A whistle followed by three clicks caught the *fiilee's* attention. It abandoned its exploration of her side and prowled toward the king; its long wing briefly brushed her leg. She blinked as the beast knocked its large head into his chest, and he pressed his forehead between the feline's ears before giving the creature rough scratches.

From the outside, it looked wholesome, but Mer knew better.

Bile rose up her throat at the display of affection. How could he act so kindly with a beast and yet act like such a savage to Ream?

Because he sees your worth to be less than that of an animal.

The anger that permanently had taken up residence in her chest burned brightly at the reminder.

The Methian king would pay. Mer blew out a breath. She'd have to extract her revenge carefully.

The king released his hold on the *fiilee* and stalked in her direction. Mer braced herself for a fight, but he hesitated just out of reach and then held his hand out silently.

She stared at his large, calloused palm and then raised her brows. "What do you expect me to do with that?"

"Take my hand." A clear command. "We are leaving this place."

She glanced from his hand to the feline and back. Understanding dawned.

He wanted her to willingly get on the *fiilee*.

Mer shook her head no just once. She would not go into the skies. "I think not."

His gaze flattened and he rushed her. Mer yelped, fighting him off. He manhandled her and tossed Mer over his shoulder. The air was knocked out of her as his shoulder slammed into her stomach. She screeched, throwing decorum out the window, and clawed at his back, tearing his shirt from his trousers and slicing bloody furrows into his back.

He slapped her on the rear. Hard.

Mer's eyes watered, but she gritted her teeth against the pain. How. Dare. He.

"Remove your hands from my person, or I'll remove your hand from your arm," she promised.

"Then pull your talons from my back," he growled in return.

"Do you think that is a good idea?" a blond warrior with bright blue eyes asked as they passed him.

The king grunted, managing to get them both on the back of the *fiilee*.

"Put me down immediately," she shouted, pummeling his back with all her strength as real terror pushed past her indignation and anger. "I do not consent to this."

He didn't waver.

"Try not to fall, vicious one," he murmured a second before he clicked once, and the *fiilee* lunged forward.

Mer lifted her head and braced herself against his back, meeting the smug gaze of the dowager queen. The older woman smiled and mouthed, *Have fun.*

Dread churned in her belly, and Mer knotted her fingers in the king's wet shirt as the meadow disappeared, a maze of trees whizzing past them. She lifted her body slightly higher and glanced over her shoulder.

Mer's eyes rounded and her stomach dropped.

They were headed toward the cliff's edge.

"No!"

The king yanked her down into his lap, pinned her legs with one muscled thigh, and secured her arms with his left hand.

"Shall we, my dear?" he crooned as they plunged over the edge.

A scream tore from her as they plummeted.

A moment of weightlessness and her heart flew to her throat as they fell toward the trees below. Her teeth cracked together as the *fiilee's* wings snapped out, stopping their descent. Quickly, they rose toward the black clouds, rain pelting them.

Her body shook as they climbed higher. Depths below, she hated heights.

"Why did you do it?" the king shouted.

She looked up at his face. Was he really asking her why she tried to kill him? Why was he playing dumb? "Because it was deserved!" she managed to get out, clinging to his arm with everything she had.

His silver eyes flashed to her face, and a grim smile curled his lips. "Well, then let me return the gesture."

All at once, he shook her off, and then, much to her horror, he shoved Mer right off the back of the *fiilee*.

Chapter Twelve

MER

M ER GRABBED FOR THE LEATHER HARNESS, BUT it slipped through her wet numb fingers.

A terrified scream burst past her lips as she tumbled in the air, plunging toward her death.

Sky. Forest. Sky. Forest.

This was how she died.

His revenge was better than yours.

She caught a blur of movement a second before she slammed to a stop. Mer gasped, the wind knocked out of her, a band of steel wrapped around her waist. She clung to the king's massive arm. Her eyes were wide as she gaped up at him, her legs kicking in the air as the *fiilee* caught the wind and swooped upward.

"What are you doing?" she wheezed, trying to dig her

toes into the feline's fur. The wind tore at her, and the rain sliced against her skin. All she had to do was fight past the panic.

"Why did you do it?" he shouted, his eyes hard as flint.

"Let me up!" Her limbs shook as she tried to find purchase against the side of the flying feline.

"Why did you do it?"

She glared at him through the rain, and Mer let her pride get the best of her. "Because it was deserved."

The Methian king leaned down into her space and bared his teeth, real hate glittering in the depths of his silver eyes. "No one deserved that fate. Especially not the children."

Children?

He shook her off. Mer caught the edge of the *fiilee's* wing but lost traction in the rain, flailing uselessly. Another terrified scream tore from Mer as she free-fell again, the wind tearing at her destroyed silk dress. Mer clawed at the air as if it could save her from what was coming. She tumbled until she faced the land. Bile burned at the back of her throat. The ground approached too quickly. She closed her eyes, praying that her death would be quick.

I'm sorry, Ream.

A roar caused her eyes to snap open.

The king darted beneath her, and Mer crashed into him right before she hit the trees. Pain ricocheted through her body, but she barely registered it. Panic had Mer wrapping herself around the king like an octopus. Somehow, her legs found their way around his waist and her arms over his head and around his neck. She locked her ankles together and knotted her fingers around the harness he wore.

"You deserve death!" he hissed in her ear, trying to push her away.

Oh, no, he didn't.

Mer released his harness and wrapped her fists in the chains of the manacles before leaning back until the metal bit into his neck. He growled, and she noted with satisfaction that more blood trickled down his throat. "It's not me who deserves death!"

He dug his massive hands into her thighs, attempting to pull her off, but to no avail. She gritted her teeth and held on despite the pain. There was no doubt in her mind that if he dropped her again, there would be no rescue.

He abandoned prying her off and reached for a blade strapped to his chest.

I don't think so.

Mer headbutted him as hard as she could, her limbs shaking with adrenaline and fatigue. Stars danced across her vision, and she swayed, barely holding on as he cursed. Maybe that wasn't her best idea. She plastered herself against his chest, tightening her hold, and bit him on the neck just above the scarf as the world rolled. Still, she didn't let go, even as the force threatened to tear her from the dreaded king. She could be sick later. Now was life or death.

The king froze, his fingers still biting into her ribcage. He panted hard into her ear.

"If you tear out my throat, I'll throw us both over the edge," he rasped.

Mer believed the crazy bastard.

She bit a little harder, but not enough to break the skin. He was in no position to make threats.

As if he heard her thoughts, he said, "We're at an impasse."

The feline banked to the left as Mer continued to shake. Bile flooded her mouth as the salt from his skin registered. She swallowed hard, her vision going in and out of focus.

Just hold on. Keep fighting.

Time ceased to matter as Mer clung to her enemy like her life depended on it.

Because it did.

The wind howled and clawed at her until she pressed her face into the king's neck, her eyes closing.

This was not in the plan.

Her temper had gotten them there.

Her stomach lurched as the *fiilee* descended, its speed picking up. Her eyes popped open as the beast's wings snapped open. She caught a glimpse of a city, and then the flight stopped abruptly. Mer swallowed as she glanced to the left. They'd landed on a wide black stone balcony, big enough to be a landing pad for the *fiilee.*

Her stomach rolled at the sheer cliff face it was built into. The world tipped and she swayed slightly.

All you have to do is get away from him without being tossed over the edge or stabbed.

In one smooth motion, she released his neck, whipped her chains over his head, unlocked her ankles, and rolled backward off the feline. Her head spun, and the drop was farther than she expected. Mer's right ankle wobbled with the impact, and agony shot up her heels and calves, but she'd managed to stay on her feet.

The king caught the chain of her manacles and hauled her against the *fiilee.*

He sneered down at her, looking every part the villain of her nightmares. "You will pay for what you've done."

Mer laughed, the world tipping slightly. "And you will . . ." Her stomach rebelled, and she vomited all over his lap and leg. The king cursed and released her, while the *fiilee* hissed, raising the scales along her forearms.

She stumbled away from the feline and its horrible owner, making it to the glass door. She yanked it open and limped inside. The king slowly lifted his head, his face a mask of disgust.

"Do you think a little glass would keep me from you?"

"You're demented," she spat, the words coming out slurred.

"You struck first. I strike back harder."

Mer cackled, grinning at his slightly crooked nose and the black eyes that were already forming. The king was in rough shape. "And yet here I stand."

His lips thinned. "Don't worry, I'll rectify that soon."

"Looking forward to it."

"I'll be seeing you soon, wife. You started this little game, but I always finish it."

Chapter Thirteen

RAZIEL

"You going to tell me the story of how you got these wounds?" Levay, the middle-aged healer, asked.

Raziel grunted and continued to stare into the fireplace, shifting slightly on the clean cot. The scent of herbs, hyssop, and lye filled the air. He'd spent much of his time as a child in the infirmary. First, because he always managed to get hurt. And second, because the Mirror Plague had almost taken his life.

Just like you almost took the Sirenidae's life.

He hung his head, and the healer hissed.

"Stop moving, or these stitches will be uneven."

He complied, staring wearily at the clean brown stone floor.

Raziel, the king of Methi, had purposely dropped his

new bride two times from Skye's back. And if she hadn't stopped him, he might have done it a third time.

Shame curled in his chest as he thought about how she shook in his arms. The way her terrified screams cut through the storm. Even now, he could hear the echo of them in his ears.

The little Sirenidae was scared of heights, it seemed.

How idiotic.

Raz huffed when the healer pierced his neck, tying off another stitch. He hadn't bothered with numbing. He didn't deserve it after his loss of control. His new bride had tried to kill him, and in return, he *tortured* her. With the scent of ash in his nose and the taste of rage upon his tongue, he'd lost all sense. It had taken every bit of self-control he had to keep calm until he had her on Skye's back.

He darkly chuckled at himself. As if the princess would break at the threat of death. Despite her obvious fear, she hadn't given him what he sought.

The truth.

From the moment she stepped up onto the dock, he could sense she bowed to no one. If he'd kept his cool, he could have seen that a little trip through the storm wouldn't give him what he wanted. Raziel would have to be strategic with his new wife. He'd have to break her walls down little by little to get what he wanted. Scaring her would get him nowhere.

The needle dug deeper and Raz gritted his teeth.

"This cut is deeper than I'd like," Levay commented. "And it's a clear cut. What caused it again?"

Raziel peeked at the healer from the corner of his eye. Levay was as skilled as she was nosey. "I didn't say."

She sighed, clearly annoyed with his antics.

The healer had been with his family since his birth. She was one of his most trustworthy and loyal companions. She'd bandaged all his scrapes and cuts, nursed him back from the brink of death, and never judged him.

Might as well admit what you've done.

Raz sighed. "My new queen tried to slit my throat." He tapped the sharp ornate shell blade in his sheath, his fingers lingering on the elegantly curved handle. "With this."

Levay whistled. "You must not have made a very good impression."

A snort escaped him as he rubbed his hands over the tops of his thighs. "I hadn't even spoken one word to her."

"And the black eyes, claw marks, and bites?"

His lips turned down. Those he deserved. "She head-butted me."

"Why would she do that?"

Time to tell the truth. "Because I threw her off the back of Skye," he admitted in a rush. Levay paused in her stitching, her disapproval evident. Raziel stared down at his calloused palms. "You examined the bodies from the *Zephyr*, did you not?" he rasped.

"I did," she replied softly.

"The attack was an act of war, but I don't know how to fight the enemy, let alone find them. My new queen is accountable for her people's actions. Someone has to pay. I did what I had to in order to get the information that I needed." It was a weak excuse, even in his own ears.

Levay hummed and continued her stitching with steady hands. "And did you learn what you sought?"

Shame and guilt surged again. "No."

The healer tied off the last stitch and then set the needle and thread aside. His neck ached, but that was to be expected.

Levay edged around the cot, her loose linen pants swishing as she took a seat on the cot in front of him. She groaned, rubbing her lower back before studying him with her metallic sage-green eyes. He forced himself to hold her gaze, even though it felt slightly accusing. Like she was scolding him without a word.

"May I speak freely, my lord?"

A small smile lifted the corner of his lips. "Whenever have you not?"

"True." She paused as if gathering her words. "Loss and fear are powerful motivators. Take it from me. Our minds aren't equipped to deal with tragedies, especially the ones you've seen. That being said, choosing cruelty in the name of justice is a slippery slope, my lord. Most times, the ends do not justify the means. You are our king. It's unfair to ask perfection from an imperfect person, but it comes with the title. You are the best of us. You must be."

Her words pierced him.

Today he let his emotions get the best of him. Raziel had made a cruel, rash decision that could have cost him everything, all because he'd been drowning in grief, fear, anger, and self-loathing. He'd already made the decision to punish the Sirenidae princess for what her people had done. It hadn't mattered whether she deserved it or not.

"I made a mistake," he murmured. Raziel wasn't afraid to admit when he was wrong.

"As you say, my lord." Levay pushed her silver-streaked braid over her shoulder and laced her fingers between her knees. "Do I need to pay a visit to your new bride?"

An image of the Sirenidae, bruised, bloody, and shivering, flashed through his mind. He nodded. "She may be concussed and possibly needs stitches."

Levay sighed and shook her head, then slapped her thighs and stood. "That's a rocky start to a marriage, my lord."

"She attacked first." Raz still didn't understand it. Surely, the sea king wouldn't send an assassin to him, especially one of royal blood. So why all the violence?

Levay scowled. "When you questioned her, did she give you any explanation?"

It was deserved.

"No, but she seemed to think it was warranted. I managed to knock her out before she could do more damage." He rubbed his forehead, trying to sort through his memories on the dock. They were foggy. His mother had warned him about the Lure, but he'd never imagined that it would be that powerful or potent. He'd lost his bloody mind as soon as he scented her.

Even now, thinking about it, his mouth watered.

Raziel shook his head and grimaced. "What do you know about the Sirenidae Lure?"

Levay shrugged and began cleaning up her mess. "Not much."

He watched as she bustled around the infirmary, putting things away as well as gathering herbs, tinctures, and bandages into a basket. Presumably for his murderous wife.

"What have you heard, then?"

"There are many myths about the Lure, but what I have surmised is that it's a biological protection for the Sirenidae people. In stories of old, they were hunted for their scales and the herbs of the trenches." She added needles and thread to the basket. "Their Lure fogged the minds of their attackers so they could escape."

True, his body had felt as if it wasn't his own, but it was more than just mental fog. He'd experienced . . . overwhelming desire. "And the desire?" he said roughly.

"Depends on the person. Individuals react differently to the pheromones." Levay paused, eyeing him. "How did you fare?"

Raz licked his lips as a blush tinged his cheeks. He

swallowed down the embarrassment and cleared his throat. "Lust stronger than anything I've ever felt."

"Interesting," the healer commented. She popped one last tincture into her collection and then slung the basket over her arm, the glass jars clinking softly together. "Where is this wayward bride of yours?"

Raziel flinched, not wanting to say. Levay arched her brow.

"My rooms."

She blinked at him, and then a slow smile crossed her face.

"What?" Raz questioned.

She sauntered toward the door. "Can I offer some advice, my lord?"

"You always do."

"First, shower before your mum sees you."

Raziel stood from the cot. "And?" There was always an and.

"And remember the line between love and hate is thin."

He flinched. "I feel nothing for her. She's a means to an end."

"If you say so, my lord. But I wouldn't put my enemy in my rooms, especially if they tried to kill me."

Chapter Fourteen

MER

M ER WAS PULLED VIOLENTLY FROM HER nightmare.

She blindly swung toward the person shaking her shoulder. A firm hand caught her wrist.

"That's enough of that," a firm feminine voice chastised.

Yanking her wrist from the stranger's grip, Mer blinked repeatedly as the world bobbed and dipped. She launched to her feet, stumbling toward the fire, her right hand catching on the mantel. Using it as an anchor, Mer focused on the extremely tall woman wearing linen trousers and a frown.

"What do you want?" Mer asked, wishing the pain from her skull would stop.

"To stop the pain."

If only that were possible. She'd been in constant pain since Ream's betrayal.

Mer swayed, eyeing the basket stuffed full of bandages and tinctures. "You're here to heal me?"

"Yes. Do you really think anyone would let you languish in the state you're in, my lady?"

Why yes, that was exactly what Mer had thought. Once she'd been sure the king had gone for good, Mer had moved to the main double doors of the suite looking for an exit. When she'd opened them, six warriors had been stationed outside. She'd taken one look at them and slammed the doors in their faces. Then she'd locked them and moved a chair in front of them for good measure.

Her eyes narrowed at the broken chair and the pristine door. Someone had a key to her room. That wasn't optimal, but there were better ways to barricade a room. Which she'd do once her infernal head stopped pounding and the dizzy spells ceased.

The woman tsked when Mer swayed again, her legs almost buckling at the wave of pain that crashed over her. "Enough of this nonsense." She set her basket on the large tufted chair by the fire and then invaded Mer's space, slipping an arm around her waist. "You need to lie down."

There were many times to be stubborn, but this was not one of them. Saliva flooded Mer's mouth as they shuffled across the massive gothic room. Any moment and she'd throw up. Again.

Tears sprang in the corners of her eyes as the healer pulled back the deep purple coverlet and helped Mer lie down on the four-poster bed. The plush mattress alone soothed some of her aches and pains.

"Don't go back to sleep," the healer warned, pulling the coverlet up to Mer's chin. "I'll be right back."

Mer nodded and closed her eyes, listening to the woman stride across the room and back. The mattress dipped as the healer sat beside her and gently pulled Mer's tangled hair away from her throbbing temple.

"He got you good," the healer muttered, disapproval in her voice.

"He looks worse," Mer retorted with a small smirk, cracking one eye open.

The healer rolled her eyes. "What a pair you make. Now, hold still. This might hurt."

Mer flinched when the healer cleaned her temple, the nausea rising up. "I think I'm going to be sick."

"Not on me, you're not." A leafy plant was shoved unceremoniously between Mer's lips. Mint. "Chew it and then swallow."

Mer did as she was told, slowly chewing the fibrous leaf, the bitter minty flavor coating her tongue. Her eyes closed, and she focused on the mint. She hissed when the healer poured a tincture on her head and swallowed the bitter leaf.

"That stings."

"Yes, it does, but it cleans the wound. Wouldn't want you to die from infection."

"Only by extreme heights," Mer deadpanned. She opened her eyes, watching as the healer began threading the needle. "Stitches?"

"Only a few. Significantly fewer than the king." The woman gave her an unamused look. "I would offer you something to drink to dull the pain, but judging from the drained decanter on the floor, I dare not give you anything more."

It hadn't been the best idea to start drinking, but she had needed something to take the edge off the pain. Her head had felt like it was going to split open. Plus, she'd been so cold, and the shivering wouldn't stop. It was only when the spirits took effect that they'd finally stopped.

"I can handle it." She stared at the ornate stone ceiling. It had been carved to look like wrought iron filigree. It was stunning. Her eye twitched at the first prick of the needle and tug of the thread. The healer worked swiftly; her motions were steady and efficient and gentle. Human healing was barbaric but effective at times. What she wouldn't give for a jelly sedative.

"What's your name?" Mer asked.

"Levay."

An interesting name for an interesting woman. "Where exactly am I, Levay?"

"Not a chance, my lady. I will not give you information that you can use against my king."

Levay tied off the last stitch and cut the thread.

Mer turned her head to the side slightly, meeting the woman's metallic green eyes. "Am I not your queen?"

The healer smiled. "Not until you prove yourself worthy."

A sentiment that Mer agreed with. She smiled at Levay. "Very well." The healer was loyal to the king, but she sensed that the woman had a mind of her own. If Mer played her cards right, perhaps she'd gain a confidant in the healer, which would prove very useful. "Do you have something for the pain in that bag of tricks?"

The healer snorted. "Would you take it if I gave it to you?"

Mer blinked slowly. It was very possible that the king had sent the healer to Mer to drug her. But then why the stitches? "Perhaps."

Levay smirked. "You're concussed, my lady. Even if my king had sent me to drug you, my oath comes before the monarchy. It's too dangerous for you to go into a deep sleep." She pulled a small green bottle from the basket and uncorked the top. "Decide now if you wish for some relief. I haven't got all day."

That settled it. Mer nodded and parted her lips. Levay poured the sour contents into Mer's mouth, and her eyes watered as she swallowed it. "That swill is disgusting," she gasped.

"Yes, but it does the job." The healer shifted on the

bed. "Get some rest. I'll wake you in a little bit to check up on you."

Mer's eyes fluttered closed. She didn't think she'd be able to fall asleep with a stranger watching her.

SHE AWOKE WITH AN ACHING BODY AND sunlight streaming into the bedroom.

Mer slowly sat up and then immediately lay back down, noting Levay was asleep in one of the chairs by the fire. Her head still hurt, but it was significantly less than the prior day. She exhaled and peered up at the ceiling.

She'd tried to kill the Methian king.

He'd thrown her off the back of his *fiilee*.

Twice.

And they'd both survived.

Tipping her head to the right, she scanned the space. A side table, candelabras, a door leading to what she presumed was the bathing room. Mer rolled her head to the left. Another side table, a large desk and chair.

Ever so slowly, Mer sat up until her back was leaning against the velvet headboard. Her head pulsed softly, but the dizziness abated quickly. She stiffened as she focused on the unwanted woman by the fireplace.

It was not the healer but the dowager queen.

The regal older woman had her long legs crossed at the knee and leaned an elbow on the arm of the chair while she studied Mer. It was a fight not to reach for her hair and smooth down the short tangled locks that surely looked like a knot of eels.

They said nothing as they appraised each other.

Mer didn't know much about the dowager queen, only that she'd ruled most of her adult life by herself while raising children alone.

"To what do I owe the surprise visit?" Mer asked. She didn't want to play games. She was too bloody sore and tired.

"I came to check on my new daughter. You've been sleeping for three days."

No wonder she was so weak.

Mer snorted. "I doubt that. I might have been concussed, but I haven't forgotten how you looked at me on the dock. If you could have killed me, you would have struck me down right then."

"A mother's love. You'll understand soon enough, my dear," the dowager queen commented.

Mer flinched. One point to the old queen.

She'd die before she gave the Methian king heirs.

"What I don't understand," the dowager queen continued, "is why jeopardize the treaty between our kingdoms? It doesn't make sense to send a royal assassin. Nor does the Sirenidae attack at sea. Just what is your grandfather after?"

Attack at sea? Mer cocked her head, forcing her expression into one of serenity while she processed the information that the dowager queen had given her. Sirenidae couldn't survive the cold water of the north. "Sirenidae attacks here?"

The queen nodded.

That wasn't right. "Where did the attacks happen?"

"North of the Wasting Corals."

Mer's brows rose. "Why do you believe it was a Sirenidae attack?"

"Because the fishing vessel had been run aground on the poisonous coral beds, and their hearts had been torn from their chests. They were way off course."

"Torn from their chests?" Mer echoed. That was brutal. The strength necessary for such an act of violence would have to be substantial. Even the strongest Sirenidae wouldn't have enough strength to accomplish such a thing. "Not possible."

The dowager queen's eyes glittered with anger. "I assure you it most definitely is. I saw the bodies with my own eyes. The bodies of children."

Mer flinched. Sirenidae cherished children. Anyone who hurt wee ones was punished by death. It was not tolerated in their culture and extremely rare. "It was not Sirenidae then."

"This is not the first time your kind has targeted our ships, but this will be the last." Her voice held a threat.

Mer's eyes narrowed at the queen. She threw back

the covers and slowly climbed to her feet, toes digging into a soft fur rug. Staying in bed any longer felt too vulnerable. "My grandfather desires this union. He would not have risked it for the lives of a few fishermen." The dowager queen opened her mouth to respond, but Mer held her hand up. "What's more, as a whole, our people cherish children. Even *if* a rogue Sirenidae had theoretically attacked your fishing vessel, they would have left the wee ones alone. That was not us."

It was obvious the Methian had heard horror stories about the Sirenidae. While she wouldn't perpetuate the notions, she wouldn't put herself at a disadvantage by admitting her people couldn't travel through the cold Methian waters. Unfortunately, fear did lead to power at times.

"What's interesting," Mer continued, "is the fact that you didn't strike me down the moment I climbed on the dock. You thought we'd committed an act of war, and yet here I stand." The dowager queen didn't react, which was telling in itself. "You must need something desperately from us."

Her mind ran over the dowry her grandfather had sent. Riches, yes. Herbs from the trench, which wasn't a surprise—everyone wanted to extend their lives. And healers—a plethora of them. She pursed her lips in thought. The healers: that's what they were after.

"Who is ill?" she asked. "Is it you?"

The dowager queen stood from her chair. "I'm in excellent health."

"Then the king." Mer smiled. Perhaps the king would die of natural causes. Well, hopefully after she'd made his life a mess.

The dowager queen scowled. "Don't look so gleeful. He's healthy." She frowned. "Why do you hate him?"

Mer picked at the silk nightgown she presumed Levay changed her into. "He took something precious from me."

"To my knowledge, you've never met." Her gaze was shrewd.

Mer wished she hadn't met the king. "And yet he still managed to destroy my life."

"Because of the arranged marriage?"

"Something like that."

"Did you not choose this path?"

Mer smiled bitterly. "I was given an ultimatum. Marriage to your son was the lesser of two evils."

The dowager queen walked across the room and stood before Mer, smelling of lilacs. She appraised her, making Mer want to shift, but she kept her head held high. "You have demons haunting you, but you're not the only one to suffer. We need your healers, but not enough to keep you alive if you try to kill the king again. You are replaceable."

"You threaten the queen?" Mer murmured. That was bold.

"It's not a threat but a promise. You almost took my

son from me. It won't happen again." The dowager queen cupped Mer's cheek, her hand surprisingly warm. "I had hoped we'd be friends, daughter. Test me again, and I'll be the last thing you see in this world."

Mer grinned at the vicious older woman. She liked the way the dowager queen was no-nonsense. "Understood . . . *Mum*."

The older woman smirked. "A sense of humor . . . you'll need it here." She dropped her hand and stepped away. "Be prepared. You have a special dinner tonight to attend. Those of the Onyx Palace wish to celebrate your nuptials."

"Oh, those? The ones I never attended?"

"Your lady's maids will be here shortly."

"My handmaidens?"

The dowager queen laughed. "After your little display? Do you really think we'd let more Sirenidae into the palace?" With that, she exited the room and closed the door behind her, leaving only the scent of her lilac perfume.

What just happened?

And who the hell was killing fishermen?

Chapter Fifteen

RAZIEL

King Raziel slouched in his chair, a silver goblet of wine in his right hand dangling loosely from his fingers.

The buzz of one hundred voices filled the cavernous dining hall. He took a sip of the rich wine and scanned the room. He tipped his head back against the chair and stared upward. Walnut beams crisscrossed the high-arching stone ceiling, making it look as if it were a woman's coronet. It was a masterpiece of architecture. One could whisper from the opposite side of the room, and Raziel could hear their conversation.

He wasn't sure what his ancestors exactly had in mind when they'd designed the dining hall, but it had proved useful over the years. Anyone brave enough or stupid enough to speak of personal life would be sharing with the entire assembly. But it worked both ways. Anything Raziel and his companions spoke of would be shared with those on the opposite side of the room.

His mother said it fostered respect, and while Raz agreed, it was bloody inconvenient. Every time they hosted an event, Raziel was on pins and needles. He had to watch every single thing he said. It got even trickier when his courtiers purposely asked him inflammatory questions.

Luckily, his sour mood had kept everyone away from him so he could drink in peace.

Long sturdy wooden tables filled the room, adorned with plates of savory food, smooth wine and brew, and vases full of colorful wildflowers. A mixture of high and common born sat together, partaking in the feast. Not many kingdoms mixed between ranks. Even though he'd enjoyed his time in Aermia, the banquets only hosted those who were highborn with a few esteemed lowborn attending.

A thread of pride wriggled in the king's chest. Methian culture was different. All were welcomed, no matter their status or the blood that ran through their veins. What mattered was loyalty, kindness, and their bonds with the *fiilee*. It was beautiful to see. All were here to partake in the banquet to celebrate his new marriage. And yet his wife was nowhere to be found.

Levay had kept Raz up to date on the state of his new murderous queen. She was much improved. Even his mother had spoken with the queen. She should have been here. And yet . . . he glanced at the empty seat to his right. There'd been speculation as to where she was, but most had swallowed his explanation that his new wife was under the weather.

He rubbed at the tip of his nose with his left hand. It throbbed, sending pain across his bruised left cheekbone. Slowly, he lifted the cold goblet and gently laid it against the tender flesh. He'd give her one thing, the Sirenidae surely knew how to pack a punch. If he hadn't been so irritated with the whole situation, he might have been a little proud.

Valen and Gideon abandoned their table from the left and approached Raziel. They paused at the first step of the dais and bowed respectfully.

The two brothers were a study in opposites.

Where Valen was thick and bulky, Gideon was wiry and graceful. Valen's hair and skin were dark, Gideon's fair. No one underestimated Valen and everyone underestimated Gideon. What they had in common was loyalty, pure hearts, brilliant minds, and long friendship with Raziel. Plus, they were brilliant riders.

Gideon's reflective ice-blue gaze ran over Raz, noting the claw marks on his arm, the stitches on his neck, and the black eyes. The man never missed anything. His attention turned to the empty seat at his side, and he arched a brow.

"It's too bad the queen wasn't feeling well," he said softly. Translation: *what did you do to your wife?*

Raziel said nothing, just took another sip of his wine.

While it suited him to not have the Sirenidae there, it prickled part of him that she'd never showed.

Appearances mattered, and his new wife was making him look weak. Even now, he could feel a few speculating gazes running over him. Gossip would be circulating full force by the next morning.

Just what he needed.

The council had been challenging him since his mum had passed the crown down to him. Every move he'd made had been questioned, especially since he'd returned from the Warlord's War. His mother had chosen to involve them in the battle, but the blame for the loss of life fell upon his shoulders.

An ache flared in his chest. They'd lost many *fiilee* and riders. In fact, he'd almost lost Gideon, in addition to his bonded.

He took another deep sip of his wine as his friends watched him quietly.

Gideon cocked his head. "When was the last time you . . ."

The murmur of the crowd rose in volume.

"The queen!"

"A Sirenidae."

"What is she wearing?"

Raziel sat up straighter, Gideon and Valen stepping

aside. He blinked at his wife, who'd stepped into the banquet hall. His tongue stuck to the roof of his mouth at the expanse of skin she showed. His admiration was quickly followed by annoyance. She was practically naked.

"Are those your . . . curtains?" Valen grunted.

Indeed they were.

He knew for a fact that his mother had delivered an appropriate dress for the occasion, and yet his bloody wife was wearing his curtains. She'd managed to wrap the black damask fabric into a mockery of a dress. Her entire left leg was exposed, along with the upper part of her midriff showcasing a marking between her breasts. The makeshift straps wrapped around her neck and tied at the back. She turned to the right, taking Chancellor Ortunge's hand, and her musical laugh echoed in the room, filling his ears.

His breath caught as she turned to whisper something in Ortunge's ear, revealing her entire exposed back. The fabric clung to the base of her spine, and he stared at the dimples winking at him from her lower back.

His chancellor would have a field day about her behavior at their next council meeting. Just what he needed.

Valen whistled. "What a charming dress." His tone said anything but.

The Sirenidae smiled as the crowd stood and bowed when she made her way farther into the room, causing a stir in her wake.

Not once did her gaze land on Raz. Instead, she fluttered her lashes at old men, laughed at lame jokes, complimented women on their dresses, and smiled brightly at all.

She was an actress. Both an asset and a danger.

His wife finally made it to the dais. Valen and Gideon both bowed to her.

Raziel held her gaze and kept his mask in place as she smirked at him, batting her long lashes, which had been tinted a deep purple.

"My lord," she murmured.

"My lady," he replied. "What a fetching . . . dress."

Her smile widened. She cocked her hip, exposing more of her left leg. He blinked slowly as he finally noticed the marks. She had bruises on her thighs.

In the shape of his hands.

His lips pressed together as he took a closer look at her outfit. Sure, he assumed she had wanted to shock his assembly, but she had wrapped the fabric purposely to show off each and every mark she'd sustained from their fight.

It was a challenge.

A declaration.

One that said *'you can't control me.'*

"Sorry I'm late," she said. "It took me longer than I expected to get ready." Her attention moved to the empty chair at his side. "Is that for me?"

Raziel set down his wine. "It is."

"It's lovely but it won't do."

He gritted his teeth, knowing that each and every

person was listening to their conversation. She ascended the three steps of the dais and dropped into his lap. Raz's hands reflexively went to her waist, shock widening his eyes.

She wiggled, slipping farther into his lap. She threw one leg at a time over the arm of his seat before draping one arm around his shoulders. Her fingers caressed the stitches along his neck, and he stiffened. She was taunting him.

For once in his life, Raziel didn't know what to do.

Per their customs, Methians didn't engage in public affection. Hand-holding, yes. Maybe a chaste kiss, but never something this bold.

"Ah," she sighed in his ear, the ghost of her breath causing the hair to rise at the back of his neck. "This is better, isn't it, my king?"

Hundreds of pairs of eyes watched them, waiting for his response.

Play her little game.

Raziel released the tension in his body and purposely lifted his left hand and placed it on her bare thigh. He squeezed gently over the bruised imprint of his hand, ignoring the titters of the crowd. She stiffened slightly before he felt her melt back into the role she was playing.

"Naughty," she murmured into the side of his neck. "What fun we will have."

By fun, he presumed she meant bloodshed.

Hyperaware of her pointed nails stroking his stitches

almost lovingly, he turned his face until they were nose to nose. Her magenta eyes glittered with malice and a touch of the devil. She enjoyed torturing him and causing a scene.

He planned to return the favor.

Raz brushed his nose against hers. "What fun we can have right here."

His mother gasped, but she stifled it with a cough.

If this Sirenidae thought he'd balk, she was sorely mistaken. Raziel wouldn't let her have all the fun.

He could feel the disgust coming off his bride as he caressed her thigh in a long fluid stroke, his fingertips running over a few delicate scale patches. She did a good job of hiding it though. By all accounts, they looked like a couple ready to tear each other's clothes off.

The only thing they wanted from each other was pain.

"You recovered well," he said softly, squeezing her rounded hip. He glanced at her bruised temple.

"I did. I wasn't as ill as everyone believed." Translation: *you didn't hurt me.*

Part of him was relieved, even if it was from bravado. Raziel might despise his new wife because of what she represented, but after the moment of rage had passed, all he'd felt was shame and crushing guilt for what he'd done. Raziel had gone over the line.

"I'm glad to hear it," he replied. And he meant it.

He intentionally flicked his gaze down her neck to her

breast, eyeing the intricate trident tattooed on her fair skin. "Will you tell me what it means?"

She laughed, dipping her hand inside his shirt and caressing his own markings. "You are first."

"I received them when I was crowned king. They represent my domain over the heavens."

"My goodness...I didn't know the heavens belonged to anyone."

"No one can own the skies, but it is my birthright."

"*Ours*, darling."

"As you say."

She squirmed in his lap, and Raz hissed, his stomach bottoming out.

Despite everything, his traitorous body still reacted to his enemy.

"Stop wiggling," he almost begged.

His wife froze, loathing flittering through her magenta gaze. "Why am I not surprised?" she crooned, purposely wiggling. "You just can't control yourself with me."

He released her thigh and caught her chin, his thumb near the corner of her plush mouth. "Don't start something you will not win."

She slipped her tongue out and slid it up his thumb. "I always win, my lord."

More whispers exploded through the room, but Raziel ignored them. He was about to give them something to really gossip about. "We'll see." He closed the space between them and pressed his lips to hers. The

Sirenidae stared back at him, shuddering in his arms. She bit his bottom lip. *Hard.* And held on. Raziel flicked his tongue against her teeth, and she jerked back with a gasp.

That was all the opening he needed.

Rising to his feet, he hoisted his wife into his arms bridal-style and strode purposefully down the steps and through the assembly. Her nails pressed into his stitches, but he managed to shove down the pain. Hoots and hollers followed them as he made their escape with a painted-on grin.

"To heir making!" a bold man called as they reached the doors.

Cheers exploded and echoed around the dining hall as they exited the massive room.

Warriors peeled away from the walls as he stomped down the carpeted hallway, an angry Sirenidae burning a hole in the side of his face.

"Leave us," he commanded.

"So forceful," the Sirenidae crooned in his ear before biting his lobe so hard, he thought she'd taken a chunk out of it.

He swung around the corner, dropped her legs, and slammed her against the wall. The Sirenidae yelped and swung, but he caught her right hand and pinned her wrist to the wall. Raz leaned all his weight into her and pried her hand from around his neck, trapping that wrist above her head.

A drop of liquid dripped down his neck.

He was bleeding. Again.

"Why?" he growled.

"You'll have to be more specific," she snapped.

"Why the display?" He shuddered as the heat from her body sank into his own.

"Because it was fun."

Raziel's eyes narrowed. "You're smarter than that. You put on a good show, but I could feel how much you hated being in my lap, despite your words and actions. So why the games? Just what are you about?"

"Haven't you heard? Wives are supposed to torment their husbands."

"But to bloody them?" he retorted. "That's something altogether different. I saw the hate in your eyes before the Lure overtook me. Why agree to this marriage? What could I have possibly done to make you hate me so?" She stayed silent. "Tell me!"

"You killed my husband!"

Raz frowned at the vehement words. "You were married before?" That hadn't been information his mother had divulged. The Sirenidae was a widow?

The Sirenidae bared her teeth at him. "Like you don't know."

His mind scrambled for information, coming up blank. "How could I kill someone I've never met? I only knew of you before our marriage."

Her gaze darted across his face, and her mouth gaped open for a second. "You truly don't remember," she whispered. "How could you not remember taking someone's world from them?"

Rage creased her face, and she struggled against his hold. Raz released her and quickly stepped back to give her space. She looked like a *fiilee* protecting its nest, hair and eyes wild, beautiful but terrifying.

"What do you want from me?" he asked, crossing his arms.

"Your suffering."

"The joke is on you because I have enough of that on my own," he spat. She shoved him and angrily stomped down the hallway.

Raziel followed his wife, annoyed by the lingering glances of the warriors stationed throughout the hallway.

"Leave me alone," she growled, glaring over her shoulder at him.

"Not until I know you're not going to cut anyone down on your way to your room."

Her scowled deepened. "The only person I want to kill is you."

He was tired of this charade. "Then why not do it." Raziel stopped and held his arms out.

Mer swung around, her chest heaving in a way he should not be noticing. She didn't move from her spot but glared at him, her fingers clenching and unclenching.

Raz slowly spun in a circle, giving her his back. It was as good a chance as any.

"What? Not so brave when you're not using your Lure to disarm your victims?"

The Sirenidae shook. "If you were struck dead right now, I would dance on your corpse and wear your bones in my hair."

Raziel grinned and sauntered forward, eating up the space between them. He leaned down, almost touching her nose with his own. "I didn't know you cared that much to carry me with you wherever you go."

Her nostrils flared. "It wasn't a compliment, you dimwit."

"By the way," he pointed over his shoulder, "Your room is that way."

Mer hissed and swung around him in an angry cloud of black velvet. Little did she know he'd sent her toward the commodes.

Chapter Sixteen

MER

"Time to go!"

Mer glanced over her shoulder to the dowager queen, who swept into the suite like she owned it. She spun slowly and slung a hip against the stone banister of the balcony despite her pounding heart. The fear of heights had always plagued her, but fear was just part of the mind. A person could work through it. Or so she told herself.

"To what do I owe the pleasure?" Mer asked. After her little appearance the night before, she'd hoped that they would leave her to her own devices for a few days. She had hoped that the king might show up so she could give him a tongue lashing for the trick he'd pulled last night.

Do you really want to see him?

She'd tipped her hand. The bloody man just made her

see red. He ruined every carefully well thought out plan by just breathing.

It was annoying.

"Come inside, daughter," the dowager queen called, walking to Mer's breakfast platter and eyeing the spread. "Does the food not meet your expectations?"

It was clear the older monarch wasn't going anywhere.

Mer left the open balcony and trudged back inside, missing the fresh air already. She padded to the fire and held her hands out to warm them. "It was sufficient."

"You hardly touched a thing."

She turned and met the queen's narrowed gaze. "I ate the fruit."

"You need protein. You must build your strength."

"I agree, but not cooked ham and eggs." Her stomach rolled just thinking about the cooked greasy meat.

The dowager queen cocked her head. "Too heavy?"

"Not exactly." She appraised the older woman. "I come from the sea, my lady. We don't have cooked meat as your land does."

Understanding dawned across the dowager queen's face. "Would you like fresh fish brought to you?" The older woman looked slightly ill as she asked.

"I will survive on bread and fruit in the morning. If I desire fish, I will obtain it myself."

"A queen does not fish."

"A queen doesn't try to murder her husband, and yet here we are." Mer grinned.

The dowager queen rolled her eyes in a very unladylike way. "You're just as bad as my son. You mustn't say such things."

Like the king. Mer's smile turned into a frown.

She didn't want to be compared to that blackguard in any way. Crossing her arms, she arched a brow at the older woman. "Did you come here to critique my eating habits, or is there a reason for your visit?"

Clasping her hands together, the dowager queen smiled, but it was a touch devious. "I'm here to help you acclimate to your new schedule. We're already late. Your ladies are waiting just outside. Shall I call them in to help you dress?"

So that's why the dowager queen was here. To make sure she dressed appropriately.

Mer grimaced. "Let them in."

She knelt at the chapel in Onyx Palace. Her legs still burned from all the stairs they'd taken to reach the base of the palace.

Mer stared at her embroidered skirts and resisted the urge to tug at the long forest-green sleeves that ended in points at her middle fingers. She'd always admired the fabrics above, but wearing the scratchy material was something else altogether.

She had a feeling her wardrobe had arrived at the palace but was being hidden from her. Mer smiled. It was no matter. Soon enough, she'd discover its location or make her own as she'd done for the banquet the night before. While she was now a Methian queen, she didn't have to dress like one and erase her Sirenidae heritage.

"Why are you smiling?" the dowager queen asked from her right.

She peeked at the woman from beneath her lashes, keeping her head bowed. "Should I not?"

"It looks as if you're planning something devious."

"Maybe I am," she whispered.

"Stars help me," the dowager queen muttered. "Pay attention. Soon you shall lead the morning meditations."

"This seems an odd custom. Do you really do it every day?"

"It's to bring peace to the mind. The world can be a difficult place, and as a queen, there are many responsibilities that you must carry out. It can feel like too much if you don't center yourself and distinguish what is truly important. Meditation helps with this."

An interesting practice, but why only the queens? "And does the king meditate as well?"

"Yes." A smile curled the dowager queen's lips, and her gaze flitted past Mer's shoulder.

She stiffened as Raziel knelt to her left, the sleeve of his own shirt brushing her arm. Heat soaked into her body, and she tried to shuffle closer to the dowager queen, but to no avail. The bloody skirts kept her immobile. Why did humans prefer so much fabric? It seemed like a waste.

Her musings screeched to a halt as the king reached for her hand. Mer's head snapped up when he laced their fingers together. Cold silver eyes held her own, daring her to pull away. She narrowed her eyes at him for a second.

Mer registered the queen edging away from them. The bloody traitor.

"Your head is supposed to be bowed and your eyes closed," the king murmured, a wry note in his voice.

"You first."

He blinked at her and then, to Mer's surprise, bowed his head and closed his eyes. She studied his profile with suspicion. Just what was he up to? Why acquiesce so quickly? Her gaze ran over his strong jawline, sharp cheekbones, and sooty lashes. He had an aristocratic nose that had been broken once, at least, and full dusky lips. He'd tied his wine-colored hair back, revealing several piercings along his rounded ear. Mer eyed a black marking peeking along the edge of his collar. What was that?

"You're staring." His voice was flat.

Mer dropped her head and crushed her skirts with her right hand. She had been, in fact, staring.

More like assessing her target.

A likely story.

Her fingers began to tingle, and the heat from his

hand soaked into her palm in a way that was wholly unwelcome but not completely uncomfortable.

When was the last time someone held your hand?

A memory of Ream flashed through her mind. Lying on a warm rock, hands laced together as he smiled down at her.

Mer jerked, blinking quickly as tears filled her eyes.

"Are you alright, my lady?" the king whispered.

"I'm fine," she snapped a little too loudly.

He squeezed her hand. "You're strangling my fingers."

Mer released her death grip on his fingers and got ahold of herself. After months of pushing down her feelings and focusing on her mission, Mer's emotions were rising to the surface, unruly and uncontrollable.

It was inconvenient.

She inhaled and exhaled slowly, counting her heartbeats. Mer couldn't look away from their laced fingers. Hers slim and silvery, his calloused and burnished. Her stomach twisted. It made a stunning contrast.

Squeezing her eyes closed against the sight, she let her mind drift. She'd expected the king to lock her away after her performance the night before. During her voyage, Mer had studied the Methian culture. She'd known Methians were conservative in dress and public affection before she'd even taken a step on Methi soil. Goading the king with her shocking dress and blatant display of faux interest had been a way to test his mettle. She hadn't expected him to play along.

She'd underestimated him.

Something that wouldn't happen again.

While she didn't trust the king, she had to grudgingly admit that his principles were more merciful than those of the sea. An attempt on the life of a royal would have been met with a swift beheading. And a public act of defiance against the monarchy would have resulted in severe punishment. So far, she only had a few bumps and bruises, and to be honest, Mer deserved them.

Now that she wasn't a thousand feet in the air, she understood the king's actions.

Not that she forgave him for them.

She would have done worse to someone threatening her life or those she loved.

Correction, Mer *had* done worse.

Her mind returned to the last Scythian warrior she'd kidnapped.

She finally had a name and place to start her search.

Guilt rose swiftly, but she shoved the feeling down deep. At least something good had come from the interrogation.

Ceto.

The mysterious entity was supposedly in Methi.

Glancing out of the corner of her eye at the hulking king at her side, Mer pursed her lips in thought. While a Methian queen had many duties, they weren't enough to keep her busy. She could easily slip out for a time without her ladies. And if she really wanted, she could bring them with her to explore her new kingdom. Because what new queen wouldn't want to experience all the joys of her new land?

King Raziel opened his eye and arched a brow at her. "Why are you smiling?"

Mer's smile widened. She refused to look away. "Just thinking about what the future holds."

"Something bloody, no doubt."

His dry tone pulled an unexpected laugh from her. Mer dropped her skirt and clasped a hand over her mouth at the *shhh* from the dowager queen. The king's eyes creased at the corners when he returned her smile.

Depths below, he was handsome.

At the thought, Mer stiffened and dropped his hand.

The king's smile disappeared, and furrows appeared between his brows as he scanned her expression. She turned her face away from him and glared at her skirts once again. What was wrong with her? How could such a depraved thought pop into her mind? This was the man who'd taken everything from her.

He didn't even remember taking Ream's life. Crushing hurt bore down upon her until she wanted to lash out just for some relief.

Don't overreact. Don't push him away. You need him. For now.

"I would like to visit the city," she whispered softly, her voice shaking. "I would like to see how our people live."

She could feel his intense gaze on the side of her face, but she refused to look at him.

"An escort could be arranged."

The tension between her shoulders released. "That would be appreciated."

The dowager queen sighed and lifted her head. "If you two are going to keep talking, we might as well do some exploring now before the queen has her fitting for her new wardrobe and we discuss her coronation."

Mer glanced at the older woman, who stared at them with exasperation and a touch of something else.

Hope.

The most dangerous emotion of all.

This is what you want.

She nodded to the dowager queen and blinked repeatedly as a large hand was shoved in front of her face. What was this? Why help her up? She was perfectly able to rise herself. Mer glanced around the room, noting all the attention on them.

Another ruse. To look like a gentleman.

Mer took his hand and allowed the king to pull her to her feet. Mer tipped her head back and mutely watched him tuck her arm into his. She curbed the reaction to jerk away.

"Shall we?" he rumbled.

Mer painted a fake smile on her face and nodded. He led her from the chapel aisle, smiling at courtiers as they passed, the dowager queen and her ladies trailing them.

Mer squinted at one of her new ladies that hadn't helped dress her. She just about gaped as she recognized one.

Mazie. The female warrior who'd ridden with her after the attempt on the king's life.

Interesting. It seemed that perhaps her maids weren't all they seemed to be.

Mazie caught her look and batted her long sooty lashes as if to say, *"Are you happy to see me again?"*

Mer grinned and winked at the warrior.

King Raziel leaned down and whispered in her ear, causing the hair along the back of her neck to rise. "Be careful with that grin. You might scare someone with the deviousness of it." They reached a set of immense double doors, and Mer fought not to roll her eyes.

"If anyone is devious, it's you, my lord," she murmured, nodding to a fancy-looking lady to her left who curtsied. Two footmen pulled open the doors, and she blinked at the blinding rays of sun. "Don't think I didn't notice your plant among my ladies."

The king smiled broadly, not in the least bit ashamed. "I take your protection seriously."

Mer snorted, her smile turning brittle. "Mazie is here for *my* protection? I'm surprised you could say that with a straight face."

He shrugged. "Believe what you want, but for the love of the heights, wipe that false smile from your face. It's so tight, it looks as if you're going to break your teeth."

She adjusted her smile into one of closed lips and softened her expression as he led her outside for the first time since she'd arrived in Methi. "Better?"

"It would be if it was real," he muttered, cold amusement glittering in his eyes.

If he really knew what made her smile these days, he'd lock Mer up in no time.

Chapter Seventeen

RAZIEL

THEIR EXPLORATIONS OF SKIGARA WENT OFF
without an incident.

His wife had ignored the warriors trailing them and
immersed herself in the tour. Raz couldn't trust the
queen, and she certainly didn't trust him. The moment
she could, Mer had dropped his arm and put space
between them, engaging with one of her new ladies. To
anyone else, it wouldn't have been obvious that she
wanted to get away, but he could *feel* the unease in her
body being so close to him.

While she may have let him guide her through the city
and all its charms, he certainly didn't feel like he was in
charge. Between the modistes, cobblers, markets, and
treats, she'd acted as excited as anyone to experience new

delights. Mer chatted with merchants, teased her ladies, and praised every young laborer she came across. It was impressive how she flowed from one conversation to another without missing a beat.

She had an agenda. Raziel just didn't know what it was. And it bothered him.

The only things he knew for sure after spending a full morning trailing his Sirenidae bride was that she loved sweets, the merchants loved her, and she was more observant than he had expected. After the war, Raziel had found himself always looking for exits and possible attacks from enemies. His wife, it seemed, did the same thing. Those magenta eyes were always roving, despite the smile upon her lips.

While she didn't embody the Methian standard of beauty, he could admit that her bowed full lips were pretty, and she had a stunning smile. It was the type that made you want to laugh and share a secret with her.

One he had liked too much.

When she'd seen him staring, it had disappeared.

And he mourned it the tiniest bit.

That was even more alarming.

"My lord?" Gideon asked.

Raziel snapped out of his musings and glanced at his good friend standing inside the doorframe to his room. "Yes?"

"Are you prepared for tonight?"

Raz nodded, turning to the mirror and adjusting the

sleeves of his burgundy velvet jacket. "As prepared as I can be."

Gideon closed the door behind him, giving them a moment of privacy before the banquet. His friend brushed a strand of blond hair from his fair face and leaned against the door. "And your queen?"

"I can only hope." He had only seen her during meditation for the last week. After their tour of the city, his mother had whisked the Sirenidae away. She'd not joined him for the evening meal nor engaged with the courtiers. In truth, other than a few glances, his wife had pretended not to notice him each morning as he took his place beside her. What he did discover was that his wily new queen had been making adjustments to her dresses.

A smile slipped across his lips at the memory of the slit Mer had cut from hem to hip of her last dress. His mum had fretted over the expanse of skin the queen had been showing as she knelt. Raziel had to admire the spirit of his bride. She would not be molded, which was as irritating as it was intriguing.

Part of him couldn't wait to see what she'd be wearing to the banquet, if just to watch how many feathers she ruffled.

"You both must be careful. You don't have friends here," Gideon reminded him.

That wiped the smile off Raziel's face. He turned away from the tall oval mirror and strode across the lavish room Duke Keventin had provided for his visit. He lowered himself onto the gaudy gold divan at the foot of the bed and propped his elbows on his knees, Gideon sitting down at his side.

His friend clasped Raz on the shoulder. "You're not alone."

"I know." Raziel cast a grateful smile to his friend. "Thank you for coming along."

Gideon cracked a grin, mischief in his icy blue eyes. "And miss a chance to needle our good Duke Keventin? Never."

"I have a feeling tonight will hold many vague threats."

His friend arched a brow. "Do you really think he'd threaten you?"

Raz laughed jovially. "He's been pushing against me since I was crowned. Amongst the tax cuts and time regulations for workers, he's not going to want to budge on their pay." He scowled at the rug embroidered with silver thread. "Between the fishing fleet and the orchards, his costs are going to soar when I propose this newest plan."

"Change is never easy," Gideon agreed. "But if it helps, what you're doing is right. What Keventin pays his workers is a pittance. It's practically slavery."

Raziel nodded. While Methi hadn't actively enslaved an entire race for work like Scythia, were they any better if their workers were paid so poorly that they couldn't leave the slums they'd lived in for generations?

The answer was no.

He just had to figure out how to do it without turning the entire gentry against him. The tax cuts would go a long way, as would the additional funds from his queen's dowry. It would help their kingdom adapt and not collapse while he made big changes.

"How will you address the extra tax he's been levying on his people?" Gideon questioned.

"With care." And if needed, all the brute force of a hammer.

Raziel stood, his attention wandering to the closed door next to the fireplace. The one that led to his wife's rooms. "We better get this over with."

Striding to the door, Raz rapped on the porcelain-inlaid door and waited. Technically, he could walk into any room he desired, but he wasn't keen on his new queen invading his own personal space, so would give her the same courtesy.

The door swung inward, and Mazie curtsied to him and stepped backward out of the doorway.

Raziel blinked once.

It seemed the queen had found her trousseau.

His queen donned a dress that seemed as if it were part of the sea. A shell-encrusted bodice tightly hugged her torso, pressing her breasts high enough that Raz pointedly looked away from them. Painted ombre silk hugged her curvy hips and fell in waves to her feet.

Bare feet.

He stared at the rings adorning her slender toes.

Chains dripped around her delicate ankles, crystals sparkling in the low light.

His mouth watered. Why did he want to plant a kiss on the inside of her ankle?

"What do you think?" Mer asked in her husky voice.

Raziel snapped out of his daze, jerking his gaze away from her distracting feet. Heat filled his cheeks as he met her gaze. She offered him a crooked smile as if his bride could tell what he'd been thinking about.

"You will do," he replied gruffly.

Mer chuckled. "What praise indeed, my king."

"You look lovely," Gideon added. "Like a goddess from the sea."

Raz glared at his friend over his shoulder, noting how Gideon's eyes twinkled. The lout was playing games. The king wiped all expression from his face as he turned back to his queen and held his hand out.

"Shall we join our hosts?"

Mer slipped her slightly colder hand into his, and Raz fought a shudder as he closed his fingers over hers. He led them from his room and into the cream-and-gold corridor.

Raz kept his gaze straight ahead, not daring to look down at his queen.

The night had just become more complicated.

Not only did he have to field threats from a power lord who hated him, Raz had to keep from staring at his enchanting wife.

Raziel scowled at himself.

It was just a dress. And she was just a person.

He couldn't let her distract him.

What about the other men?

Raziel cursed underneath his breath.

Tonight was definitely going to end up in a fight.

Chapter Eighteen

MER

Duke Keventin was a snake.

The man spoke like he was the deciding authority on every subject, but beneath the arrogance was cunning. And that was dangerous.

Mer spooned a little bit of savory pureed soup into her mouth and took a sip, hiding her wince at the pumpkin flavor. She'd hoped it would be carrot instead. There was something about the mushy orange gourd that rubbed her the wrong way. Was it supposed to be sweet or savory?

She forced herself to swallow the soup and set her spoon down gently while tuning out the conversation around her.

Twenty-five people sat at the long rectangular table that ran down the middle of an opulent room. Mer blinked at the gold candelabra sitting on the table, so shiny her reflection glared back at her. She leaned to her left to see around the monstrosity at the young woman who sat across the table from her—Keventin's daughter. Her olive skin shone in the light and her sleek black hair curled gently around her round rosy cheeks. She never looked up from her plate but continuously fiddled with her spoon and stared into her soup like it held the answers to the world.

Mer cocked her head, studying the girl's bone structure.

Scythian.

What was the duke doing with a Scythian daughter? Scythia had its borders open for the first time in five hundred years, and the girl looked to be all of thirteen or fourteen? That was well before the Warlord's War. Had Keventin married a Scythian refugee? It was clear the girl's mother had to be of that origin.

Just how did the duke procure a Scythian wife?

Mer sighed. Too many questions and not enough answers.

She gave up trying to catch the young woman's eye. How did humans have conversations with each other when the table decorations kept one from even seeing their dining partners? It was unreasonable, to say the least.

Picking up her crystal goblet, she slanted a glance at

the king to her left. King Raziel sat at the head of the table, looking at ease, as if this were his own home.

Mer took a deep sip of her wine and relaxed slightly. At least humans knew how to brew their spirits.

"No love for pumpkin?" the pretty man at her right asked.

Mer turned to him—Gideon, she'd heard him called. "It's vile," she confessed.

Mirth made his lips twitch. "It's not my favorite either. No gourds beneath the sea?"

"No. At least, not sweet ones."

They fell silent as servants entered the room and quietly took their bowls.

Good riddance to the pumpkin soup.

Mer sipped her wine, observing the staff over the rim of her glass. While they were all dressed in finery, it was the gauntness of their faces and the emptiness in their eyes that made her skin crawl. These weren't happy workers. She narrowed her gaze at Duke Keventin as he gestured lazily and smiled a little too broadly while regaling his story.

This man didn't take care of his serving people.

That made her dislike him even more.

The duke caught her attention, and her stomach dropped when he sent her a rakish grin, licking the edge of his glass before hiding the gesture. Mer fought not to react. The indecent man was propositioning her while the king sat between them.

While she loathed Raziel, the pompous lord did not know that.

"What do you think, my queen?" Keventin asked with an oily smile.

"Of what, my lord?" she drawled, swirling the wine in her glass. A chill ran down her spine at the way he said *my queen*. It was possessive.

Duke Keventin pushed back his thick black-and-silver hair from his square jaw and then set his glass on the table before lacing his fingers together. Jeweled rings glowed in the candlelight. She'd already known the duke was rich, but each finger had two or three gemmed rings. Mer had seen the king each morning for the past week, and he'd never worn that many jewels. Was the duke trying to intimidate Raziel with his wealth?

What an interesting turn of events.

"Of your husband's new policies."

Gideon stiffened at her side.

Mer knew nothing of the changes Raziel was making in the kingdom. She smiled at the duke and feigned confidence she didn't have. "He is a very loyal and noble king," she answered truthfully. "Wouldn't you agree?"

Keventin's metallic gaze glinted. "Of course, my queen."

"Then any new policy he's put in place would be to better our kingdom, no?"

Gideon slightly relaxed at her reply.

"Yes, I believe our dear king has our people's best

interests at heart." There was a *but* coming. "Change takes time, don't you agree?"

Mer smiled. The duke was trying to back her into a corner. Just what was he after? She glanced at the king. He looked completely cool and calm—except for the fingers of his hand curling into a fist in his lap. Mer flicked her eyes back up to her husband's face. Whatever was going on was important. Whatever she said was important. There was more to this banquet than the dowager queen had let on.

It would be so easy to fall into Keventin's trap. It was clear he was angling to humiliate the king. Part of Mer wanted to do it, but that wouldn't endear her to him. She needed to get close to him so that she could tear out his heart.

"It can take time, but it moves faster when allies work together. You're an ally to my king, are you not?" Mer sipped her wine again, feeling all the gazes around the table on them.

"I am, my queen. The changes that are coming will burden some of your dear gentry to the point of beggars. Not all are as loyal as I am."

She stifled her snort.

Keventin was as loyal as a sea serpent and twice as venomous.

Mer took her time setting her crystal goblet on the table and lacing her fingers together to mirror his position. She purposefully scanned the room, her gaze touching each gaudy display of wealth, until she landed on the jewels that decorated his fingers. Much to her satisfaction, the skin around his eyes had tightened.

One point to Mer.

"If all highborn lords are as wealthy as you, surely it won't weigh too heavily on your province." She nodded to one of the thin waiters hovering near the wall. "A little equalizing wouldn't be too much hardship."

Duke Keventin laughed. "Whatever do you mean, my queen? Are my staff not up to your liking? Does the sea kingdom have such excellent staff that it leaves something to be desired among us land dwellers?"

One point to the duke for making her seem like a spoiled Sirenidae.

"No, my lord," she said, batting her lashes, her smile turning a bit more predatory. "I have found so much to love and admire about Methi. It already feels like home." A lie. "What I was referring to was the state of your servants. They are positively wasting away. I've never seen such a thin group of workers in my life." Mer's smile froze as the king reached underneath the table and squeezed her left thigh. A warning that she was about to ignore. She giggled and played with the stem of her wineglass. "Surely such a lofty lord as yourself could afford to fatten your people up a bit. It's a travesty just looking upon them."

Another point to Mer.

Duke Keventin's lips pressed together momentarily before a forced laugh exploded out of him. The table joined in, and he sat back in his chair, his calculating eyes never leaving her face. "What a generous creature you are to care for those who are so far beneath your notice." He grabbed his goblet and held it up. The table followed suit, toasting her. "How lucky are we to have gained a magnanimous queen."

A creature, not a woman.

A chorus of, "Hear, hear!"

Mer's attention never left Keventin's as he drank deeply from his glass.

She had a feeling she'd just made an enemy.

The servant's door swung open, breaking the moment, and waiters filed in. The scent of roasted meat, savory roots, and buttery bread filled the air. Mer sat back in her chair, avoiding the king's gaze. She brushed his hand off of her thigh as a servant placed the next course in front of her.

Mer glanced at the waiter, thanks upon her lips, and froze as she locked gazes with another pair of magenta eyes.

A Sirenidae.

She blinked at the young servant, who dropped her gaze immediately and stepped back, moving to Raziel. She felt Keventin's gaze before she looked at him. He smiled in a way that made her skin crawl. He had a Sirenidae in his employ, and he'd sprung her on Mer to get a reaction.

Duke Keventin gestured to the Sirenidae servant. "A pleasant surprise, no? You're not related are you?"

Indignation had her sitting up in her seat. The insinuation that someone was related just because they were of the same race was disgusting.

"As much as I would like to claim her, unfortunately no," she gritted out.

The duke took a heavy swig of his brew, and swung his hand out, not seeing the Sirenidae servant stepping forward to place his plate before him. The duke knocked the plate out of the servant's hands and into his daughter's lap. She squeaked, a whole plate of hot food splattered on her dress.

The duke pushed from his seat and backhanded the Sirenidae, knocking her to the ground. Mer gasped at the brutality of the action, finding herself on her feet as Keventin kicked the servant twice for good measure.

All eyes turned to her as she glared at the duke's back.

King Raziel had reached out and caught her skirts in his hand, discreetly tugging so she'd sit. Righteous anger filled her for the poor servant on the ground. The duke had been the one to cause the accident, not the waiter.

All she wanted to do was vault over the table and beat the horrible lord with one of his shiny candelabras.

Keventin spun around with a bright smile and smoothed his hair back from his face. He blinked slowly at Mer. "My queen, is everything alright?"

No, it was not. Mer was about to show him how much of a *creature* she could be.

Mer looked at the king, who was as blank as a white

canvas as he stared up at her. The only thing that gave him away was the fist he'd buried in her skirt to keep her in place. What a joke. Little did he know she'd destroy the dress in seconds to get to the Sirenidae servant.

Be smart.

"My king," Mer murmured. "I must take my leave so I may help Duke Keventin's daughter. Please excuse us while we freshen up." She caressed his bicep, ignoring the tension that filled her king at her touch.

She kept her eyes from the servants, who helped the younger girl from the floor and dragged her from the room.

Keventin's smile grew sharp. "You mean my wife."

Mer froze, her gaze resting on the *Duchess* Keventin before she pasted a pleasant smile on her face. "As you say."

The rest of the men and women rose from the table. The king released her dress and stood as well. She flinched as he dropped a quick kiss on her cheek.

"See you soon."

A promise or a threat? She couldn't contemplate either.

Mer woodenly walked out of the room, followed by an entourage of ladies and one rumpled-looking Lady Keventin.

Who was only a bloody child.

It looked like Raziel wasn't the only one who needed to pay for his sins.

Chapter Nineteen

MER

Duchess Keventin's salon was cozy.

Mer stood at the glass doors that led outside to the veranda, half listening to the chatter of the ladies. The sound of the ocean was music to her ears. She could taste the salt in the air. Even as goosebumps ran down her arms from the chilly breeze, she couldn't find it within herself to move.

Huge waves crashed against the cliffs below. She grinned as she spotted luminescent jellyfish floating through the dark water.

Home was calling her.

What she wouldn't give to swim peacefully among the jellies.

Home was calling her.

"Here, my queen, something to keep you warm," a familiar honeyed voice said.

Mer turned to Mazie and took the fur cloak and tossed it over her shoulders, the heat enveloping her immediately. "Thank you."

The duchess had rejoined the group, cleaned up and dressed in a new green gown.

"How old is the duchess?" she asked softly so only Mazie could hear.

"Fourteen."

Mer's stomach churned. Just a child. "How long have they been married?" she forced herself to ask.

"For a little over a year."

Depths below, she was going to be sick.

Mer studied the gathering of women.

Women was generous. They were girls. All fresh-faced and young.

Too young.

"They're all children."

Mazie grunted but said nothing else.

Revulsion filled her the longer she stared at the group of girls. "Is this a common practice among your people?" Mer rasped. Half the girls didn't look old enough to have had their first bleed.

The warrior's lips thinned. "It's more common among the highborn than lower classes. You'll see families sell off their daughters to others, but they're not married until they come of proper age."

"And what is proper age?" Her stomach lurched as Lady Keventin caressed her belly.

Trenches bite. No. Please no.

Mazie hesitated for a second. "Fourteen."

Bile burned the back of Mer's throat, and she stumbled farther out onto the veranda. Mazie caught her elbow, but Mer shook her off. "Fourteen is too young," she rasped, clutching the stone railing. "Lady Keventin is with child?"

"She is." Mazie's voice was flat.

Mer tilted her head back, staring at the crescent moon that gave just enough light to illuminate the waves in the distance.

"How are you so calm?" she asked fiercely, glaring at Mazie.

The warrior turned lady-in-waiting leveled a heavy gaze upon her. "Don't mistake my stoicism as acceptance for what is happening. But some things are out of my control, my queen."

"And your king allows this?"

"It is not for me to judge what my king does and doesn't do."

"If the duchess is fourteen, how is it that she's been married to the duke for a year?"

"Nobles always find a way to get what they want," Mazie practically growled. Her gaze flickered to the salon and back to Mer. She bowed her head. "Duchess Keventin comes."

Mer snapped her mouth shut and schooled her expression as the young girl floated to her side, the green silk dress outlining her little protruding belly. The duchess wrapped her arms around herself and stood quietly beside Mer. Mazie melted into the background, leaving them alone.

A shiver wracked the girl, and Mer found herself pulling the cloak from her shoulders and laying it over the young woman's thin frame.

Lady Keventin's large brown eyes widened, and she shook her head. "I couldn't take th-this from you, m-my queen." A light accent to her voice.

So Mer's suspicions were right. The duchess was Scythian.

"Nonsense," Mer replied, securing the clasp at the girl's throat. "You're caring for more than yourself."

"Th-th-thank you."

"How are you feeling, Your Grace?" Mer asked as the cool air ruffled her short hair, locks falling in her face.

"I am w-well, my queen."

"How is the sickness?"

The duchess blanched. "F-fine."

Mer cocked her head. "There's no wrong answer, my lady. You don't have to fear me." She'd had a friend who had a tricky tongue growing up. His stutter always grew worse when he was nervous, scared, or excited. Was this something similar?

A flush crept into the girl's olive cheeks. "I don't f-fear

you. I've been t-ton-tongue-tied since I was a ch-ch-child, my queen."

"You speak beautifully. Thank you for your words." She smiled warmly at the girl and took Duchess Keventin's hand in her own. "I have a feeling we'll be fast friends. You may call me Mer in private."

The duchess smiled shyly. "Thank you. I'm Sienna."

No stutter. It felt like a reward.

Sienna stepped closer to Mer, her gaze flitting from the group of girls and back to Mer's face. "Th-thank you for what you did, M-mer."

"I've done nothing." She frowned at Sienna. What was she referring to?

"For Phia. Th-the servant." The girl shifted on her feet, the cloak dragging on the ground. "You distracted the l-l-lord from his rage."

Mer squeezed the girl's frail hand, hate for Duke Keventin burning hot in her gut. "Is he often like that?" she asked softly, trying not to scare the girl.

"If y-y-you get in his way," she whispered.

"Has he hurt you?" Mer murmured softly, scanning Sienna's face.

"Not since . . ." Her hand dropped to her rounded belly. "I'm his th-third wife."

Mer stiffened but tried to keep her fear and worry for the young woman off her face. Duke Keventin was an abusive brute and quite possibly a murderer. Lady Sienna wasn't safe, and neither was her unborn child.

"How did you two meet?" Mer asked gently. After all the genetic tampering the Scythians had pursued over the past millennia, they'd almost doomed themselves to extinction. They never let their women leave the country. So how was Sienna here in Methi?

"A long s-s-story, one I d-don't speak of, my queen." Her words were firm.

Mer wouldn't be wheedling the story out of the young duchess this night. She needed more time with the girl to gain her trust. Something was clearly wrong but the poor girl was too afraid to speak up.

She nodded to Sienna. "I understand. There are parts of my past that I would like to forget as well." She gave the girl a soft smile. "Our time at your keep is almost up, but I've enjoyed your company tonight. I would like you to come back with me to court once our husbands have concluded their business."

Sienna's eyes widened further. "I-I-I cannot possibly . . ."

"Nonsense. I am the queen. Duke Keventin would never deny my request. Plus, I know humans have confinement, but you can't possibly be close to that time yet." Two birds, one stone. Mer could keep an eye on the duchess's safety, and gain more information on what the duke was up to. There was something rotten about Laos Keep and its duke. Mer just needed to find more proof.

A little glimmer of hope filled Sienna's eyes. "You really wish me t-to go with you?"

"I do." She squeezed the girl's hand. "It's settled, I'll speak with your husband tonight."

"Thank you, my queen."

"My pleasure." Mer smiled at the girl, her chest heavy with the revelations of the evening. "I do have a question about your servant girl. Phia, was it? How long has she been here?"

"Before m-my marriage."

"And you are . . . close?"

"Phia helps me stay calm when the l-lord loses his temper. She hums for me."

Part of Mer's soul bled at the admittance. Just what sort of hell was Duke Keventin's keep? "Has she said how she came to be here?"

Sienna's brows furrowed. "No. Phia is mute."

"Mute?" Mer had never met a mute Sirenidae.

"Yes. Her tongue was cut from her mouth."

Mer nodded, dropping Sienna's hand so she didn't crush the girl's fingers in her rage.

A Sirenidae's voice was sacred.

Someone had mutilated Phia's.

And Mer planned to find out who and return the favor.

Chapter Twenty

RAZIEL

Each day spent in Laos was more oppressive than the last.

Duke Keventin was playing games with him. He'd taken great pains to show Mer his fleet of fishing vessels, his orchards, and the fancy part of his province. What he had neglected to show the queen were the slums and poverty that clung to his province like a disease. The Mirror Plague ran rampant among those living in the shanty worker towns.

Raziel kicked off his boots and left them in the sand as he picked his way through the beach littered with porous black rocks. He rounded the bluff and spotted his wife standing in a tidepool at the edge of the jetty. He pushed his trousers up his calves and clambered up the slippery rock, avoiding the green patches of algae.

The farther out he moved, the higher the waves became, crashing around them. Sweat dotted his brow, and his hands trembled. He forced them into fists, trying to control his fear of the water.

He edged around a cluster of sharp mussels, the thunder of waves in his ears. He paused, watching Mer as she stood in the crux of the rocks, the ocean on either side. The water lapped around her knees, her dress floating in the water, salt in her short wild hair.

A sea goddess.

It looked as though if she only lifted her hands, the ocean would obey her commands.

Every morning, she visited this spot.

Each day, he joined her.

The first day, he hung back, wary of the Lure.

The second day, she ignored him completely as he crept closer.

The third, she'd stared at him as if willing Raziel to leave.

The fourth day, the queen had sighed and silently accepted his presence when he'd gotten close enough to experience the Lure but not enough to overwhelm him.

Raz didn't know why he kept coming back. They weren't friends. He hated the ocean.

And yet, here he was again.

Hoping maybe she'd speak to him.

Like a bloody fool.

Her words a fortnight ago haunted him.

Raziel had reached out to Samuel Ramses, the Spymaster of Aermia, about his new queen. The information he'd received had been surprisingly vague, and it seemed Samuel would be visiting quite soon.

Mer Thalassan had indeed been married before. Her husband, Ream, had been a healer, but there wasn't much on his death, only that he'd died during the Warlord's War. What confounded Raz was the fact that the Sirenidae had been their allies. He didn't understand how he could be responsible for her husband's death. When Raz took a life, it tended to haunt him at night.

No Sirenidae faces visited him during his nightmares.

That's not true.

He gritted his teeth.

Mer visited him in his dreams. Ones where skin slid against skin, and she sighed softly in his ears.

Raziel shook the image from his mind and focused on important matters. Like communicating with his queen so they could move forward in harmony.

She hadn't brought her husband's death up again, and he didn't know how to broach the subject without incurring her considerable wrath.

He'd wed a feral little bride.

Like calls to like.

Wading into the cool water, he tiptoed past sea anemones, starfish, and tiny crabs watching him with large eyes. His toes became buried in the sand as he stopped, standing beside the Sirenidae. Her eyes were closed, lips slightly apart.

Once again, she was only half dressed.

Raz shook his head and soaked in the salty air, breathing through the Lure that perfumed the air. His mouth watered at her tantalizing scent, and his hands trembled with the need to run them across her skin.

Maybe this was a bad idea. His dreams of the night were too fresh in his mind.

He eyed the ocean, a small smile lifting his lips as dolphins played in the water. They sped through the side of waves and leapt out of the sea in arcs like they weighed nothing. It was incredible.

"WHAT ARE YOU DOING HERE?" SHE ASKED, NOT opening her eyes.

"Meditation, my queen."

Mer snorted, her nose wrinkling with the movement. "Your custom." A pause. "Don't you think we're past honorifics in private? I did try to kill you."

Her blunt words pulled a booming laugh from Raz. Tears sprouted at the corners of his eyes, and he bent in half, bracing his hands on his knees. Stars, she was brash.

"Are you done yet?" she drawled.

Raziel glanced at his wife, who scowled down at him. He laughed harder. Swiping the tears away, he straightened, shaking his head. "Only you would say such a thing . . . Mer."

"And only you would laugh at a death threat, Raziel."

They stared at each other for a beat before she cracked a smile and snickered.

Something inside his chest loosened at the sound. She really was lovely.

That's the Lure talking.

She caught the look on his face, and her laughter was gone as soon as it came. Mer regained her composure, all traces of mirth wiped from her face.

His smile disappeared and he sighed. For a moment, they'd both forgotten what each had done, or at least they could laugh about it.

He turned his attention back to the rolling sea, unease rising as the waves did. What if one got too big and swept them away?

Breathe. Calm your mind.

Instead, he started babbling, distracting himself from the fear and her scent.

"Why do you come here each day? There are better views elsewhere." Silence. "Why don't you swim?" Silence. "Do you miss home?" Silence. "Why is the Lure not as strong as it was that first day?" Silence. "Do you want to be miserable for the rest of your life?"

Mer twisted to look at him, something haunting in her gaze that he'd seen in his own eyes after visiting a funeral pyre. He longed to reach for her, to soothe the pain from her face.

It's the Lure.

"What is misery but penance?"

That struck a chord. "What do you have to pay for?"

She stayed silent, her mesmerizing magenta eyes holding a wealth of pain before she shuttered them and looked away. A broken soul if he'd ever seen one.

"And yes, I do miss home."

He gestured to the water. "Then go. No one is stopping you."

A hollow laugh fell from her lips. "If only that were the case."

The Sirenidae dropped to her knees in the tidepool, the water rising to her waist. She hissed out a breath but bowed her head and closed her eyes.

Conversation over.

Raziel stared down at her short silver hair, and his fingers twitched at his sides. Her Lure swelled, and he almost dropped to his knees and wrapped his arms around her body, maybe to even taste the skin of her neck right by her gills . . .

Warning bells went off in his head, and Raziel forced himself to take one step at a time back from the deadly alluring female he'd married.

He finally pried his eyes from the Sirenidae and turned his back to her, striding down the jetty.

"When do we leave?" Mer called.

Raz peered over his shoulder. "As soon as I settle matters with Keventin."

Mer bared her teeth, her incisors slightly longer than his own. "Be quick about it, or I might kill him."

He grinned back at her. "So bloodthirsty."

"You have no idea."

Turning back around, he clambered down from the rocks, the smile slipping from his face. Raziel didn't know if he should take that as a warning or not. Even though she hadn't tackled him into the ocean and drowned Raz . . . or fed him to her pet beasties he'd seen swimming around the jetty at night . . . it meant nothing.

She rarely showed him her true self.

Raziel snorted.

They really were quite the pair.

When was the last time he'd been honest with anyone about what he wanted? Or who he was?

Chapter Twenty-One

MER

Phia had all but disappeared from the keep.

Mer had questioned Sienna, but the young duchess had not seen her friend since Duke Keventin had beaten her. She'd even asked the duke outright where the girl was, and he'd told her she'd been dismissed for her incompetence and sent home to her family.

Mer didn't believe him.

A Sirenidae wouldn't have been able to return home to her people through the ocean. Mer was sure Keventin hadn't sent her along with any money to make her way home.

Either Phia was in a watery grave, or she was being kept somewhere.

Mer guessed the latter.

A Sirenidae held value, and with the proclivities of the duke, she doubted he would let something he deemed valuable slip through his fingers.

That evening, she sat on a plush divan listening to a bard sing about love as Keventin had his pregnant wife rub his shoulders. Mer stared, feeling her hackles rise.

Sienna had dark bruises beneath her eyes as if she hadn't slept all night and a beard burn along her neck and shoulder. The poor girl looked as if she were about to pass out on the spot.

"If you stare any harder, you'll turn him to ash," Gideon whispered in her ear.

Mer scoffed. "He's lucky that I don't lunge from this couch and rip his heart out."

Gideon dramatically gasped, blue eyes flaring wide. "My queen, how could you say such things?"

She quirked a smile at the ambassador. She'd met many people since arriving in Methi, but the fair Gideon was one of her favorites. There was something so likeable about him.

"Hush, you two," the king rumbled from her left, his face a mask of boredom. "Or you'll offend our host."

As if Raz really cared about that. Mer had been listening carefully over the last week, and he'd had no problem putting Keventin in his place. If anyone had offended the duke, it would have been the king.

The duke in question pulled his wife into his lap as the bard changed his song.

"I thought your culture didn't accept public affection?" she hissed, wanting to tear the man's hands off of the girl.

"This is not public, and Laos is more . . . relaxed," Raziel answered, sipping his brew from the silver chalice. "In fact . . ."

She squeaked when he wrapped his arm around her waist and hauled her against his side.

"What are you doing?" she hissed.

"Cuddling my wife as everyone expects me to," Raziel grouched softly.

Mer shifted, aware of each place they touched. Her skin warmed and hummed, and the desire to lean into him was almost overwhelming.

Until she glanced back at the duke.

He caught her eye and winked while laying kisses on Sienna's shoulder.

"Deep breath," Raziel murmured. "Ignore them."

"Is that what you do?" she whispered back. "Ignore the child brides around you?"

The king stiffened. "No, but I can't control everything, even though I wish to."

"You are the king," she whispered harshly. "It is your duty to protect your people, especially those who cannot protect themselves."

"I agree, but it takes time."

Time girls like Sienna didn't have.

Mer swallowed hard and focused on the bard's song, knowing she would do something drastic if she watched the duke's display any longer.

The young man sat on a stool, his voice ringing out clear and pure:

A MERRY DANCE ABOVE THE WAVES
 Frolicked the ladies of the sun.
 Ceto plotted from his dark palace,
 Wishing for the touch of fair skin.

MER STRAIGHTENED. *CETO.*

HE TRICKED AND FLATTERED,
 Stealing her into his den.
 She cursed her fate
 And slowly wasted away.
 Desperate to save his love,
 Ceto returned her to the surface.
 A promise that he would return
 When the tide rose,
 So did the dark king only to find his love,
 Hanging from the gallows.
 Tarnished she was by sea,

Broken and battered by her people's unholy glee.
He raged and swore his revenge.
So sweet maiden, listen to his tale
And never dance by the sea.

WHEN GIDEON BEGAN TO CLAP, MER STARTLED out of her reverie, the words of the song ringing in her ears. A soothing movement along her hip registered as her mind tried to pick apart the song. She glanced at the king, but he was looking at Keventin. It seemed he didn't even know he was running his thumb along her hip.

She should have been repulsed.

But it felt nice . . .

Ignore him. Focus on Ceto.

It was a unique name. It was a coincidence, wasn't it?

She wanted to believe that it could be something more. It could be the clue she'd been looking for. Songs and poems usually were rooted in truth.

Mer needed to speak with the bard.

"Wonderful!" Mer clapped and rose to her feet, the king's arm dropping. Raziel watched her, his brows rising in what seemed like surprise.

The bard blushed and bowed deeply to her. "Thank you, my queen."

"Where did you learn such an enchanting song?" Mer sauntered toward him, lowering her lashes. "It reminds me of home."

The bard's smile grew at her attention. "It's a fish-man's song that originated in the villages along the coast. I stayed with a family there once, and they taught me. It's a warning to those about cavorting with the sea. It can be enchanting but cost you your life."

"Very true," she murmured. "And Ceto is meant to be the sea? It's a unique name, no?"

The bard set his lute on the floor and nodded. "In our kingdom, Ceto is an old myth. A dark god of the sea. Fishermen bless or curse him according to their luck. Many believe he pulls ships down into the North Sea to appease the bloodthirstiness of his people."

"His people? Do you mean Sirenidae?"

The bard shook his head, eyes widened. "No, my queen. Demons."

MER STARED AT THE CEILING OF HER DARK ROOM, the moon hidden for the night.

She couldn't take her mind off the song.

It was as if it spoke to her. Like the meaning was just out of her grasp.

One thing she did know was that she needed to travel to the fishman's coast. Lilja had traveled the world, collecting songs and stories like trophies. She shared them with Mer. Not once had she ever mentioned this story or a character with the name Ceto.

If this story originated in the fishing villages, there was a high chance that Ceto was associated with the Pernicious who had passed through that area or even been raised there.

She kicked off the blankets and rolled onto her stomach, hugging a feather pillow to her chest. Sleeping in a bed on land was an adjustment. Between their seaweed cocoons and floating moss beds, it was as if the ocean had coddled her almost every night of her life.

Here, her body cramped and sagged into the bed uncomfortably after a few hours, and she was constantly too hot or too cold.

Her eyelids finally drooped, and sleep began to claim her.

The bed groaned, and she shifted a second before her scales stood on end.

Mer's eyes snapped open as her face was shoved forcibly into the pillow and mattress. She tried to scream but only ended up sucking fabric into her mouth as a heavy weight settled over her bare legs. A large hand squeezed the back of her neck, pinning her in place, unable to breathe.

She bucked her hips and swiped at her attacker, not able to reach them. Mer changed tactics and pinched the hard thigh straddling her with all her might. A man hissed above her.

"Get her hands, you fool," Keventin whispered harshly.

Mer tried to push herself upward, only to have her arms yanked roughly behind her back and tied. Dizziness washed over her as she tried to inhale, panic rising higher and higher.

"Leave us," Keventin commanded. He leaned down. "Now I have you where you belong, you sanctimonious wench. Hold still as I show my queen a proper welcome," he sneered softly in her ear like a lover.

Her eyes widened as a calloused hand caught the hem of her nightgown and yanked it over her hips, cold air washing over her skin.

This couldn't be happening. This couldn't be happening.

Mer struggled against his strength and cried out into the mattress, wildly flailing.

"Won't it be fun to see if the next heir looks like me or Raziel?" he murmured. "You've been asking for this since the moment you stepped into my home. Always challenging me. Always glaring at me."

She registered a belt being undone and an eerie sort of calm settled over her.

This is happening. Fight. Remember your training.

"You want this just as much as I do. Stop playing hard to get."

Mer pushed past the terror and dizziness and disgust, wiggling a little to get a sense of his position.

One right hand on the back of her neck, left hand fumbling with his pants.

A body off balance.

She lifted her left thigh and hooked it over his left one.

A soft chuckle rumbled out of Keventin. "I knew you wanted me, but a little punishment first for trying to steal my wife away, huh?" He groaned softly, tracing his fingers over the scales on her left thigh. "You're just like the other one. So soft, pliant. Exactly how you should be."

That was it.

Mer threw herself to the right with all her strength, reversing their positions. She spun onto her knees.

Make every blow count.

She knelt and slammed her knee between his legs. Keventin doubled forward, and she headbutted him, knocking him back into the bed. Mer breathed hard, her pulse hammering in her ears. Mer wrenched her arms, clawing her way out of the bonds around her wrists.

A knock sounded at her door. "My lady?" Mazie called, her voice sleepy.

Mer sucked in a full breath ready to scream when Duke Keventin rasped.

"I'll kill her if you call for help."

She paused, staring down at the monster in her bed cupping himself, face red. "Who?"

"You know who," he wheezed. "I didn't miss the way you looked at that half breed. Her death will be on your hands if you ever speak of this. You will kill Phia."

"Don't you dare say her name." She bared her teeth at him. "If I scream, you will be stripped of your title and hung. Phia and Sienna will be rid of you."

"My lady?" Mazie's voice grew louder.

Mer grabbed Keventin by the throat. "Tell me where Phia is."

"She's somewhere you'll never find her." He smiled at her through his pain. "Do you really think her torment will be over if I die? She'll cry for death and beg for the pain to stop, but it will never end."

It wasn't a choice.

"I'm fine," she choked out to Mazie. "Just nightmares."

"I can fetch some warm milk," the warrior offered through the door.

"I am okay. Go back to bed." She trembled.

"Okay. Good night, my queen."

"Good night," Mer replied, her voice raspy. All she had to do was get this man out of her room and then get to the king. They would find Phia and destroy Keventin.

The duke whispered, "I know what you're thinking. That perhaps you can get the king to turn against me, but it won't happen. I've heard the stories about you, my queen. The woman who hates the king so much, she tried to kill him on first acquaintance. The woman who wears revealing clothing and flirts with the entire court. The shameless slut who got jealous when a duke showed his wife affection."

She stared down at the snake who'd slithered his way into her bed, her shaking increasing with each insidious lie. "You know nothing."

"You might hold a title, but you are nothing. No one would believe a murderous foreigner over a respected member of the gentry."

She could see how this fight would play out. The king held no love for her, and he needed Keventin. Her gaze darted over his face as the horrid truth dawned. There was nothing she could do.

"Now, get off me."

Every part of her wanted to kill him.

Think of Phia.

Mer leaned into his face, her wrists bleeding from the rough rope. "Mark my words, I'll kill you one day."

He grinned, his teeth bloody. "Not before I have you."

Over my dead body.

Bile burned the back of her throat and before she could think it through, she whispered, "Don't scream, your grace, or your ruse will be over."

"What . . ."

She released his throat and slashed him across the face, her nails digging in deep.

He clamped his lips together, groaning.

Mer jumped to her feet and kicked him in the crotch and then the ribs for good measure before scurrying from the bed. "Get out."

Duke Keventin hauled himself out of her bed, limping to an open panel in her wall.

A secret entrance.

He tipped his head to her, a vile grin on his face that made her skin crawl. "See you in the morning for breakfast," he crooned.

She stared as he disappeared from sight. The door shut without a sound.

She scrambled forward and wedged a chair against the panel before backing away.

Blood dripped down her right hand.

There was part of him still on her.

With trembling hands, she poured water into the bowl and scrubbed her hands furiously until they burned. But it wasn't enough. She still felt him everywhere. Mer tossed the water into the cold fireplace and poured more water into the basin before scrubbing her whole body.

It wasn't enough.

The keep creaked, and she jumped, her heart pounding.

Tears flooded her eyes, and she abandoned the rag and water. Mer moved as far as she could from the secret door, her back meeting the door between her own suite and the king's. Mer snatched a heavy candlestick from the mantle above the fireplace and slid to the floor.

Her wet fingers pressed into the cold metal, and she retched, bile filling her mouth.

You did well. You fought.

It almost hadn't been enough.

Tears tracked down her cheeks one after another as she cried silently, feeling dirty and scared.

You're just as soft as the other one.

Mer cried harder, wishing that Phia was dead so that she wouldn't experience whatever horrors the duke had planned for her.

Chapter Twenty-Two

RAZIEL

Something was wrong.

Duke Keventin had suggested they'd go for a stroll to the markets around the docks and take the women shopping. Not once during the week he'd been at Laos Keep had the duke shown one iota of interest in his wife's wellbeing.

The outing was a ruse.

Keventin just wanted to show Raziel how much influence he had over the navy and how profitable his province was. He was trying to intimidate Raz.

It was laughable really.

While Duke Keventin could be a powerful enemy, his entire province had been bestowed upon him during

Raziel's grandfather's rule. It would be just as easy to oust the man and replace him.

But he really didn't want to do that.

It would create more problems.

He needed to do this carefully and get Duke Keventin on his side.

Gideon strode by his side as they meandered through the open market, his ever-loyal spymaster. No one ever suspected his friend of being deadly with a blade. He was underestimated at every turn because of his fair looks, which suited them both. Gideon could gallivant around as Raziel's ambassador, gossiping and flirting, all while protecting the king's back and collecting information without seeming threatening.

The scent of fried dough, roasted meat, sweet fruit, and incense perfumed the sea air along with hints of brine and fish. Exotic fabrics waved in the breeze, and jewelry sparkled in the sunlight, gleaming from velvet trays. His warriors mingled with the crowd, ever close but not over-bearing.

"Did you see Keventin's face?" Gideon muttered underneath his breath. He smiled and winked at one of Lady Keventin's ladies, who trailed a little ahead of them with the queen. She batted her lashes and glanced away coyly, pretending to admire a painted scarf.

Raziel nodded, eyeing his wife and the way she drifted through the crowd, barely engaging with any of the merchants. She'd certainly not been herself this morning.

He'd gone to the beach for their early meditation, and Mer hadn't been there.

It bothered him more than he'd wanted to admit.

Over the last week, Raz had thought they'd made some progress. Maybe she hated him a little less or had come to terms with the fact that they were stuck together for life.

Apparently not.

Trying to catch her eye proved unfruitful. Why the cold shoulder? All the life seemed to have been drained out of her. After Mer's excitement over the music last night, he procured the bard to visit them at the palace. She seemed to be fond of music, and if it made things a little more peaceful between them, so be it.

Frustrated, he glanced away at Keventin on his right, and the four deep cuts across his cheek, jaw, and neck. The man chatted with a goldsmith and gestured to his face.

"Subdued the vicious thing before it had a chance to take another swipe at me." The duke grinned cockily at the merchant, puffing out his chest. "Would like to have another go at the beastie."

"It would be entertaining, to be sure," the goldsmith replied.

Raziel brushed a small braid from his cheek and tucked it behind his ear. He didn't think that was the whole story. The tight skin around Keventin's eyes and the anger that he held just beneath the surface told Raz something different. If only he'd been around to see what actually happened.

The older man was as vain as they came.

If the cat story was true, then he hadn't expected to be attacked, or else he wouldn't have engaged. The duke liked winning. He always stacked the odds in his favor. The fact that he'd lost to a beast seemed . . . odd or rather fortuitous.

No, Raz suspected something else altogether had occurred. But what?

"They're pretty ugly," Gideon breathed, flashing a smile at a buxom merchant's wife, who blushed furiously and set about organizing their carved candlesticks.

"That they are." He kept from rolling his eyes and smiled at the old carver, who glared at his wife, unabashedly fanning her face. Raz stifled the chuckle that threatened to escape at their display. Gideon always had that effect on the fair sex everywhere he went. It didn't matter their age either.

His friend pursed his lips. "Do you believe him?"

"It doesn't matter what I believe, only that he agrees to enforce the new changes I've proposed." Pushback wasn't an option. He peered over his shoulder at Keventin, who untangled himself from his wife and winked at a servant girl carrying a box.

Irreprehensible.

"If he's smart, he will," Gideon replied. "He's been taxing the people more, and none of that has gone to the royal coffers but into his own pockets. Some could construe that as embezzlement."

Raziel grunted in agreement.

The markets grew crowded, people bowing and curtsying as they passed by. A woman with a decorative curtain formed of sea shells and underwater trinkets caught his eye. The queen had slowed, her fingers gently running over gilded shells, pearl hairpins, ocean jasper rings, and coral bracelets.

Her fingers lingered on a soft green pearl hairpin for a long moment before she reached up to her short hair. A flash of regret crossed her face before she moved on. If she hated her hair short, why cut it?

More questions and no answers.

His wife continued on, speaking softly to Duchess Keventin who had caught up.

Raz approached the stall, and the windswept woman with dark brown hair and skin bowed low, her eyes on the ground. He picked up the hairpin and studied it.

It was simple.

A large pale green pearl sat at one end of the gold pin. Waves were engraved into the pin itself. It ended in a sharp point.

Simple. Beautiful. Sharp.

Just like his wife.

He didn't understand the *need* he felt to procure it for his wife. It seemed like it belonged with Mer. Nothing more.

Liar, liar.

"Gideon?" he called.

His friend arched a brow at Raziel but silently placed the coins on the artist's table, plus a little extra for good measure. "Your work is stunning."

The woman beamed. "Thank you," she blurted out, glancing up at Raziel before looking back to the ground. "Would you like me to wrap it?"

"No." Raziel pocketed the object, his thumb running over the pearl. Satisfaction settled over him at the purchase. It was a good gift—no, *peace offering*, lest Mer get the wrong idea.

"If I might be so bold," the woman said softly, "our lady might like these." She pushed a set of dainty silver hair clips with small purple-and-orange shells, accented with peach seed pearls. "These are good for shorter hair," she explained, lacing her fingers together.

He eyed them and fiddled with the hairpin in the pocket of his sleeveless robe. Her hair wasn't long enough for the pin, so she'd have to wait to use it, but the clips . . .

"Wrap them," he demanded gruffly, feeling too many eyes on him, including Keventin, who had turned around to see what held them up.

The woman quickly packaged the clips and set them on the table. Raziel scooped up the small parcel and shoved it unceremoniously in his other pocket while Gideon paid the merchant. He continued on, smiling to those who met his gaze, ignoring the annoying boasting of Keventin as they perused the wares.

Gideon caught up with him and shoved his hands in his pockets but said nothing.

Raziel's jaw clenched, wanting to explain himself but knowing he didn't need to. "I couldn't go to the market and not support my people." A logical explanation.

"You don't have to explain yourself to me."

Except he felt the need to. "They were pretty," Raz admitted, feeling a little vulnerable.

"Like your wife?" his friend teased gently.

He scowled at Gideon but didn't refute his words. It would make him a liar if he did. Raz had expected her to be cold like the sea, but she was all flames and fire like the sun. Despite her prickly nature, he was inexplicably drawn to her. It was off-putting and inconvenient.

Sighing, Raz shrugged. "She needed them." Which was true. Over the course of the last few days of meditation, her hair was constantly tangled and in her eyes. It made him want to smooth the wavy locks out of the way. That was not something he could indulge in. Their marriage was an agreement made for the better good. He had no plans of forming any attachments.

"They suit her. You chose well."

Raz shoved down the burst of pleasure at the compliment. It didn't matter if she liked them or not. She had a need, and as her king, he was duty bound to provide her with what she needed.

Keventin smiled widely at Raziel, the wounds pulling on his face. "Are you ready to tour our newest warship, my king?"

"I am looking forward to seeing what you've done to my fleet," he replied.

The duke's smile was sharp. "I aim to please." He turned his back to Raz and strode ahead.

"He didn't like your reminder that the fleet is yours," Gideon muttered. "He's going to be a problem."

"Keventin is already a problem," Raziel growled.

The market gave way to the naval docks. Magnificent warships bobbed in the harbor. Seagulls screeched from the skies, circling high above. Uniformed officers stood at attention at the end of the closest dock. Raziel spotted Captain Velicu standing on the warship, her signature long navy coat fluttering in the wind. She'd been given command of the new ship. At least the duke had listened to Raziel in his suggestion for the outstanding female captain to be rewarded.

Keventin paused next to Mer, and for some reason, it made the hair along Raziel's arms stand at attention.

"Shall we, my queen?" Duke Keventin asked, bowing grandly to Mer.

Don't take his hand.

He missed a step at the thought and stumbled before catching himself. Where had that come from?

The queen stiffened, staring Keventin down.

The duke smiled wider. "Come now, let me show you all the strength of our navy."

Raziel's eyes narrowed at their backs when she slowly accepted his arm.

"Easy there," Gideon advised. "You're looking a little jealous."

That wouldn't do. Raziel wiped a hand over his face and spotted Duchess Keventin gazing after her husband and the queen, her hand curled around her belly. Disgust filled him. She was too young for Keventin. Hell, she was too young to be anyone's wife. She was just a girl. A pregnant girl.

That was his next project. Changing the marriageable age. It had been a long time coming. The horror on Mer's face at the banquet when she discovered Sienna was the duke's wife haunted Raziel. It was hard to even look at her without wanting to beat the duke bloody.

One thing at a time. Be patient.

With unease churning in his gut, he approached the little lady and held his elbow out for her. She blinked owlishly up at him before curtsying and placing her dainty hand lightly on his forearm.

"Th-Thank you, my k-ki-king."

"My pleasure," he answered. He took small steps so that she could keep up.

Lady Keventin made him feel like a brute. She didn't even reach his sternum. Most women didn't with his height.

Except for your queen.

His gaze was drawn to Mer once again. Most of her smooth back was exposed, her body swathed in a baby-blue watered-silk dress. She reached his shoulder. He didn't have to angle his neck to look at his Sirenidae wife.

It would be easy to kiss her.

Raziel blanched.

There would be no kissing.

"She's lo-lovely," Lady Keventin whispered, following his gaze. "K-kind too."

Kind? When had the queen shown kindness to the little duchess? From the girl's tone, she liked Mer. That connection could prove useful. "I hear that you will be returning with us to the Onyx Palace. You must have made a good impression on the queen as well."

The duchess smiled but said nothing.

With Keventin's wife and heir in the capital, perhaps it would keep the duke from doing anything he might regret.

Like start a civil war.

His lips thinned as Keventin released the queen's arm and placed his hand on her bare back to help her up the ramp to the new warship. She jerked and twisted slightly out of the way, her feet catching on the long skirt of her dress. Mer grabbed the duke, a scream falling from her lips as she lost her balance.

Calculating magenta eyes met Raziel's for a second before the pair tumbled into the bay.

Chapter Twenty-Three

MER

MER SUCKED IN A DEEP BREATH AS THEY
crashed through the water.

Icy prickles shot through her body at the frigid
temperatures of the bay. Fish darted away from them, a
few inky shadows of sharks lurking about, sensing the
commotion.

Her gills flared, inhaling water and shoving the air
from her lungs, but she hardly felt the burn.

The duke thrashed in her hold, but Mer managed to
wrap her legs around his arms and waist, locking her
ankles together so he couldn't move. The vile man tossed
his head back as if to headbutt her, but she caught it
between her palms.

Fear and disgust writhed in her gut from just touching the man.

A song of hate and prey rose from her lips as they drifted down the sharp slope of the bay toward open water. Tears burned her eyes.

Don't kill him. Think of Phia.

Her last straw had snapped when he'd caressed the skin of Mer's lower back. She'd dealt with his wild stories of taming a seacat and all the innuendoes the entire morning.

The veiled threats were the worst.

Familiar shapes appeared in the distance, advancing toward them.

Keventin convulsed in her arms, fighting harder as the largest leviathan Mer had ever encountered swam closer. She shivered, trying to keep her mind from fogging. The water was just so cold.

A pregnant female with many scars along her sleek striped body.

The beast hummed in reply, its rows of sharp teeth visible. She was hungry and looking for a fight.

Mer held the duke tighter and whispered in his ear, "You came to me in the dark like a coward. You may think you hold power but know that I hold the ocean in my hand, and you're fortified Keep hovers over my domain. There is no place you can go to escape me. If Phia or Sienna are harmed in any way, I will make sure you suffer the most gruesome death imaginable."

He shook, the stench of his fear in the water.

She dismissed the man and locked eyes with the leviathan, turning her song into something softer, pleading, peaceful. The beastie didn't retreat. Mer released her hands and held them out, making herself bigger. They would not become the creature's meal. Her fingers tingled, moving slowly from the icy water.

A different tune reached her ears, and Mer fought not to break the stare off with the leviathan. Lack of dominance could get her killed. The song grew sharper.

Another Sirenidae?

The beastie darted forward and passed them, chasing a smaller shark that had come too close.

Mer released the duke, who clumsily clawed for the surface, his movements sluggish.

She pushed her short hair from her face and searched the depths for the song, which had abruptly cut off.

Just the creatures of the sea feeding off bay scraps.

It was only your imagination.

Grief and exhaustion crashed down on her, and all she wanted to do was lie down on the silt sand and sleep. The shivers increased, the skin around her gills aching from the cold.

Move.

Mer pushed off the bottom of the bay and swam toward the surface. The duke had slowed, his movements sluggish.

Don't let him die.

Catching him underneath the armpits, Mer gritted her teeth and towed Keventin up. Movement near the docks caught her eye. The king hovered in the water just a few feet beneath the surface, his silver eyes narrowed as they neared the surface.

A thread of panic wound around her heart. How much had he seen?

Human eyesight was poor in saltwater.

Mer pointedly ignored the king and helped the duke reach the surface. He coughed and spluttered, gasping for air when she pushed him against the slick dock, holding them both up, her legs gently kicking to keep them afloat.

The dock was pure bedlam.

Warriors were shouting at each other, and court ladies were crying in dismay. Mer locked eyes with King Raziel over Keventin's shoulder. He held onto the edge of the dock, his wet red hair so dark it looked like spilled ink.

No worry creased his brow. Only anger.

He'd seen what she'd done.

That didn't bode well for her plan of winning him over just to destroy his heart.

With her gaze still on the king, she whispered in the duke's ear, "I keep my promises. Remember what I said. Return Phia to the keep."

"As you wish, *my queen*." He leaned into her body with a groan, his hand reaching for hers. "I am a man of my word too. I'll have you soon."

She jerked away, bile burning the back of her throat as

he turned in the water, grinning, his pupils blown wide from the Lure. Nausea churned in her belly. He reminded her of a shark. Cunning, smart, and dangerous.

"Everyone onto the ship," Gideon ordered.

The warriors followed the command, ushering the ladies up the bridge onto the warship. Sienna paused watching Mer tread water, no emotion on her young face. The girl tipped her chin to Mer, a small act of defiance before hustling onto the warship.

Mer's teeth began to chatter as Gideon helped Duke Keventin out of the bay. The hulking duke stumbled away from the water's edge and brushed off his help. He spun to smile at Mer, and her blood went cold. This was not nearly over. She wanted to shrink under his gaze, but somehow, Mer managed to keep her head up.

Duke Keventin held his hand out to her. "Let me help you out of the water, my queen. What an adventure!"

The thought of touching him again just about made her retch.

"Your Grace," Gideon called, flashing his bright smile. "Come and get warm. The captain tells me they have dry clothing for you on the ship."

Annoyance crossed Keventin's face before he masked it. "Of course."

She watched as he disappeared onto the massive ship.

That just left Gideon, the king, and herself.

King Raziel hauled himself up, water pouring down his wide shoulders and muscular back. An unwelcome flicker of heat surged in her belly. He was too handsome for his own good.

He knelt and held his hand out to her, his face an impassive mask. "Gideon, you need to move back, away from the queen and me."

His blue eyes widened. "Of course. Be careful. I don't want to go in after you."

They thought she was going to drown him. While the idea always had merit, not today. The only one who deserved a horrid drowning was the duke.

Slowly, she bridged the distance between them, assessing the king as his pupils expanded. He coughed, and a shudder ran through his body when she slipped her hand into his large calloused one. A squeak flew out of her when he yanked her from the cold sea and into his arms. She stumbled, catching herself against his chest. Water poured from her gills and then sealed shut.

"Cloak?" the king grunted, pulling her fully against him. "Why are you always almost naked?"

Gideon handed over his own, and the king brusquely slung it over her shoulders.

She blinked up at him, shivering. "I'm wearing a full dress."

"One that is *see-through*."

Her teeth chattered together, and everything hurt, but she managed to shrug. "It's just a body."

"One that doesn't belong to *them*," he muttered.

"Nor to you."

He stilled. "As you say."

She scanned his features, and the urge to cup his face nearly overwhelmed her. He was upset, and she wanted to soothe him.

What is wrong with you? Remember who he is. Stick to your plan.

The plan to capture his heart and then break it. Maybe she should just touch his face anyway... all in the name of vengeance.

Mer stamped out the desire and yelped when the king swept her into his arms bridal-style, holding her close as he stalked down the dock, Gideon in tow. His wet robe slapped against his boots.

"I can walk," she objected, not wanting to be close to anyone. At least he wasn't touching her skin. Just the large cloak that cocooned her.

His fingers flexed against her body just as his nose brushed her temple. "I couldn't let you go even if I wanted to," he growled in her ear.

Right, the Lure.

"Where are we going?" she asked, shivering and hating herself as she cuddled closer to the king's warmth, glancing over his shoulder. Captain Velicu hovered by the railing and lifted a hand in goodbye. Mer smiled at the formidable woman, but her smile dropped as the duke stepped up to the captain's side. There would be consequences for what she'd done today. Keventin's eyes promised retribution.

"Home. Where you can't try to kill anyone else."

She stared out at the open ocean, wishing she could have said a proper goodbye to the sea.

Something out of place caught her eye.

It looked almost like a face?

She blinked and it was gone.

Wishful thinking on her part.

Chapter Twenty-Four

MER

AFTER HER STUNT AT LAOS KEEP, THE KING HAD unceremoniously locked her away as soon as they reached the Onyx Palace. It had killed her leaving Phia behind, but the duchess promised to arrive within the week with her friend in tow.

If Keventin hadn't killed the Sirenidae.

Mer believed he was smarter than that. Phia was the key to controlling Mer. He wouldn't be that shortsighted, or at least Mer hoped so.

It seemed like the duke hadn't made any accusations against her, but Raziel had seen something of the interaction between her and Keventin that made him believe she tried to kill the duke.

Any trust they had been building disappeared with her actions.

They hadn't even let her out for meditation.

Even the dowager queen had shown up to give her a tongue-lashing about modesty, propriety, and attempted murder. Surprisingly, the older woman had focused on Mer's dress, not Keventin.

Humans were odd.

Sirenidae had always hated clothing. For most of Mer's life, she'd worn hardly anything but her sealskin, and that covered very little. There was never shame associated with anyone's body or skin. A body was just that. A body. Something to be appreciated for the life and support it gave.

Her lips thinned as she played with the short ends of her hair.

Humans were a little different when it came to modesty, and it seemed Methians even more so. Every single person she passed seemed to be covered head to toe.

During the welcoming feast, she'd taken great delight in leaving the stodgy Methian gown in her room and tearing the curtains from the wall. The final look had been beautiful, even though the color hadn't been right for her. What she'd enjoyed even more was the look on the queen's face when she'd entered the dining hall.

That night felt like a lifetime ago.

When she'd left for Methi, Mer had painted King

Raziel as the worst of men. While he still needed to pay for what he'd done, Duke Keventin was worse.

Her heart raced and her breathing accelerated.

For the last three nights, Mer had barricaded the doors and then slept on the floor with a knife she'd stolen from Laos Keep. Nightmares plagued Mer, so she was just as tired when she woke up in the morning.

Mazie had even commented on the dark circles beneath Mer's eyes. The warrior knew something was wrong but couldn't figure out what it was. Mer wouldn't be telling her either. While she really liked Mazie, she knew the king had planted her into Mer's lady's maids to spy.

She growled and pushed out of the large chair by the fire. Mer paced, feeling like her skin was too tight for her body. Too many things were spiraling out of control.

The king didn't remember Ream. His death had been so insignificant that the king didn't even know he'd destroyed Mer in the process.

Phia was still missing and in the clutches of Duke Keventin.

Mer had no way of reaching the coast to continue her inquiries about Ceto.

The dowager queen expected Mer to become a Methian queen.

She had no true friends.

And . . . she felt herself softening toward Raziel.

It was a betrayal to Ream.

Mer leaned heavily against the back of the chair and squeezed her eyes shut. Grief came in waves. Some days, she only ached. At other times, the pain was so excruciating, Mer could hardly function.

Just breathe.

With difficulty, Mer slowed her breathing and managed to calm her racing pulse. By the time she'd come out of the spell, the fire had burned down to coals.

A knock sounded at the door, and she quickly wiped the tears from her face. Mer walked to the door and opened it.

Three Methian lady's maids, including Mazie. Mer barely kept from rolling her eyes. The dowager queen had sicced them on her once again. They were a good source of information, but Mer wasn't in the mood for engaging in idle gossip. She had plans.

"I am about to lie down and rest for a bit," she said with a small smile.

The youngest of the lady's maids, Mariah, nodded a bit too vigorously, her light brown curls bouncing around her round face. "Of course. We will visit later, my lady."

Mazie arched a brow. "Can I bring you some tea, my queen? It might help."

Mer shook her head no. The last thing she needed was the warrior poking around in her room. "No, thank you."

"Alright. We will visit you once you've rested," Mazie said, her tone somewhat begrudging.

Translation: *you're not getting rid of me.*

Mer smiled gratefully and closed the door, locking it. She turned and leaned her back on the wood, sighing. She had to move quickly. Mazie was as suspicious as they came.

She glanced at the huge four-poster bed. While she would love a nap, there was much to do.

A grin curled her lips.

Today, she'd steal a *fiilee*.

After the last few weeks of teasing information out of her lady's maids, servants, courtiers, and merchants, Mer settled on one irrevocable truth.

Being bonded with a flying feline was *everything* to the Methian people.

While Mer had no plans to leave the king without exacting her full vengeance, she thought it wise to have a means of escape. Especially after the last few days.

Being locked away with one's own thoughts was torture. She needed something to keep her mind occupied. She'd already searched through all the books on Raziel's shelves, and none held any hints or information on the Ceto legend.

Mer pushed away from the door and sidled toward the bed. She lifted the mattress up and yanked out the makeshift rope she had been working on.

It had been laughable that the king thought to lock her away like a wayward child.

The first thing Mer had done was create her rope.

Hundreds of balconies covered the face of the mountain. And twice she'd been able to sneak out using her new rope to explore the palace under the guise of a nap. It was a labyrinth of hallways. She'd imagined the Palace of Skigara would have been gloomy as it was carved literally from the mountainside. But surprisingly, she'd found the gothic palace warm and charming.

Unlike its king.

She didn't remember much of the flight from Laos Keep. The numbness that had settled over her had combatted the fear of flying. They'd flown for hours, and the king hadn't said one word. He hadn't even looked at her.

Mer knew this because she'd stared at his face the whole time. Much to her shame, he'd become her lodestone in that moment. He'd kept her curled in his lap, safe and secure.

Forget him.

With the rope hanging from her forearm, Mer made her way outside. She secured the rope on the stone balcony and gave it a couple of expert tugs. It held, thanks to Lilja and Hayjen. As a child, she'd been fascinated with nautical knots. Her aunt and uncle tirelessly taught her knot after knot.

A true smile lifted her lips at the memory, and she threw the rope over the edge.

The wind ruffled her hair, and she tipped her face up, eyeing the clouds. They hung low and were dark gray as if rain would break any moment. Not a second to lose. And if memory served, she could drop down onto the balcony below, skulk through the rooms and into the hallway, take the stairs down several flights, and then make her way to the *fiilee* nests.

A full grin broke across her face.

There was no trapping a daughter of the sea.

Mer peeked over the balcony and calculated the distance from the end of the rope to the balcony. It would be close to a ten-foot drop. She looked to the left, eyeing the mountain. True, she could have climbed down the mountainside, but she wasn't that stupid. One small mistake or a change in the weather could mean the end for her.

A long jump it is.

She took a small breath, swung her leg over the railing, and began to shimmy down the rope before she could talk herself out of it. The wind swayed the rope back and forth, but Mer kept moving hand over hand.

A raindrop hit the top of her head.

"Not now," Mer grumbled, trying to curb the anxiety rising in her chest. "Please hold off."

As if the heavens mocked her, the sky opened up, and the downpour began.

"I'm cursed," she huffed, moving quicker, her breath puffing from her lips.

The rope dampened, and her hands became slippery. Mer peered over her shoulder. She still had so much distance to cover. Her fingers ached as she clung to the rope. They gave the tiniest bit.

No, no, no, no, no.

This had been a bad idea.

Her fingers gave out, and a scream caught in her throat as she slid down the rope with no sign of stopping. Mer wrapped her leg in the rope and squeezed. It burned the inside of her thighs, but she jerked to a painful stop.

Her heart pounded and she swallowed hard, swaying in the wind. Mer leaned her cheek against the rope and stared down at the balcony beneath her.

Only a few more feet before she made the jump.

Move now.

Ever so carefully, she edged down until her legs hung from the rope, only her arms holding her up. The wind tossed her backward until there was nothing but a thousand-foot drop beneath her. Mer squeezed her eyes shut and shuddered. Depths, she hated heights.

You can do this.

Swallowing hard, she forced her eyes open and waited until the rope swung back to the balcony.

Now.

Mer let go of the rope.

Chapter Twenty-Five

RAZIEL

Somehow, Raziel's council always managed to make him feel like a child.

Like he'd done something wrong and was going to get in trouble.

His wife had ruffled more than a few feathers in the last few weeks. And he was paying for her actions.

"Is this what we should expect from our Sirenidae queen?" sneered Chancellor Ortunge.

Raz pinched the bridge of his nose and blew out a calming breath before addressing Ortunge. "The queen's culture is very different from ours," he reasoned. "It will take time for her to acclimate to our customs. Plus, would you ask her to give up her customs, her way of dress? She's already given up the comfort of friends, family, and kingdom to become your queen. Can we not be a little gracious in this transition?"

The chancellor's eyes narrowed, and Raz arched a brow at the disrespect. Ortunge quickly averted his gaze and asked, "What transition is that, my king? Our new queen didn't seem like she wanted to make any sort of transition to the Methi way when she showed up for the celebration feast. If anything, it seemed like a statement. That she wasn't here to fit in."

Raz opened his mouth to respond, when his mother cut in.

"Queen Mer has only been in our kingdom less than a month. Did you really expect her to fit in seamlessly?"

Raziel nodded in agreement. "Royalty is meant to stand out, not to blend in."

"As my king says," the dowager queen replied. Her sharp gaze was pinned to the chancellor. "And from what I recall of the banquet, she was kind and generous to everyone. Isn't that the very basis for our Methian culture? She shook hands and spoke with highborn and commoners alike without batting a lash. Outside our kingdom, that is not common practice. So instead of focusing on a few pieces of clothing and criticizing her for the fabrics that she wore, how about you show some appreciation for the healers and dowry she's enriched our kingdom with?"

Raziel glanced at her from his left eye as she stared stonily at Ortunge. He hid his smile at how defensive his mother had become. If he didn't know any better, he'd have thought she liked the Sirenidae. "Well said, my lady."

His mum blushed and smoothed her hands down her silk tunic. "It's nothing you haven't already expressed to me."

A lie to make them look good and to have a strong united front. His mum was brilliant.

"Discussion of my wife's ensemble is off the table," he announced, eyeing each of his councilors. "We will not speak of it again. What's next?" He locked eyes with Levay. The healer nodded once, her movement sharp, her lips pressed thin. Raziel braced himself. She needed to speak, and it wouldn't be pleasant.

"Do you have something for us, Master Healer?"

Levay held her head high, ignoring some of the looks shot her way. While the Methian people believed in unity between high and lowborn, it seemed that the council he'd inherited was mostly highborn. His mother had appointed Levay some years earlier to her council position. They accepted her begrudgingly because of her skills, but despite her humble origins. Her father had been an apothecary with no sons to continue his trade. He'd trained Levay, unwilling to leave his business vulnerable without an heir. The man had a terrible gambling problem and lost his business anyway, leaving Levay with skills she couldn't use.

Until she helped Queen Osir when she unexpectedly

went into labor in the countryside after her *fiilee* was injured.

"I do, my lord." She sighed. "There's no easy way to say this, and I do not wish to alarm anyone or incite panic."

His arms broke out in goosebumps at the tone of her grim words. "Please continue," he rasped, dread filling his belly.

She scowled at the pages in her hands and then pressed them against her knees before she soldiered on, addressing the room. "It seems the Mirror Plague is mutating."

Sharp gasps echoed through the room, followed by suffocating silence.

"Are you sure?" he asked.

"Yes." Levay cleared her throat. "There have been several cases of those who have survived the original sickness and yet they are now also getting sick."

Raziel cursed, running his fingers through his hair. The only good that had come from contracting the Mirror Plague was that once someone survived it, they couldn't contract the disease again. It gave them immunity.

"How many is several?" the chaplain asked, his hands twisting anxiously in his lap.

"Less than fifty, more than thirty."

Raziel's stomach dropped. This was not a fluke. He exchanged worried glances with the dowager queen. The kingdom could not afford another strain of the plague.

Methi was still suffering from the first bout. They were on the brink of civil war already. This could be what pushed them over.

"How long have they been sick?" his treasurer asked, her amber eyes wide and almost glowing.

"A fortnight. Our healers caught on rather quickly," Levay answered. "All infected were moved to a separate camp."

"Where did this new strain start?" Chancellor Ortunge snapped.

"A village outside the west of Laos near the Caves of the Lost. The village is quarantine now. No one will go in or out."

The chancellor tossed his hands up in frustration. "We thought our queen's healers were supposed to prevent something like this!"

Raziel glared at Ortunge. The man was going too far. It seemed like he was still bitter that Raz had not chosen his granddaughter to be his wife.

"I understand you're frustrated," he bit out. "We are all frustrated and afraid for our families. Once again, the Sirenidae healers have only just arrived. Our healers have been trying to find a cure for the Mirror Plague for almost thirty years. Do you really think the healers from the sea would figure it out in a handful of weeks?"

The chancellor snapped his mouth shut, looking mulish.

The king's words seemed to penetrate but did nothing

to soothe. All of them had been living with the threat of the plague hanging above their heads for years. Everyone had lost a loved one. The Mirror Plague had left its mark on each and every one of them.

"Is there anything else that can be done?" he questioned Levay.

The Master Healer shook her head. "No. I've put all the protocols into place and redirected a few Sirenidae healers to the village. Hopefully with time, patience, skill, and a little bit of luck, we will have answers soon."

"Thank you for your insight."

"My pleasure to serve," Levay answered in the customary response.

Raziel's marshal crossed his arms, his face a mask of anger. Not that the man was angry. Whether he was happy, sad, frustrated, or joyful, he always looked as if he were ready to tear someone's face off. "My king, what about the attack on the *Zephyr*? Have you gathered any news from your new bride?"

Raz nodded. "She claims it was not the Sirenidae."

His words were met with disbelief.

The chaplain blinked slowly. "And do you believe her, my lord?"

The dowager queen sat forward in her chair. "I interrogated her myself at the behest of our king. Whether or not it was a Sirenidae attack is still yet to be seen. But if it was one of them, the queen has no knowledge of it. She firmly believes that it was not her people."

The marshal scoffed. "That's the first trick in the book. To deny, my lady."

Raziel cut in. "You have a valid point, but one fact remains. The Sirenidae do not wish to make war with us. The sea king has made that abundantly clear."

"But we cannot ignore evidence," the chancellor added.

The king nodded. "You're right. And we will not ignore evidence, but for now, we wait."

"And if there are more deaths?" the marshal said, scowling.

"Then we will deal with it as we always have."

Gideon sat back in his chair. "And what of the duke?"

Raziel gazed at his spymaster evenly. They'd discussed at length what they'd tell his council. Someone was bound to bring up his recent trip. It was better if Gideon did it so they could control the information. "Our visit was so well received that the duke and duchess plan to visit court within the week."

The marshal huffed. "To cause mischief or to give support?"

"A bit of both, I assume," Raziel commented. "The man is not eager to give up his gold. But between Gideon and me, I believe he is on our side. For now."

"What of the queen's health?" the chaplain asked. "There's been talk she's been in her rooms for the last three days."

"She's not feeling well." A lie. She was staying in her rooms until he could trust her to not try to kill someone.

The chaplain paled. "The plague?"

"No, just a cold."

Another lie. One he wished was true.

Chapter Twenty-Six

MER

THE FREEFALL WAS FAST AND THE IMPACT HARD.

Mer stumbled backward, her spine hitting the rail as she tumbled.

She clutched at the balister, her nails scraping against the stone.

Her vision dipped in and out at the height. Mer threw herself away from the handrail, her whole body shaking.

That had been terrifying.

An incredulous laugh escaped her. For the first time since the duke's attack, she felt something other than anger and fear.

She edged to the glass door, opened it, and stepped inside, praying she wasn't going to scare some unsuspecting victim. She froze as an old Methian woman stared back at her, blinking slowly.

Mer wrung some of the water from her linen trousers. The old woman didn't scream or demand who she was but continued to stare at her with pale silver eyes. Eyes that were eerily familiar.

She released her clothing and gave a little wave. She smiled for good measure. "Hello." Might as well be friendly.

"Have you come to steal from me?" the old woman asked, her voice raspy and low, her tawny forehead creased with age and suspicion.

"No," Mer replied.

"And yet you came through the window like a thief."

"Well, technically, I came through your door. Don't all riders visit through the balconies?"

The old woman snorted. "You came from the mountainside in the rain. I smell no *fiilee*."

"I like climbing in the rain," Mer offered. A lie. "Now, if you don't mind, I'll be on my way."

The woman tsked, pushing a heavy lock of wiry white hair from her grizzled face. "Don't run off so fast. Come here so I can look at you properly."

A demand that brooked no argument, and for some reason, she listened.

Mer sighed and shuffled to stand in front of the old woman, feeling time slip away from her. She flinched when the crone, quick as lightning, grabbed her hand and hauled her close so she was bent over almost nose to nose with the old woman.

She gaped at the woman and then shut her mouth when gnarled fingers traced over Mer's face, exploring.

The old woman was blind.

"I knew you were different," the old woman whispered, brushing her fingers lightly over the scales on Mer's shoulders. "I could smell the sea on you."

Mer didn't know what to say to that. She hadn't been in the ocean since the day they left Laos. "Thank you?"

The woman sighed and released Mer, leaning back in her chair and tugging her blanket up further on her lap. "It's nice to finally meet you."

"Finally?"

"I've always wanted to meet a Sirenidae in person, and now I have." Her gaze was unfocused, and she pursed her lips. "So, what is the queen doing here? Skulking about my rooms?"

Mer blinked down at the old woman. How did she know she was the queen?

As if the crone could hear her thoughts, she said, "Dear girl, do you really think there are any other Sirenidae in the palace?"

"There are healers." Or there could be servants like Phia of mixed heritage.

"True, but what would one be doing in my room when they should be in the plague camps? They wouldn't be sulking around the palace running away from their duties, would they?"

Plague camps? Interesting. Everyone had been pretty close-lipped about the sickness. Even young Duchess Keventin had been scared to speak of it, as if mentioning it would bring the disease upon you.

"It seems like you have me at a disadvantage. What is your name?" Mer redirected, feeling altogether more seen than she would have liked.

"You may call me Ravielle or Ravi for short. Now, what are you doing here?"

For a brief second, Mer debated telling her a lie but ultimately decided to be honest. "I'm in search of the nests. I've been cooped up too long in my room with nothing to occupy my mind."

"So Raziel has you tied to his bed, does he?"

For some reason, Mer blushed. Hard. "No, he doesn't want to see me."

"I see. A lover's spat. It will be over soon, pet."

"It's nothing like that."

"Then tell me what it's like."

"He doesn't trust me." Why was she telling the old woman this? "And he shouldn't."

Ravi's white eyebrows arched high. "And so, you're seeking a bond for yourself?"

"Your culture surrounds the *fiilee*. I figured it would be a good way to start my new life. I must fit in." A lie. One she truly felt guilty over.

"I don't think so," Ravi retorted with a chuckle. "I can sense the wildness about you. You crave freedom, and our *fiilee* offer that. I'll humor you, little Sirenidae. There's a set of stairs outside my rooms right across the hall. Take them down five levels and turn left. You'll smell the nests before you see them."

"Thank you."

"Don't thank me. This knowledge is not free."

Mer shifted on her feet. "What do you want of me?"

"Another interesting visit."

That was easy. "I can do that."

"With you and the king."

That would be harder. "I will do my best."

"I'm sure you will." Ravi grinned. "And remember one thing."

Mer nodded and then rolled her eyes at herself. The bloody woman couldn't see. "What is that?"

"Don't get eaten, little fish. Bonding with a *fiilee* is more difficult than you can imagine."

"I'll try not to."

"We shall see."

Mer walked to the door, leaving wet footsteps behind on the carpets. She eyed the cloak hanging near the door and threw it over her shoulders. She'd return it. Eventually.

"You don't happen to know where the library is?" she called over her shoulder, clasping the cloak at her throat. That was her next project. She needed more information on the legends of Methi and on the fishing villages. They were the key to finding the Pernicious. She could feel it in her bones.

"I'll tell you on your next visit."

Wily old woman.

As she reached for the handle, Ravi called from her chair. "Come back and see me *soon*, my dear. I enjoyed our talk."

"Only if I survive." She pulled the hood over her head.

Ravielle cackled. "Something tells me you will."

Chapter Twenty-Seven

MER

I T WAS RELATIVELY EASY TO GET INTO THE NEST.

She'd slipped down the stairway and ghosted through the halls until the scent of hay, animals, and leather reached her.

Mer had been expecting that the Methian's most important resource would be guarded fiercely. And yet, she'd waltzed right into the nest without anyone stopping her. She looked left and then right. No guards here. Odd.

She stepped to the right and leaned against the curved stone wall, taking in the breathtaking view. It was as if a giant sphere had been carved inside the mountain. Stalactites hung from the ceiling like vicious rotten teeth. A rectangular opening to the face of the mountain let in a weak shaft of light.

Stepping farther along the wide walkway, Mer slowly made her way to the abrupt drop. A lump of fear lodged in her throat as she stared down into the gaping maw of the cave. It was so deep that it seemed as if there was no bottom to the chasm. Chills ran down her arms, causing the scales near her elbows to quiver. There would be no coming back from a fall like that.

Fiilee nested in every nook and cranny, their eyes crawling over her skin. Several hissed, raising the hair along the nape of her neck.

Gently.

Feline eyes reflected back at her, and she spotted a few *fiilee* creeping a little closer. It was time to move back. Mer crept away from the edge, feeling a little dizzy. Leviathan's bones, she hated heights.

And yet you plan to fly.

Mer grimaced and slowed her movements as not to spook the predators. Her back touched the stone wall, and she sighed with relief. No beasties would be sneaking up on her, and she was far from the drop. A leather strap brushed her right shoulder, and she glanced up.

All sorts of riding paraphernalia hung on the wall.

Harnesses, bridles, ropes, reins, and saddles.

She eyed the saddle, noting the metal notch at the front. Brilliant. She could only assume it was used to tie oneself to the saddle, negating any possibility of falling. That's what she needed. But there was no way she was actually flying today.

"I'll come back for you," she whispered, not wanting to disrupt or agitate the *fiilee* that were observing her with interest. Mer pulled a sturdy-looking leather strap from the wall with stones knitted into each end the size of her fists.

A snare.

She was familiar with the tool. Mer gave it a couple of expert swings. If a *fiilee* attacked, she'd at least have the option of capturing one by its legs.

Mer crept down the wide stone walkway, flinching each time a flying feline circled above roaring or screeching. She clambered around the rough protrusions in the wall, ever watchful of the beasties, searching for a small place to survey the cavern.

Her plan was simple.

Find a spot to watch the felines.

Call one to her.

Bond with it.

While she was no great rider, even when it came to horses, bonding with a *fiilee* would be similar to a leviathan in her mind. They were both taciturn, fearsome creatures. She was just exchanging one of the seas for one of the sky.

She popped her head up over a rock and froze as a *fiilee* emerged from the dark, its lips pulled back, long ivory teeth on display. Mer's eyes rounded, and she retreated quickly. She certainly wasn't going to bond with that one.

A few more precarious situations led her to a high and deep ledge with a great view. She skittered back from the edge and checked the ledge above. No *fiilee*.

Perfect.

Mer plopped down with her spine pressed against the stone wall. She sighed, closing her eyes for a moment. She'd made it without falling to her death or being eaten. That was something.

Movement from her right caught her eye, and Mer cursed.

Another rider.

She maneuvered onto her belly and spied on the Methian.

The woman stood at the edge of the walkway, her toes hanging over the drop. A wailing sound burst from the rider like she'd been shot and then she leaned forward.

"NO!" Mer screamed, reaching her hand out as if she could help the woman.

But she was gone.

She began to shake, her mouth hanging open. Why had the woman done that? Why had she taken the plunge? Why had . . .

A *fiilee* burst from the chasm with the woman on its back. Mer gasped as the rider lay on top of her *fiilee*, hugging the beast lovingly as they flew out the exit of the cavern.

What the devil?

"They're all mad," she muttered. Who in their right mind would do such a thing? It was idiotic.

She backpedaled to the stone wall, breathing hard. Her hands shook, and she fiddled with the lasso, learning its weight. Her nerves slowly faded away, as did the shaking, and soon wonder took its place. The *fiilee* seemed to lose interest in her presence. Some bathed, others ate, still others napped or flew. But her favorites were the wee *fiilees*. The little flying felines were the cutest creatures she'd ever laid eyes on. Fluffy little bodies with stubby wings.

The creatures came in all patterns.

Dappled. Striped. Spotted. Black, white, brown, gold, orange.

A sense of peace settled over her. Mer unlaced the cloak and spread it out over the ledge before lying on her belly. She crossed her arms and pillowed her cheek on her bicep, just enjoying the experience. This wasn't something she'd expected. The joy. The peace. The contentment in this moment.

But on the coattails of that was the guilt.

Guilt because her husband couldn't be laid to rest until he was avenged.

Guilt that she hadn't gained any new information on the missing girls.

Guilt over the fact that she was safe for a moment, and Ream's child was not.

Guilt that she'd softened to the Methian king.

Guilt that girls like Phia and Sienna weren't safe in their own homes.

Too much guilt. It felt like drowning.

The smallest whisper of a sound caught her attention.

Dread ran down her spine.

She slowly pushed to her knees, scanning the area. Nothing seemed out of place.

A small huff.

Right behind her.

She spun around, lasso in hand, as a *fiilee* lunged for her from above. A blur of orange and white filled her vision as she was slammed against the ledge. A huge paw pinned her in place, the other on her left arm. Mer panted as golden eyes came into view along with very long teeth that snapped way too close to her neck.

Enough. You will not die like this.

Mer narrowed her eyes at the beastie and bared her own teeth in response. Predators never liked eye contact. She hissed, earning another growl from the *fiilee*. Its cream-and-light-orange ears lay back against its skull, the whiskers of its snout quivering.

Mer fingered her lasso. She'd only get one chance at this.

She swung the rope and released.

It did not wrap around the feline's muzzle but around its chest. It skittered to the side, clawing at the rope snugly wrapped behind its two front legs. Mer scrambled out of the way and rolled to her feet. She eyed the distracted *fiilee*, so close she could sink her fingers into the caramel-and-cream lynx-like fur.

When will you ever get another chance like this? Claim your fiilee.

It was stupid and more than a bit reckless, but before Mer could think twice, she'd launched onto the feline's back, wrapping her hands in the lasso. The *fiilee* twisted, snapping its teeth at her, but missed. Mer dropped down onto her belly, holding on for death as the beastie spat, hissed, and tried to throw her off.

"Not today," Mer gasped, ignoring the bite of the rope. She couldn't give up now.

The feline threw itself toward the ledge, and Mer's eyes rounded as they dropped over the edge. A terrified scream burst from her lips as her legs lifted off the *fiilee's* back and into the air.

Fear had her tightening her hold and scrambling to wrap her legs around the beast. She pressed her face into its fur, her arms trembling with adrenaline as they soared in the cavern. Mer popped her head up and then ducked back down just as they passed a stalactite. The tip caught the back of her leg, and she grunted in pain. The infernal creature was trying to scrape her off.

"You have to do better than that," she spat at the *fiilee.*

The feline banked toward the entrance of the cave, and they burst free from the mountainside. Bile flooded her mouth as they climbed higher, the trees looking like a smooth green carpet. The wind tore at her as the beast accelerated to incredible speeds.

A deranged laugh spilled from her. Part from terror, part from amazement.

She was flying alone on the back of a *fiilee*.

The feeling quickly fled as she felt the rope give a little.

Without any warning, the beast barrel-rolled. Mer's body was tossed one way and then the other. Something gave in her right shoulder. She screamed in pain, still holding on. The *fiilee* righted itself, and Mer panted heavily against the back of its neck.

Tears streamed down her face at the intense pain. She blinked the water back, noting how her hands had turned an odd shade of gray where the rope dug into her skin. A large splash of blue pulled her attention, and she gasped as they soared over the largest lake Mer had ever seen.

The *fiilee* dove low, almost touching the water, and then back upward, dragging a groan from Mer. She'd definitely dislocated her shoulder.

"Is that all you got?" Mer shouted, high on pain and adrenaline. "You're not going to get rid of me."

The beast's ears twitched as if it understood the challenge.

The feline dove, but this time barrel-rolled not just

once but twice. Mer screamed in pain but managed to hold on the first time . . . but when the second roll came, the rope loosened, as did her grip.

Mer gasped, terror seizing up her muscles. A scream caught in the back of her throat as she was airborne.

Not again.

Chapter Twenty-Eight

RAZIEL

The meeting had gone on too long.

Raziel was so tired. All he wanted was a hot bath, a snack, and his bed.

Except there was a murderous wayward woman in his bed. His own wife.

He frowned for a moment and then outright scowled when Valen stepped into the room and leaned against the wall, crossing his ankles. His friend locked eyes with Raziel and jerked his chin toward the door.

Valen would never interrupt a council meeting unless it was dire.

Great. Just great. He would not be seeking a bed anytime soon.

The king stood from his seat, his councilors following

suit. "I am needed elsewhere. We will convene again tomorrow morning."

With that, he strode through the room with his head held high.

Valen fell in line as they exited the stuffy council room and walked down the hallway. His friend kept pace, eyeing the guards that were trailing them. Raz nodded to them, and they fell even farther back. It must be truly horrible if Valen was worried about his guards overhearing the news.

"What is it?" he barked, feeling like he was about to come out of his skin.

Valen's lips thinned, looking grim. "Er . . . your wife seems to have decided to explore the palace."

Raz stopped, glaring at his friend. "You pulled me from a stressful meeting to report that my bloody wife went on a walk?"

"Not exactly. As you remember, you ordered her to be contained to your rooms after her little stunt in Laos."

He rolled his eyes. "It wasn't because of a little stunt but because of her murderous intentions."

Valen snorted. "Would it have been so bad if the duke died from an *accident*?"

"Convenient, yes, but also bad. Our people are divided about Mer. Half think she's our savior, the other half our enemy. Even *if* it hadn't been her fault, she would have been blamed. She's part of the monarchy. What she does reflects on me. We need the support of our gentry.

Too much is at stake. Methi is one stone away from crumbling."

"And yet you are obsessing over your wife."

Raz ground his teeth. "That is not true."

"And yet here you are with me when you could have gone right back into that council meeting."

He sped up, feeling like his skin was too small for his body. To his ever-loving shame, Raz had grown to like her outlandish dresses and the feel of her skin against his own. What he did not like was the mind games and how blood-thirsty she was. Plus, the fact that she never did anything he asked of her.

Liar.

Feeling frustrated, Raz shook out his hands, his mind looping back to the fact that his wife was roaming the palace. He glanced at Valen. "How the devil did she manage to escape? I had guards stationed outside the doors, down the hallway, and even in the stairwell. How did she get past you?"

Valen winced. "She sent away her lady's maids to rest. That wasn't out of the ordinary since her return, but when dinner was sent up, her maid couldn't find her. It seems she created a rope and used it to scale down to the balcony beneath yours." A look of awe crossed Valen's face. "It was brilliant, really."

Ravielle.

Raz swiped a hand down his face. "Did she hurt my grandmother?"

"No. Lady Ravi is just fine." Valen smirked, his eyes glittering. "In fact, it seems she wants your wife to come back and visit again. She liked the Sirenidae."

This day could not get any worse.

"Well, where did she go? The armory? Pick the lock to my office? The courtyards to shock more of my courtiers?" Raz could just see her waltzing into the courtyards soaking wet and blowing kisses to all the old men and women, giving them heart palpitations.

You'd like it just as much.

"The nests."

Raz almost stumbled. "How did she know where to go?"

"It seems our new queen has many questions about her new kingdom. Her lady's maids have shared all they know to accommodate their queen."

By blood and stone. He'd taken her Sirenidae handmaidens so that they couldn't conspire, and yet he'd given his enemy queen three informants with all the gossip and knowledge of the palace.

Raziel kept underestimating her. She was a commander. He needed to start treating her like one.

Raziel began to jog, veering to the right toward the nests. "Has anyone seen her there?"

"One rider said your wife was on the top of a high ledge watching the *fiilee* a few hours ago. When she returned, the queen was gone."

His stomach bottomed out. There were so many bad scenarios.

She could have fallen and broken her neck.

The queen could have been attacked and fallen and broken her neck.

She could have tried to claim a *fiilee* and broken her neck.

All he could imagine was her broken pale body at the bottom of the chasm.

What would he say to her grandfather? The Sirenidae king would surely revisit the idea of waging war on Methi.

"No one else has seen the queen?"

Valen hesitated. "One other rider claims to have seen someone of the queen's likeness."

"Where?" he growled.

"On the back of the *fiilee* outside the nest, headed toward the Lake of Springs."

That was a short enough flight, but it would still be several kilometers of searching for the body.

"You should know which *fiilee* she tried to claim."

"Who?"

"Skye's mate."

Raziel's jaw clenched. Of course, she chose Feather. As if his day couldn't get any worse.

Now they'd truly be bonded for life.

That's if Feather hadn't killed the Sirenidae.

Chapter Twenty-Nine

MER

WATER WAS A CURIOUS THING.

It could be soft and gentle. Or hard and cruel.

This time, it chose to be hard.

Mer crashed through the water, her legs taking the impact.

She screamed in pain as her injured arm was jerked away from her body. Her gills flared open, forcing the rest of the air out of her lungs. Mer clutched her wounded arm to her chest as she sank in the water, eyes stinging with pain.

Her brows furrowed as the scent of salt filtered through her gills. It wasn't strong enough to be seawater, but there was no mistaking the salty taste of the ocean.

And . . . the water wasn't cold. It was almost as warm as bathwater.

Just what was this place?

Mer glanced toward the surface, floating in the water, her hair twisting like small snakes around her head. She needed to return to the palace before someone noticed she was gone. But there was something curious about the lake that called to her. If she managed her time well, she would be able to explore, seek a healer and shelter, and sneak back to the palace before she was missed.

Just a few minutes.

With care, she swam toward the bottom of the clear lake using one arm, the pain agonizing. It was deeper than she expected. The lake was circular in shape, and all the sides sloped toward the middle like a gigantic crater. Mer swam around a large boulder, startling a school of multi-colored fish. She gasped, smiling as they scattered at the sight of her. It wasn't uncommon to discover something new in the sea. The ocean had its secrets, and if someone was curious enough, they'd reveal a few.

A sense of giddiness filled her stomach, and she smiled at the few fish who were hovering uncertainly just out of range. There were always friends to be found if one was willing to look.

Mer moved extremely slowly toward the boulder and sat upon its surface. She ran her hand over the light purple algae that softened the rock's rough exterior. She criss-crossed her legs and waited patiently for her finned friend to come and investigate as she took in the foreign landscape of the lake.

A bed of deep blue seagrass stretched out before her, only broken up by round rocks. A forest of chartreuse seaweed waved in the distance like pagan dancers reaching greedily toward the surface. Small clusters of spiny white flowers grew out of waterlogged trees, long forgotten.

Her eyes closed of their own accord, and Mer inhaled slowly and then exhaled. For the first time in months, she felt the smallest seed of peace. She'd found a refuge. An escape that would see her through the coming years.

If you last that long.

Opening her eyes, she froze as a little red guppy edged closer, his large black eyes seeming almost comically wide.

"It's okay," she whispered, holding her pointer finger out. She wiggled her fingers through the water, beckoning the little fish to come closer. The little guppy approached cautiously, touching her finger before darting back.

"I won't hurt you," she crooned and wiggled her fingers in invitation once more.

The brave little fish swam up to her hand and bumped the tip of her finger. Mer held still as he investigated her. She held in a laugh as the guppy soon became comfortable, running his side against her finger as if he had an itch.

"Brave wee thing you are," she hummed, massaging his translucent fin.

The fish swirled through her fingers once more as if to

say goodbye and then returned to his school, which had gone back to nibbling on the blue seagrass. It always amazed her how all creatures craved connection. One just had to be willing to meet on their terms.

She slipped off the side of the large boulder and floated down to the bottom of the lake. Sand and dirt swirled through the water until she reached the seagrass. The fine strands of plant life tickled the bottoms of her feet while more fish came to greet her.

Mer savored the experience.

The light ahead shifted, reminding her of the passing of time, but Mer ignored it. What was the worst that could happen if they discovered her missing?

Reaching the forest of seaweed, she stepped inside.

Mer wove through the stalks, lazily touching the large fronds and bulbs along the winding spindles.

This felt like home.

Her arm throbbed in pain, reminding her of its presence, but Mer ignored it. All she wanted was to savor this moment. The forest thinned out, and she stopped in her tracks.

An ancient-looking structure sat in the dead center of the lake.

Excitement bubbled inside her, and she abandoned walking to swim toward the structure.

It appeared to be an amphitheater in the shape of a birdcage. A large chunk was missing, as if a giant fist had punched through the roof, damaging one of the walls. Narrow winding broken stairs led to the bottom floor. Three stories of columns held up the soaring roof that were so white they looked to be whalebone. Benches lined the upper stories as if awaiting guests.

Mer softly dropped to the top of the stairs at the entrance and took her first step into the amphitheater. A thrill went through her as she ran her hand over a thick column. The smooth marble was slick beneath her palm despite cracks here and there. Little plants grew out of the fissures, which made her smile widen.

Life would find a way.

It was utterly perfect in its imperfection.

"Who built you?" she asked, her question swallowed up by the silence of the lake.

Mer pushed away from the entrance, making her way toward the center of the pavilion. Her brows slashed together as she noticed that the algae on the floor grew in peculiar patterns. She bent low and ran her finger over it, and it wiped away, revealing markings carved into the floor.

Her eyes rounded.

Constellations . . . but why?

Mer spun slowly in a circle, her hair fanning out as she tried to take in the grandeur of the space. It was ancient, to be sure, but not Sirenidae. She didn't know who had built the structure, but it wasn't her people. No shell, bone, sparkly stones, precious corals, or gold decorated the amphitheater. Each line was clean, simple, and elegant . . . very human.

She tapped her chin as she considered the building. How had the Methians built such a thing underwater? And most importantly, why?

Tilting her head back, she squinted up toward the surface of the water. There were secrets here, and she wanted to discover them.

Mer explored the entire structure and continued on. She startled a little eel, who blinked at her with large eyes and a mouth gaping from its crevice.

"Sorry, my friend," she whispered before moving on.

To her knowledge, eels didn't live in freshwater. Then what was that one doing here? Perhaps there were freshwater eels as well? Mer hadn't spent enough time in fresh water to know.

The water warmed, and large pink flowers grew from the rocky bottom, the lime-and-pale-pink leaves swaying lightly in the current.

Her nose wrinkled. A current . . . there wasn't supposed to be a current in lakes, was there? She'd have to do research when she returned to the palace.

She followed the source of it, the ground tilting slightly upward. A blast of cold water hit her, causing her scales to rise and then it dissipated. She blinked and smacked her lips, tasting the water. That had been pure saltwater.

Chasing the source, she swam faster and halted as a massive stone wall rose from the lake bottom. It was black, porous, and pockmarked. Some holes were large enough that she could have stood inside. Movement caught her eye to the left. Mer squinted at the hole and drifted closer. The water grew hotter until Mer stopped, watching as the sand roiled in front of the wall, glistening iridescent water rising upward. Carefully, she reached toward the water and paused when she could get no closer. Mer snatched her hand back, gaping at her reddened palm.

The water had burned her.

She blinked at the bubbling sand once more.

A natural hot spring.

Another blast of frigid saltwater made its way through the wave of hot acrid water, and she froze as a pair of gleaming eyes met hers from one of the holes in the porous rocks. She stiffened when a pair of black-and-blue striped lips turned up into a smile.

Mer blinked and it was gone. She rubbed her eyes and squinted harder. Mer drifted as close as she could to the boiling water, searching the rock face for any sign of life.

Nothing.

She pushed back, feeling a little queasy from the heat, and shook her head.

Perhaps she'd imagined it all. Her attention moved to her arm, which still throbbed in pain. Perhaps her injury was causing her to hallucinate. She couldn't ignore her dislocated shoulder anymore.

Mer turned her back to the wall and swam back toward the pavilion.

Her skin crawled, and a chill ran down her spine. She whipped around and scanned the wall once more. Someone was watching her, and it felt . . . sinister.

Chapter Thirty

MER

NO MONSTERS OF THE LAKE HAD REVEALED themselves to Mer.

Her uneasiness drifted away as her right arm had made itself known again. She couldn't put off dealing with it any longer.

Taking a deep breath, she eyeballed her contraption. Mer had managed to tie a length of seaweed around her wrist one-handed. She dug her heels into the sand and leaned back, putting tension on her wounded shoulder. The seaweed stretched but held. If she pulled hard enough, her dislocated shoulder would go back into place. Pain sizzled up her arm, and her teeth gnashed together. It still wasn't enough to put her shoulder back in.

More pressure.

Mer pulled harder, and much to her frustration, the seaweed popped from the soil, and she tumbled backward. She scowled at the spiderweb-like roots of the seaweed that floated through the water.

Well, that didn't work very well.

She eyed the amphitheater over her shoulder with narrowed eyes. The columns were sturdy enough. If she rammed her shoulder into the stone, perhaps she could fix the dislocation.

Or make it significantly worse.

Mer sighed. It was time to return to the surface.

She untied the seaweed from her wrist and tucked her arm gently against her chest. She pushed off from the bottom of the lake, leaving a soft cloud of sand, algae, and silt behind her. It would have been easy to ascend to the surface rather quickly, but Mer savored the last seconds of her time in the warm water. She hovered right below the surface, reaching up and skimming her fingers along the reflective water pane that looked like a broken mirror.

If only she could stay.

Mer made her way toward the edge of the lake, the sides gently sloping upward. Her feet touched the pebbled bottom, and she walked until her head broke through the surface and her eyes were above the water. She scanned the bank, searching for trouble. Her eyes rounded and then narrowed as she spotted a familiar *fiilee* who lay in the sun, licking its paw like it had all the time in the world.

Mer took a couple steps closer to the bank until her

gills were fully exposed to the air. Water poured out of them, and they sealed shut along her neck. She gasped, the cool air rushing into her lungs. Gravity weighed her down as she stomped out of the water toward the troublesome feline.

She stabbed a finger from her left hand at the beast and then gestured to her damaged right shoulder. "This is your fault!"

The *fiilee* gave her a droll look as if to say, *"Whatever you say, human."*

Mer stomped from the lake, sharp stones digging into the bottoms of her feet. She ignored the pain, keeping an eye on the feline. Water dripped down her torn dress to pool at her feet.

There were nipples along the beast's belly. A female then.

The *fiilee* tracked her movement and stood. They stared at each other, and she stiffened, almost taking another step back when the feline approached her steadily. First, she sniffed Mer's feet and then along her legs, slowly circling. Mer forced herself to stay still as the *fiilee* inspected her.

A large wet nose pressed at the bottom of her spine and huffed. She yelped and leapt forward, only for the beast to dart around her. The *fiilee's* tongue slipped out of her mouth, and she licked Mer from knee to hip bone. Mer gaped at the beast. Was this a taste test to see if she was worth eating?

The fingers of her left hand flexed anxiously. "How do I taste?" she grouched. "Like fish?"

The *fiilee* cocked her head. Her peachy ears perked up at Mer's voice.

"Not so hostile now. So what? Are we friends?" she asked as the feline pressed her wet, cold pink nose into the palm of her hand.

Mer stared in amazement at the display of trust. She wiggled her fingers, and the large cat leaned into her hand. Excitement suffused her limbs. Had she managed to bond with one of the legendary creatures?

Her excitement was soon eclipsed by dread. If she had bonded with the *fiilee*, that would surely mean flying again. Her stomach churned at the idea. She was not ready to fly. In fact, if she never flew again, it would be too soon.

She shifted slightly and her arm twinged. Mer gave the feline one cautious scratch along her snout before stepping around the beast and cupping her elbow. She winced.

"It's time we head back," she murmured.

Mer glanced around the forest that surrounded the lake, noting that the sun hung low in the west.

Her brows furrowed, and she tried to remember everything she could about the kingdom. To the east was the Bay of Laos. To the west were the mountains and the city of Skigara. To the north, the Northern Sea.

After the hazardous flight from the mountain to the lake, she knew the palace wasn't horribly far. If she was diligent, she could get back in half a day. There was only farmland, forest, and a few villages along the way. Someone would be able to help her.

Mer stared at the Hollow Mountains, and instead of walking toward them, she spun on her heel and headed north. The stones turned to dried leaves, pine needles, dirt, and dainty weeds. Each step hurt, but she continued on. Walking on her tender feet was something she'd still not gotten used to. Life in the ocean never created calluses. Each day she spent time on the land, her hands and feet would toughen up just in time for her to go back to the sea and have them disappear.

A small sad part of her mourned that this might be the last time she ever had tender feet.

"Let's go find some help," she called over her shoulder. She listened for the *fiilee* and heard nothing. Mer shrugged. It was not as if the feline owed her.

Mer picked her way along the lakeside just inside the tree line until the lake was firmly behind her. She dragged her palms along the rough bark of trees, admiring how strong they were. The sun shone through the boughs of the pine trees, casting long streams onto the forest floor. White-and-purple wildflowers grew along the ground, creating winding pathways. Woodland creatures scurried about the pines, playing and chasing each other. Birds sang, trying to out-trill each other.

But then, all woodland sounds stopped.

Mer froze and scanned the area warily before turning around.

The breath in her lungs froze.

The *fiilee* had crept up on her.

Yet she'd never even heard the blasted thing move.

"What are you doing?" she asked, exasperation in her voice.

Her beast's peachy ears perked up, and her long tail swished through the underbrush lazily.

No aggression.

"So, you decided to come." Mer waved her left hand at the beast. The *fiilee* chuffed. "Let's go.'"

Mer turned her back to the feline and continued on. Her gaze kept flickering over her shoulder at the *fiilee* in wonder. This was not what she expected.

They made their way through the forest until the thunder of waves reached her ears at last. Her steps picked up speed. She ignored the sharp bite of a pinecone in her left heel as she practically sprinted toward the sound.

They were calling her.

Home.

Tears flooded her eyes as the trees abruptly stopped, and the dirt turned to stone.

She slowed to a stop, the porous rock warm beneath her feet. Mer shuffled forward until she stood at the edge of a cliff. Blue-green waves crashed below her as if raging.

The cliffs formed a huge V that stretched out to the

open ocean. Large black rocks rose from the water like rotten teeth. It would have seemed dreary to some, but to Mer . . . it was everything.

Staring down at the roiling waves and seafoam, it took every bit of self-control not to jump. Her arm couldn't handle it. The waves spoke of dangerous churning tides. The inlet was a death trap, but she still wanted the comfort of the ocean. After several nights of nightmares about the duke and little to no sleep, all she wanted to do was climb into the loving embrace of the ocean.

But not here.

Mer forced herself to continue on, the sea spray coating her skin as she walked west. Wisps of smoke rose in the distance. A village, to be sure.

The *fiilee* stop trailing Mer and padded next to her, her amber eyes darting everywhere in interest.

Mer couldn't help the smile that curled her lips. This moment was surreal. She would never have dreamed of having her own Methian mount. Nothing would stop her now.

She slipped on a particularly slimy rock and scrambled. She caught herself, jarring her shoulder and cutting the bottom of her right foot. Mer kicked up her foot and stared at her bloody arch. Her brows furrowed in frustration. This was just what she needed.

The sun sank low as she limped her way toward the smoke trail curling in the sky, leaving behind the rocky inlet for the forest once again. They had to make it to the village before dark, or she would have serious problems. Shivers had begun to wrack her body as her damp dress clung uncomfortably to her skin.

The sky turned from orange to pink to periwinkle and then a dark blue.

The *fiilee* pressed closer to Mer's left side, her left hand resting on silky soft fur. Mer found herself brushing her fingers through the beast's coat as they maneuvered their way through the woods.

As the stars began to appear in the sky, Mer spotted a familiar constellation and adjusted their course. She almost wept in gratitude when she saw a fire in the distance. The trees thinned out until a small coastal village was revealed. Little stone houses dotted the main road, and the black sand beach stretched out to the north, waves crashing calmly against the shore.

Mer limped her way toward the large bonfire at the other end of the village, passing a few homes on the outskirts of town. She frowned at the blue paint swiped across their door. What the devil did that mean? Was it a sign? Or a Methian form of decorating?

The *fiilee* pressed her nose into Mer's palm before loping back into the forest. Mer stared after the feline and then shrugged. She didn't blame the beast for not wanting to deal with any more humans.

"I'll see you soon," she called. "I hope."

It was an easy walk into town. Some lantern light filtered through curtains and windows in a few homes, but many were dark. Did the fishing village seek their beds so early? It seemed so.

The closer she got to the bonfire, the stronger the scent of something burnt became. She couldn't put her finger on it. It wasn't food, but something that made her stomach turn. Mer kept to the shadows, not sure how the people would take to a Sirenidae. She hovered near the porch of the house closest to the fire and blinked at the sight that greeted her.

There were Sirenidae here, and they were wearing face coverings.

She frowned.

So, this was where the king had sent her dowry.

A twinge of foreboding filled her as two humans carried a wrapped bundle between them. She swallowed hard as they tossed it into the fire.

Bodies.

They were burning bodies.

It was the worst of sins to the Sirenidae. The ocean was to claim back what it was given. Not to burn it away.

She shoved away from the home and limped toward the fire. A Sirenidae caught her movement, and his eyes widened. The lanky coral-skinned male loped toward her, holding his hands up.

"Stop!"

Mer froze, not able to take her gaze from the fire. "Why? What's going on?"

"My lady, we're quarantined."

A chill ran down her spine. "For what?"

"The plague."

Chapter Thirty-One

RAZIEL

He'd killed his queen.

Isn't that what you wanted just a few weeks ago?

Raziel scowled at the forest floor and kicked a pinecone. He hadn't truly wanted her dead, but he had wanted answers . . . and perhaps to scare his new vicious wife.

"Mer!" he yelled, his voice startling the birds. Raz had given up calling her by her title and had begun using her name.

Half the city of Skigara was out looking for the queen. She'd been missing for over three days. It was a bloody political disaster. He stomped forward, making sure to keep his line so that no part of the forest went unsearched. Part of him wondered if she had done it on purpose. The woman seemed determined to torture him.

For the husband you killed.

His scowl deepened. The husband he *supposedly* killed. To be honest, the king didn't remember such a confrontation. He'd been racking his mind late at night as he lay in bed, trying to figure out what the devil she'd been talking about.

Even during the Warlord's War he'd rarely had any interaction with Sirenidae. The Methians had been aerial support. The Sirenidae, naval support. The two hadn't mixed.

He stepped over a large root and continued walking, the silence only broken up by the echoing calls of his men. They'd covered a lot of territory in three days but still no sign of the queen.

Skye's mate had returned to the nest without a rider a day after Mer's disappearance. Raziel had even braved the vicious female to communicate with her, but she wasn't having it. After a few hisses, swipes of her claws, and a new gash on his forearm, Raz left the *fiilee* alone.

Usually, *fiilee* only bonded with one person and loosely communicated with them. They tolerated the bonded of their mates. He'd hoped she would be amiable, but she'd been more hostile than ever. What he had found interesting was the fact that the *fiilee* slipped out each day and disappeared for a few hours, leaving their young with Skye. It wasn't typical for the females to leave their cubs so soon.

Raziel had her followed the second time she left. His

scouts had lost her near the Lake of Springs, but it gave him an idea. If by some miracle the queen had managed to bond with the *fiilee*, perhaps the feline was returning to her rider.

If she's alive.

His stomach churned at the possibility.

What would be the consequences for his kingdom if she'd died? The sea king would no doubt seek recompense if not revenge. Their truce was uneasy as it was. And while Raz still believed the Sirenidae to be responsible for the *Zephyr*, he wasn't willing to drag his people into an all-out war over speculation.

His worries morphed into anger as he pushed through the tree line at the edge of the Lake of Springs. The back was covered in small pebbles glimmering in the sun. He glared at the water's edge, lapping gently at the bank.

It could all be a game.

"You better not be in there," Raziel grumbled, staring at the gentle waves.

They'd finally searched all the land between Skigara and the lake. This was the next section to cover. His eyes narrowed on the water. None of his people had ever been able to reach the bottom of the body of water. It was just that deep. The hair along his arms rose, and he angrily rubbed at them.

He hated that water affected him so. It was a reminder that he was weak.

The king lifted a hand over his brow to block some of

the glare from the sun as he scanned the lake again. At one time, an enormous ancient amphitheater had sat at the center of the lake surrounded by hundreds of little warm springs. If the stories were to be believed, it would have been a place of celebration. One day, hundreds of years ago, the earth began to tremble so hard that the ground cracked open and swallowed up the amphitheater along with all the springs, leaving only a gaping crater. It quickly filled with water, becoming the Lake of Springs, erasing all evidence of the holy place.

That's what water did; it took.

He sighed and dropped his right hand, the sun warming his face, his anxiety rising.

What if the queen wasn't playing games? What if she'd fallen from the *fiilee* and had been knocked unconscious on impact with the lake? What if she'd sunk beneath the water and . . .

He pinched the bridge of his nose and exhaled heavily at his flawed thinking.

Sirenidae couldn't drown.

Raz pursed his lips.

Well, he didn't know that for a fact. What if they couldn't tolerate fresh water? He didn't know how her gills worked. Hell, Raziel didn't know much about his wife as a person or her culture.

He found himself touching the healing cut along the side of his neck. What he did know was that she hated him, she was cunning and reckless, and that his grandmother liked her. Unfortunately.

Raziel pulled a face and took two steps into the water, the lake lapping at his boots. Familiar fear rose up his throat, but Raz shoved it down deep. His square jaw flexed as the sensation of water in his lungs rose to the forefront of his mind. The memory of clawing at the water and then sinking helplessly to the bottom of the ocean while staring at the light above.

The sense of impending doom settled over his shoulders like a cloak, and he physically shook it off. His fingers curled into fists at his sides as he trembled. With the sound of waves in his ears and the taste of bile in his mouth, Raz vowed to conquer his fear of water.

He turned his back to the lake and stomped back into the trees. Raziel wouldn't explore the lake until they had finished securing all the surrounding area.

If she was dead, there was truly nothing he could do for her.

If his queen was wounded, then she would have found a secure refuge or sought help.

And if she were hiding in the lake, then he'd let her cower a bit longer before dragging her home.

Where she belonged.

ANOTHER TWO DAYS PASSED.

Still no Sirenidae.

Raziel sat on a rock eating a piece of cheese while staring down at the rolling waves that crashed on the black sand beach before greedily sucking backward as if longing to inhale the land. His attention turned to the giant pyre at the far edge of the village.

This was the center of the newest strain of the Mirror Plague.

He'd sent his men away, but Raziel stayed to watch the healers bustle between tiny stone homes. He swallowed the salty cheese and brushed his hand off on his leather pants.

The sun was sinking, the hint of night-time approaching from the east. The Hollow Mountains towered in the distance, calling him home. Skye chuffed behind him and plopped down, whipping up the dirt around them. Raz scowled at the unapologetic beast over his shoulder and wiped his eyes with the sleeve of his black shirt.

"That was unnecessary, and you know it."

Skye huffed before laying his massive head on his criss-crossed paws. The beast closed his light blue eyes, completely ignoring him.

Raziel crooked his left leg and leaned his elbow on his knee, propping his chin on his palm. The council and his mother were riled because of the missing queen. No one had anticipated her stealing the *fiilee* and then disappearing completely.

Several of his council believed her to be dead.

If Skye's mate hadn't tossed the Sirenidae to her death but she'd been injured and unable to seek help, Mer would also be dead. The forests of Methi weren't safe places. All sorts of predators stalked the trees looking for an easy meal.

He leaned back into Skye's warmth, his *fiilee* lifting his wing so that Raziel could get comfortable. Staring at the sunset, Raziel debated what to do next. He couldn't call off the search yet, but it wasn't possible for him to be searching for the queen every day. He had to run a bloody kingdom, and yet . . . his conscience wouldn't allow him to stay in Skigara. Each night, he'd gone to bed saying to himself that today would be his last day of searching, and yet each morning, he rose with Skye and joined the search.

Skye chuffed, and Raz glanced to his right as his *fiilee* lifted his head, his ears perked high.

The beast was curious.

Raziel sat up and followed the feline's gaze and blinked slowly.

A Sirenidae bustled through the village below.

A familiar one with short hair.

The queen.

Raziel was on his feet, sprinting down the hillside before he knew what was happening. She had been playing tricks. All this time, she'd been hiding out in the village while everyone had been worried about her safety.

He stormed into the village after Mer, who walked toward the pyre. When he got his hands on her, Raz was going to kill her.

Catching up to her right before the fire, he caught her elbow and spun her around. Mer's eyes rounded as he grabbed her other bicep.

"Where the devil have you been?" he exploded.

Her shock disappeared, and in its place rose an anger to match his own.

"Let go of me!" She yanked her left arm out of his grip as if to escape him, soiled linens falling to the ground.

"Oh no, you don't!" The king caught her around the waist and pulled her against his chest. "Do you know how long you've been gone? The whole kingdom has been looking for you. *I've* been looking for you!"

She braced her left hand against his chest and leaned away, yanking her mask down and baring her teeth at him. "How dare you speak to me that way!"

"How dare I?" he hissed, leaning into her space until they were almost nose to nose. His wine-colored hair fell around their faces, creating a curtain of sorts. "I am the king, and you are my wife. You were sold to me, Mer. By all accounts, you belong to me." The ugly words came out, but he didn't take them back fast enough.

Her gaze flattened, and her nails dug into his chest. Instead of leaning away, she pressed into him, a wicked smile on her lips. Raziel blinked, feeling the power shift as she brushed her lips against his own. He'd expected them to be cold, but they were warm and plush and *sinful*.

Raziel kept his mask of disgust on his face as she pulled back. He arched a brow at her. "Was that your pathetic attempt at an apology?"

She flat-out grinned at him. "Never. Just sharing what I've been given."

His brows furrowed in confusion, feeling a trap closing in on him. "What?"

Mer nodded to the soiled linens at their feet. "Someone vomited all over me and themselves."

Realization dawned, and his hand twitched against the base of her spine. The plague village. The new strain.

"Welcome to hell, my lord. I hope you get sick."

MER

MER SCOOPED UP THE LINENS AND WALKED AWAY from the king with victory in her soul.

But her smugness didn't last long as the scent of burning bodies became almost overwhelming when she reached the pyre. She handed the linens off to the nearest man, whose face was covered in sweat and ash. She backed away from the raging heat, feeling sick to her stomach.

The men handling the bodies had all stopped wearing masks, feeling as if it were a futile form of protection. Mer scraped her hand through her hair and jogged away from the village to the sea. The tide was coming in, the waves crashing hard against the black sand.

She wiggled her toes into the wet sand, rooting herself.

A gasp flew past her lips as the cold water rushed past her legs, rising to mid-calf. In the time since she'd stumbled into the village of Vierla, she'd aged years.

Sickness ran rampant among the people.

Fevers, delusions, vomiting, and sores.

Then came the convulsions and eventually death.

Mer dropped to a crouch as the water receded, breathing hard, head hanging between her knees. The disease moved quickly. Once contracted, in five days someone could be dead. She stood as the next wave rolled in, staring at the darkening sky. They'd already lost a Sirenidae healer.

It had been violent.

And scarring.

She squeezed her eyes shut to block out the image of the Sirenidae's sore-covered face with sightless eyes.

The ocean was brutal, it's true, but their people were careful in their endeavors. Most of the Sirenidae lived hundreds of years. Between their healers, herbs, hearty constitution, and respect for life, it was unusual to lose someone from disease or to an accident.

And the healer had been young.

Tears sprang into Mer's eyes, grief welling for the life lost.

The wind picked up, and Mer wrapped her arms around herself, rubbing her palms up and down against the chill. She stared out at the dark water. While she wasn't a healer, Mer had learned a lot during her marriage to Ream. A pang of loss ran through her at the reminder.

Focus, Mer.

Every disease had a cause.

And a cure.

The five Sirenidae healers that had been stationed here had already used many of their concoctions on the ill. None had worked. It gave those sick a little bit of reprieve but did nothing to extend their lives.

This new disease had originated in this village.

Mer wanted to know why.

It was a very clean town with little to no imports.

The village of Vierla was isolated and self-sufficient.

Just what had caused the sickness?

She sighed, watching the water. She began to hum a new tune that had been stuck in her head, not able to remember where she'd heard it before.

It was very possible that there was a cure in the ocean.

They just needed to figure out how to get to it.

Since her arrival in Vierla, she'd been trying to build up her tolerance to the cold water. Every morning and night, she'd plunge into the sea and explore until her limbs began to give out. It was harrowing and miserable, but necessary.

Icy tingles ran up her heels and Mer forced herself to walk away from the ocean. As much as she wanted to dive into the water and begin searching for herbs, Mer wouldn't be able to see anything at night, nor last longer than five minutes in the cold water without the sun to warm it.

She walked from the beach, sand rubbing in between her toes as she made her way to the home she'd been given to stay in.

Movement caught her eye to the right.

Her *fiilee* was perched on a nearby outcropping of rocks watching Mer.

"Go home," she called to the beast. "I'm going to bed. I've no use for you."

As if the feline understood her, the *fiilee* stood and dropped down to the sand, prowling to Mer. She rubbed her snout against Mer's side and huffed out a rumbling purr.

Mer ran her fingers through the silky fur between the creature's ears and then turned to hug the *fiilee* around the neck briefly. "I'll miss you too," she whispered. Mer stepped away and the feline loped off into the dark.

Since she arrived, Mer hadn't met many people, but none had been a true friend. Her *fiilee* was probably the only creature she could trust. It was a sad realization.

Mer stomped her feet outside the wooden door, wiped them on a faded woven rug, and stepped inside, trying not to drown in her morose thoughts. It was harder and harder not to sink into a depression she wasn't sure she could claw her way back from. Working with the healers was a blessing of sorts. It kept her so busy she didn't have time to think about her problems.

She hung her mask on the peg by the door and smiled at the roaring fire. The people were really too kind to her.

The stone house was one rectangular room with a loft above. The fireplace was directly across from the door. A simple kitchen lay to the right with an old circular table and two well-used chairs. And to the left was a small tub with actual warm water fed from the hot springs. In the corner between the fireplace and the tub was a rustic bed made from driftwood.

It was perfect.

Mer padded over to the tub and turned the water on, running her fingers underneath until it reached the right temperature. She smiled as she spied a plate on the small counter. Bread, cheese, and smoked fish. Her stomach rumbled as she popped some salted fish into her mouth, followed by a chunk of creamy cheese.

She'd have to thank Isla somehow. The woman was in charge of caring for the Sirenidae, and she was a force to be reckoned with. Mer tore a chunk of heavy bread away from the crusty loaf and munched on it. Once finished, she dusted her hands off on her ratty skirt and sauntered over to the bathtub, turning the water off.

Peeling her soiled clothes off, she tossed them to the ground and sank into the water. She released a groan as the warm water caressed her skin and loosened her muscles. This was one of the human comforts she could get used to.

Her eyelids slowly slid shut, and she leaned her head against the edge of the tub. Over the last five days, she'd been cursing herself for not going back to the palace. Not because she didn't want to help but because she was stuck here. Sure, she had wanted to visit this area and gather more information on Ceto. But no one wanted to talk about old legends when they were fighting for their lives or bone-tired from trying to save lives.

In fact, she'd been so busy over the past few days that as soon as she lay down, she slept deeply. Which was unfortunate because then she was stuck in the nightmares.

Her eyes popped open at the mumble of voices outside. Mer sat up and clenched the edges of the tub. Her breaths came fast, and her eyes landed on her pillow where she'd hidden a blade. Nudity had never been an issue before, but after Keventin's attack, it had changed something inside her. She stood just as the door swung open. Mer dropped back down into the tub.

"Thank you so much for your hospitality," Raziel's deep voice said.

She shrank even farther into the basin when he stepped inside. His head hung low as he shut the door and leaned back against it, closing his eyes.

"What are you doing here?" she demanded.

The king's eyes snapped open, all traces of weariness gone. "I thought it was obvious. Going to bed."

Mer glared at him over the rim of the tub. "That is my bed and this is my home."

He smirked at her. "And you are my wife, so whatever is yours is also mine."

The audacity. He pulled his boots and socks off, tossing them by the front door like he owned the place. She gaped at his broad back as he explored the kitchen and even took some of her bread.

"You're not welcome here," she hissed.

"Clearly." He took another bite of the bread. "But as there is no other place to stay, and we are married, this is where I will sleep until it's safe for us to leave."

"No."

"You have no choice." He sighed, walking over to the fire, completely dismissing her.

She shook as he warmed his hands and then moved to the head of the bed, plumping one of the pillows.

"Don't you dare."

Raziel met her gaze, his silver eyes hard. "You put me in this situation. If you hadn't run away, I wouldn't have had to look for you."

"I didn't ask you to."

"No, you didn't, but as your husband, it didn't feel right doing nothing when you could be dead or dying somewhere. What the blazes were you thinking when you tried to claim a bloody *fiilee* with no training?"

Mer started to tremble. "That you'd trapped me, and I was tired of being a prisoner. I am a daughter of the sea, not some maiden you can lock in your bedroom for your pleasure."

He barked out a laugh. "Pleasure? What pleasure is there, Mer?" He moved to the end of the bed and yanked the collar of his shirt down to reveal the scar she'd given him. "Was it when you tried to cut my throat? Or the other time when you tried to tear it out with your bare teeth? How about the time you made a mockery of my court by wearing curtains to your welcoming banquet? Or when you accused me of murdering your husband?"

She trembled harder as he stepped between the tub and the door. Her breath became thready. "Stop." He was too close. She couldn't breathe.

He took another step closer. "Stop telling the truth? No. It's clear neither one of us wanted this marriage, but we had no choice. I have tried to make you comfortable, and all you have done is literally stab me. I will no longer make your life easy. I have lied for you, protected you, and made excuses for you. No more, especially after what happened in Laos." He loomed closer. "But what I can't forgive is your actions with Duke Keventin. You knew he was important, and you undermined me by trying to kill him in broad daylight?"

Not safe. Not safe. Not safe.

Mer snapped, her reality blurring when he came closer.

No one would touch her ever again without her consent.

She launched from the tub and tackled the king, water spraying everywhere. Raziel grunted and stumbled backward with the force of her attack. They crashed through the flimsy front door of the tiny little house, wood splintering everywhere.

She hissed as they hit the ground hard.

The king rolled quickly on top of her, rocks digging into her spine. Mer wrapped her legs around his waist and squeezed as hard as she could. Raziel huffed and pushed up on his hands and knees before curling his hand around the back of her head and dropping his full weight on her, slamming her against the sand.

Mer wheezed, the air knocked from her lungs. Panic coursed through her at being pinned down. She bucked, yelling while managing to wedge her arms underneath his armpits. She released her legs and tossed him up over her head.

She scrambled to her feet as the king rolled to his own. The wind picked up, chilling her bare form. He locked eyes on her and settled back into a defensive pose.

Raziel waved his hand at her, baring his teeth. "You want to fight? You want to take your anger out on me? Let me have it but know this is your one chance to be rid of me. After this, you become mine."

She saw red.

Mer attacked, charging under his right arm and trying to swipe his legs out from underneath him. He leaped over her leg and spun, catching her round the throat. It wasn't right for someone so large to be so graceful.

She lifted her left elbow and slammed it into his forearm, breaking his hold. His hair hung loose, so she managed to grab a handful and yanked. Hard.

He hissed, his head tilted back. "You fight dirty," he gritted out, grabbing his scalp. "There's no honor in that."

Mer cackled, the sound unhinged in her own ears. She punched him in the stomach, which was more muscular than it had any right to be. "And there's no honor in death."

She squeaked when instead of trying to push her away he yanked her against his body and sank his hand into her hair, holding on tightly. Her panic rose again, and all she could see was Keventin's face. Mer stepped hard on the top of his foot, but her bare foot did nothing.

He laughed, and her rage burned hotter. Mer jerked her knee upward and managed to unman him. Immediately, his face creased in pain, and he doubled over before releasing her. She kneed him in the face before kicking him squarely in the chest as he toppled backward toward the surf. He managed to grab her arm, pulling her with him.

The couple tumbled into the dark surf, and he rolled until Mer lay in the water beneath him. Chills erupted along her body, and she panted, gills flaring open. Terror froze her in place. It was like that night all over again. Being helpless. Pinned.

She screamed, doubling her struggles.

Raziel's face changed and blurred with her tears. Sobs wracked her chest. "No."

The pressure on her hips disappeared, and she found herself in the king's arms. "Hush," he rasped in her ear. "It's okay. You're okay."

Mer used the last of her strength and managed to flip them until he was beneath her. The waves crashed over them, and Raziel spluttered, his pupils expanding as the Lure took effect. He blinked the water from his eyes, the long red strands of his hair plastered to his cheeks.

Her fists curled in his wet black shirt, shaking. His hands released her naked waist, and he held them out to his sides.

It would be so easy to drown him.

The Lure was taking over. He wouldn't even feel it.

She stared down into his love-drunk face, time stilling. He no longer touched her. His body shook, and his jaw was clenched so tight. Was it the pain?

No. He was resisting the Lure. Fighting not to touch her.

Her heart cracked.

While he'd destroyed her world when he'd taken Ream's life, the man beneath her didn't deserve death. Any man who fought the Lure to protect a person from themselves was worth something. His death would not bring her peace but only more suffering.

Her knees had fallen onto either side of his thighs as the waves pushed past them. The silver of his eyes was nearly swallowed up by the black of his pupils, yet he still didn't touch her.

A sob sputtered from her lips, and tears dripped down her face. "I hate this."

She registered shouts in the distance. More chills erupted along her skin, and she cried harder. Raziel slowly sat up, leaning back on his hands, just watching her cry.

"People are coming," he whispered. "We should go inside. Get you warm."

The soft words undid her.

Mer threw her arms around his neck and buried her face in his shoulder.

"I'm going to hug you," he murmured. "Just tell me if I do something you don't like."

The king wrapped his arms around her tightly and ran his hands over her hair. He maneuvered onto his knees and rocked Mer gently. He skated a soothing hand over her spine and then stood. She wrapped her legs around his waist, and he hitched her higher.

"Do you want to stay with the sea or go to bed?" he asked gently.

Another shiver wracked her. "Bed."

He slogged out of the surf, through the sand, and into the house. Heat blanketed her back, and the sound of the crackling fire reached her ears.

"I'm going to set you down." She untangled her legs, toes touching the warm wood floor. She wavered as he yanked the knitted blanket from the bottom of the bed and wrapped it around her naked body. "I'll be right back."

The king disappeared out the door and spoke in a low voice to someone. He rustled around outside and then brought in a tall piece of driftwood. Numbly she watched as he set it up as a makeshift door. Mer blinked slowly when he approached her and reached for the blanket.

"May I?" he asked.

She nodded, feeling outside her body.

Briskly, he toweled the remaining water from her body and then squeezed out the ends of her hair. Raziel took her hand and led her to the bed. A momentary blip of panic rose when he pulled back the covers, but he only tucked her in and pulled the comforter up to her chin.

Mer blinked up at him, shivering.

Slowly, he reached inside his wet shirt and pulled out her shell blade.

He placed it in her palm and curled Mer's fingers around the handle. "So you feel safe."

Tears once again fell from her eyes. She averted her gaze, staring at the fire, unable to voice her thanks.

He retrieved her blanket-turned-towel and moved to the bathing area. She registered the sound of wet clothes hitting the floor. Raziel returned to her view with the wet blanket wrapped around his waist. They stared at each other as he sat on the floor, then began to feed wood into the fire.

His dark red hair dripped water onto his chest that

shined in the firelight. Mer studied the handsome man on the floor, noting bruises that were already starting to show.

Bruises she'd given him.

And yet, he'd still given her a blade after everything she'd done.

Maybe he wasn't the monster she believed him to be.

Maybe . . . she was the monster.

Chapter Thirty-Three

RAZIEL

SOMEONE HAD HURT HIS WIFE.

And Raziel would kill them.

His jaw clenched as he dropped more wood onto the burning pyre, his eyes watering from the smoke.

Three days since she'd attacked him.

Three days since she'd spoken more than ten words to him.

Three days since Mer had looked him in the eye.

And it bothered him. A lot.

He stepped back from the immense heat and wiped the sweat and ash from his brow, adjusting the scarf he'd wrapped over the bottom of his face. The Sirenidae healers had advised him to stay away, but how could he? The village needed more help and its people were suffering. He wouldn't hide away in his coastal cottage when he could help.

"The sun is setting, my king," a gruff fisherman by the name of Jodere said. "We have this handled. Please get some rest."

Raziel nodded to Jodere. "Let me know if you need me to take a shift during the night."

"I will."

He walked away from the pyre, his skin itching to be free from his dirty, sweat soaked clothing. Raz pulled the scarf from his nose and smiled at those who bustled through the quiet village. A smile could do much for morale and the people needed it.

Winding his way through the town, he followed the sound of the waves. Raz popped out onto the black sand beach. He yanked his boots and socks off, stuffing them in the boots and picking them up. The sand stuck to the bottoms of his feet as he trudged his way to the cottage at the end of the cove.

The door still hadn't been replaced. The large driftwood piece was set aside.

Mer was home.

He eyed the open doorway and sighed. Raziel didn't think he could have an evening of strained silence. Plus, he needed a bath. Raz pushed past the little home to the back of some rocks that curved around the edge of the cove.

Dropping his boots in the dry sand, he took one last look at the cottage before shucking his clothes and striding into the surf. A sigh escaped him as the cool water washed over his calves, thighs, and then waist. He ran his hands over the top of the gentle waves, ignoring the ever-present fear that lurked in the back of his mind.

Just breathe.

The waves rocked him gently back and forth, his feet settling into the sand. Raziel inhaled measured breaths until the anxiety receded. He watched as the water changed colors into the evening. Colorful fish darted around in the clear water as if playing tag. Sea stars clung to the bright corals along the rocks while sea anemones waved like dancers with their hands flung to the heavens.

A cream spotted snake skittered next to his left foot and he almost jumped out of his skin, a curse flying from his lips before he cracked a smile. The sneaky little creature had perfectly camouflaged itself against the sand once again.

While he feared water in general, there was something hypnotic and almost magical about the ocean, the scenery always changing and new treasures to be discovered.

He brushed a dirty strand of hair from his face and grimaced. It needed a good scrub. He inhaled deeply and dove beneath the waves, cold water closing above his head. Raziel opened his eyes, the saltwater slightly burning his blurry vision. Roughly scrubbing his scalp, he eyed the water, looking for any murky shapes. The fishmen tended to gut and clean their fish in the area which attracted larger predators.

Like the leviathan.

A shudder went through him as he gave his hair another good scrub. Bath time was over.

A flicker of movement not twenty feet to his left caught his eye. He froze, fear rooting him in place. His eyes narrowed as he registered what it was. A foot. A silvery foot.

Mer.

Curiosity piqued, he swam over to the rock shelf, sending crabs scuttling into the cracks of the porous rocks. He grasped the rock, avoiding the coral and popped his head above the water. On the other side of the rocks was a small cove.

His wife burst through the water, throwing her head back, water flipping in an arc behind her. His breath caught as the sinking sun glimmered on the scales of her shoulder. She shone like the inside of a shell—all pinks, purples, peaches, and silvers.

Silver hair dripping down the back of her neck, she stood up with her back to him and slapped the water, releasing guttural screams that made his chest ache. Scream which spoke of frustration, pain, anger, and loss.

Things he could identify with.

She turned slightly so he could see her profile and in that moment, he was sure he had never seen anything so radiant. It was as if the sunset had been captured and formed into this magnificent creature.

He watched in fascination as her gills spurted water

and then sealed shut, becoming almost invisible. Her eyes closed and she tipped her head back as if to calm herself. A huff to his left pulled his attention.

Feather was perched on the rock above him, her orange and white striped tail lazily swishing just above the water. Her gaze pierced him and a small prick of guilt hit. What was he doing? Watching his wife during something that was clearly private surely wouldn't endear him to her.

He tried to back away but a large wave crashed into him, forcing his body forward and against a sharp piece of coral. Raziel hissed and jerked back, the right side of his ribs stinging.

Blood curled through the water from the small cut.

Great. Just great.

He lifted his eyes and locked onto a familiar pair of magenta ones.

Bitter bones.

Raziel froze, not knowing if he should retreat or say something.

She arched a shimmering brow at him. "Spying on me, my king?"

A shiver of pleasure skittered down his spine at her words. He swayed toward her, his gaze devouring his wife. She wore a gray and white spotted bodice that fit like a second skin. He'd never seen anything like it. It looked slick like poured oil. What would it feel like beneath his fingers?

Raz shuddered. Why was she affecting him so much?

It's not like he was close enough for the Lure to take effect. Her other brow lifted.

Blast. She was still waiting for an answer.

"I came from the pyres," Raz replied gruffly. "I needed a bath." Like he had to explain himself.

She nodded slowly, her face losing any playfulness. "How many did we lose today?" she asked softly.

"Three." It was only one word, but it hurt to speak it out loud.

His stomach dropped as an image of a smaller wrapped body flashed through his mind. Grief rose. The loss of children cut deeper than anything. How many little bodies had been burned over the years? When would the plague decide it had claimed enough life? When would it be sated?

Never.

Mer shifted closer. "Less than yesterday."

But still too many.

His rib stung and he glanced down, annoyed at the cut that leaked blood. He needed to tend to it before it got infected. Time to go.

"You're hurt," Mer commented, her voice all too close.

His head snapped up and his eyes rounded. She'd snuck up on him and had lifted herself on the rock to look down on him. Raziel sucked in a breath and immediately regretted it, her scent sinking its claws into him. His mind fogged a little bit, but he knew he needed to leave. The last thing either of them needed was for Raziel to lose himself and try to maul her while completely nude.

He gritted his teeth and backed away, the water lowering to his hips. "I'm fine."

The Sirenidae dropped back into the water and quickly swam around the point of the rocks, her pretty eyes narrowed on him.

"You're hurt. I can help."

His wife dove into the water, flashing him her entire bare back and disappeared beneath the waves. Panic crested over him, and he dropped his hands into the sea to cover his groin. While he wasn't ashamed of his body, he didn't want to scare Mer.

It was clear someone had taken advantage of his wife. He didn't want her to think she wasn't safe with him or that he'd come out here with the intention of watching her while he was naked.

Raziel grumbled to himself, "I only wanted a bloody bath."

He glanced longingly over his shoulder at his clothes. There was nowhere to go where his nudity wouldn't be exposed. He should have gone inside the cottage.

Turning back toward the open ocean, a fissure of fear skated down his spine as he spotted a murky shape that was neither human nor Sirenidae.

A shark.

He cursed, glancing at the blood dripping down his abs and into the water. Part of Raz wanted to run screaming for the shore, but knew the movement would only rile the ocean beastie. Perhaps if he held very still it would leave him alone.

His heart pounded as it edged along the outcrop of rocks.

Mer popped back up in front of him and he shouted, nearly scared out of his skin.

She held out an orange leafy plant in her hand. "I found something for you."

His gaze had turned back to the shark which drifted closer. "Mer," he said softly. "There's a shark."

"And?" she muttered, quickly grinding the delicate plant beneath her palms.

"It's coming closer," he hissed, noticing how the size seemed to grow.

She held out the pulpy mixture. "Take it."

"But the shark."

His heart lurched into his throat as the shark darted forward. Mer spun, holding the pulpy mixture aloft. Raz gaped as she grabbed the snout of the shark and redirected it away from them with a firm, but gentle push. He barely twitched when she ran a hand down its side, crooning softly.

The shark didn't spin around but continued toward the open ocean as the Sirenidae turned back to him once again.

"You pushed it away," he said woodenly. "Like a misbehaving pup."

"She was only hunting and curious about your blood. Nothing else."

"Would the shark have attacked?" he asked, still searching the waves for any other sharp-toothed beasties.

"Their teeth are one of their senses."

"That doesn't answer my question."

Mer huffed, holding out the pulpy mixture. "She wasn't protecting her pups or showing territorial displays. She was just saying hello."

Raz didn't like it. Not one bit. "Do all sharks like to say hello to their queen?"

A small smile lifted her pink lips. "Only the friendly ones."

He exhaled heavily and chuckled, eyeing the mixture in her hands. "What is that? It looks disgusting."

"It helps purge infection and seals the wound until it's fully healed, then it falls off," she said.

He reached out slowly and took the gummy mixture from her fingers, a tingle running down his arm at their connection.

It's just the Lure.

He attempted to breathe through his mouth and not his nose, but it wasn't helping any. Her heady scent was urging him to move forward to wrap his arms around her body to pull her into his embrace. It would be so easy to gorge himself on her silky skin, wrap her legs around his waist and...

Shame crashed down upon him.

Fight it.

Raziel focused on the blood dripping down his stomach and slowly dabbed the mixture into the cut and across it. A pleasantly cool tingling sensation spread over his skin and numbed the pain almost immediately.

He smiled in awe. It was like magic. "Why have we never used this before?"

The pretty woman in front of him shrugged her shoulder. "It's an ocean herb. If you're not looking for it, you wouldn't be able to find it."

"Thank you."

She glanced away from him and slapped her hand against the water. "It's nothing."

An awkward silence settled between them.

Finally, he said, "What are you doing out here?"

She gave him an odd look, rubbing her palms along her arms. "Swimming... obviously."

Raziel rolled his eyes at the snark in her voice. "Obviously... is it very different from where you come from?"

A sad look crossed her face. "It's very, very different," she whispered. "But not bad." A pause. "The water is cold." Her tone said she didn't like it.

He grinned at that. "The water isn't cold." His arms hadn't even broken out with goosebumps.

She snorted, shaking her head. "That's because you haven't swum in the warm waters of the Thalassan Sea in the south. It's akin to the warm waters of your lake."

"I did at one point." The words just popped out.

Raziel tried not to remember his time during the Warlord's War. Nor the time he almost drowned.

Her interest grew keen, her eyes sharp upon him. "Continue."

"During the war, I was stabbed in the back." He turned slightly so she could see the large scar on his back. "I fell off the ship and almost drowned. I remember the water settling over me like a warm blanket."

"But you survived," she commented, no inflection to her voice, her face a placid mask. The Sirenidae dropped his gaze and drew patterns along the surface of the ocean.

"I did."

A shiver ran through Mer as the wind picked up and he watched as her scales lifted slightly on her arms—a trait he'd noticed was akin to goosebumps.

"You're cold?" he asked, frowning. "If you want to get out, I'll look away."

A sardonic smile lifted her lips. "You pretend that you haven't seen my naked body, nor had your hands all over it."

A flush of heat went through him, and he scowled. Bloody Lure.

"Well then, look away while I get out," Raz muttered.

She crossed her arms, the waves gently lapping at the tops of her breasts, giving him glimpses of a tattoo she kept hidden most of the time.

"You saw me naked. Now it's my turn to see you." She wiggled her brows. "We're married after all."

He huffed out a laugh. It felt good to laugh after the last few days. Raziel turned around and pushed toward the beach, swaying his hips—the water slowly lowering. Peals of laughter followed him and he couldn't help but look over his shoulder and grin at the Sirenidae who held a hand over her mouth.

It was the first moment he'd ever seen her truly free. Speedily, he scooped up his belongings and hustled into the cottage, making sure to wipe his feet at the door. He dumped his clothes into the tub and slipped on a fresh pair of pants. Raziel retrieved a blanket and then moved back to the beach. She was still in the water, watching him.

"I won't look," he said, holding the blanket out and averting his eyes. "Or I can leave it on the beach for you."

"I'm in my seal skin," she called. "It's perfectly modest."

He barked out a laugh. "Maybe for a maid of the sea."

The sound of footsteps registered and Mer pulled the blanket from his fingers, wrapping it around her body.

A flicker of heat ignited in his gut as Raziel stared down into Mer's sparkling, solemn magenta eyes.

She searched his face. "Why are you so kind to me? Do you pity me?"

He reached out and tucked a strand of starlight hair behind her ear. "I know a wounded soul when I see one," he answered. Raz had his own demons that he had to fight night after night. "No one should feel powerless. But no, I don't pity you, but I wish someone had been there to show me an ounce of comfort when I was struggling with my own problems."

She huffed, brushing off his touch and moving around him.

The moment was broken as she moved back to the cottage. He stared at his hand, the feeling of her skin permanently imprinted there.

Just the Lure.

Raziel flexed his fingers. At least he hoped it was.

"Are you coming?"

He twisted to face her. "What?"

She wiggled her brows. "Isla is grilling fish by the fire tonight and she promised me a story. I don't want to be late."

"You want me to come with you?" he asked slowly, trying to see the trap.

Mer shrugged. "It's for the whole village. You can come too if you want. You are the king."

"And you're my queen." Raziel didn't know why he said the words.

She held his gaze evenly. "So I am."

Chapter Thirty-Four

MER

MER SNAPPED THE BOOK SHUT AND SET THE
heavy medical tome on the table. She rested her elbows on
the desk and massaged her temples. "There has to be
something more."

"There isn't," Joiakim answered gravely, running a
hand through his long pale lavender hair. His gaze flicked
to the books scattered across the table in front of Mer.
"Do you really think those human texts are going to offer
us any help?"

Mer ran her left hand over the weathered cover of the
nearest book. Levay had sent it to them in the hopes it
might help. It hadn't, but Mer was looking for a clue.
They were all desperate.

"Perhaps the Methians missed something," she mused.

Joiakim tossed his head, his face a mask of annoyance. "After thirty years of searching for a cure, I doubt it." She narrowed her gaze at his snotty tone. He flinched and immediately dropped his head in apology. "Excuse me for speaking so informally, my queen."

Mer waved a hand at him before pushing back the old rickety chair and getting to her feet. Everything about the village council room was old but clean. She sighed, running a hand down her face. The loss of life was getting to them all. While the Sirenidae were masters at healing, their people hadn't suffered a deadly sickness in hundreds of years.

"We're all under a tremendous amount of pressure," she said softly, glancing at the other three Sirenidae healers. "We need to think outside the box." Mer rested her palms on the table, eyes burning from the lack of sleep. "Yes, the Mirror Plague has been around for three decades, but the new strain started here in the village. What does that tell you?"

Avalon, the youngest of the Sirenidae, twirled a piece of coral hair around her finger, biting her bottom lip. "That it mutated here. Something about this village changed the sickness."

"But what?" Reef cut in. He pushed away from the doorway and crossed his arms, standing next to his younger sister. The siblings could have been twins from their coloring. No one would know that there was over twenty years difference between the brother and sister.

"From my inquiries, nothing has changed in this village. Their food and water sources have been checked and nothing seems to be contaminated." He grimaced. "I swam as far as I could in the ocean before my body gave out. No pollutants ever filtered through my gills."

"I agree that it's not the water. I've noticed the same things in my swims," Mer added.

Silence greeted her statement and she lifted her gaze to Alanis who seemed to speak loudly while saying nothing at all. The woman's jaw was clenched tight and her eyes seemed to burn.

"Do you have something to add?" Mer drawled, uncoiling to her full height.

By law Mer shouldn't be entering the ocean at all. She was a banished one, fated to be parted from the loving embrace of the sea.

Alanis unclenched her jaw and spoke. "If you wish for frankness, I will give it to you. I hate that you were branded as a traitor. You are a hero to our people."

Mer's jaw dropped. That was not what she was expecting from the gruff healer. "You are not upset that I'm disobeying the sea king?"

Alanis snorted. "No, my queen. I'm old enough to know when an old man's pride is wounded and he's taking his frustration out on everyone else." Avalon gasped but the older healer ignored it. "From my point of view, you've always tried to help others to the best of your ability. You should not be punished for that."

Mer's eyes were suspiciously hot. "Thank you for your honesty," she choked out.

Avalon dropped the lock of hair she fiddled with and gave Mer a blinding smile—one that spoke of hope and innocence. Had Mer ever looked like that? Had she ever been that innocent?

The answer scared her.

"We love you, my lady," Avalon said brightly.

Mer smiled back at the sweet healer. They needed more Avalon's in the world.

Slapping a hand against the table, Mer resumed her pacing, determined as ever to get to the bottom of their conundrum. She wasn't a healer but she was very good at figuring out problems. Mer laced her fingers behind her back. What were they missing?

"The village is dwindling day by day," Joiakim said. "We must find a cure now or we will all die... just like Pearl."

Avalon sucked in a sharp breath and Reef wrapped an arm around his sister's slim shoulders.

Alanis teetered her head back and forth. "Have any of you noticed how the disease transmutes?"

Mer paused her pacing and focused on the oldest healer. "What do you mean? It's spread through the air, right?"

"Perhaps, but I know for a fact that a young girl coughed right into Reef's face three days ago. There was blood and mucus. It got into his mouth too because he was not wearing a face covering." She squinted at the male.

Reef winced. "A mistake I will not be making again."

"But that's my point," Alanis said. "That was over three days ago and yet you are still showing no symptoms."

"I assumed it was because my immune system is better than others."

Alanis walked to the table, messing with a corner of one of the books, brows furrowed in deep thought. "Right. We've been operating under that assumption, but what if it was something different?"

Joiakim arched a brow and yanked out a chair. "Like what?" he asked tiredly, sitting down.

"Like the fact it's not passed through the air or through blood and mucus." Joiakim scoffed at Alanis, but she continued, undeterred. "Most diseases are, but what if it's not a disease."

Mer blinked slowly, trying to follow the conversation. "What do you mean it's not a disease? We're watching people get sick and die daily."

Alanis nodded, her gaze sharp. "True, it's spreading, but not how it should if it *was* a disease."

Reef bounced from foot to foot, rubbing his chin. "So you're proposing the Mirror Plague isn't a disease and this isn't a new strain? That seems hard to believe since it's been plaguing their kingdom for over thirty years!"

"Exactly," Alana said. "*Thirty* years. That is a long

time for an illness to stay trapped in Methi. Sickness has a way of spreading no matter how careful a person is. But consider this, Methi has managed it for three decades. Merchants have had to come in and out and yet most have not contracted the plague nor spread it to the other five kingdoms. Something isn't adding up."

"So, what are you saying?" Joiakim asked, glancing out the open door toward the pyres.

"That something else is going on."

Mer studied the older healer, running her mind over what Alanis had said. The impossibility of keeping the disease contained. How the disease spread from person to person. The fact that none of their herbs were helping whatsoever. If it wasn't a disease, what was the culprit?

Avalon gasped, her eyes growing wide. Her attention snapped to Alanis. "Surely you don't mean..." she trailed off.

The older healer nodded her head once. "It fits the symptoms."

"Please share with the rest of us," Joiakim grouched. "We must get back to caring for the people."

"Poison," Avalon whispered.

Poison.

It was a far-fetched idea.

"Do you even hear yourself?" Joiakim snapped.

Mer leaned heavily against the bookcase behind her and stared at the four Sirenidae as they all turned over Alanis's idea.

"Poisoning a whole kingdom?" Mer shook her head. "How would that even work? A shared water source?"

Reef shook his head no. "We've tested the water sources all around the village. There's nothing in them."

"That you can find," Avalon said softly. "Not all poisons are detectable." She pursed her lips. "The plague doesn't present like any poison I know."

"For that I'm glad," Alanis said to the younger healer. "When you've lived as long as I have, you come across things you wish you could wipe from your mind. Poisons aren't straightforward. They present in different ways."

Mer caught movement to her left and she spotted Coven—the skittery young woman who always seemed to be helping with odd jobs around the village. The girl's hat was just barely visible above the frame of the open window.

Odd. What was she doing out there? Was there word from Isla?

Perhaps she didn't want to disturb them.

Maybe the young woman was curious about what they spoke about, but why hide? It wasn't as if what they were speaking about was a secret.

She's shy. Stop being so suspicious.

"Okay." Reef held his hands up. "Let's say for argument's sake that it is a poison. If it isn't in the water source, then what do the people have in common across the kingdom?"

"A food source? Maybe a household item?" Mer offered, dismissing the girl.

Joiakim sighed. "I'll play your game." He laced his fingers and rested them on his chest. "Surely if it was poison the Methians would have discovered it."

"Not if it came from the ocean," Mer said, the damning words falling from her lips.

The room fell silent and tension filled the air.

"Are you suggesting that our king has been poisoning the Methians for over the last thirty years?" Joiakim hissed. "It's treason to even think such things, let alone speak them aloud."

"No, my grandfather does not care for the lives of land dwellers. He never has and he never will. Methi has basically been cut off from the five kingdoms for the last thirty years. Aermia struggles with disease and civil war. Nagali is a wasteland full of minstrels and pirates. Scythia has been consumed with lust for power. But none of the other kingdoms have been able to penetrate the security of Methi's borders."

"What of ships?" Joiakim asked.

"They would have been noticed."

"Scythia could have done this," Alanis darkly muttered. "Their depravity knows no bounds."

"But as you said, this is a new strain," Mer pointed out. "Blaise is now queen. From what I've heard, she has an iron control over her court."

"And yet..." Joiakim sighed. "It's easy to plot behind a ruler's back. Haven't you successfully done so yourself?"

Mer swallowed down her retort. The healer had been close to Pearl and was taking out his grief on everyone around him. She could extend some grace to him. "True, but it wouldn't be an easy thing. A year hasn't even passed since the Warlord's War. Everyone is still walking on pins and needles. I don't think someone would do this now."

"We've cleared everyone," Avalon said. "That leaves no one and we're back to a disease."

"But what if it did come from the sea?" Mer said softly, as she moved to the table and pushed around the books until she found the one she was looking for. She stabbed a finger at the myth about sea demons she'd found. "I heard a bard sing stories about these creatures. He'd even studied about them in his travels. I've spoken with Isla. The whole village believes them to exist. They believe them to be Sirenidae."

Reef burst out laughing and then choked it back when he realized everyone else was quiet. He threw his hands up in the air. "That's preposterous." He waved a hand toward the ocean. "That water kills Sirenidae. We cannot survive in the cold. It's just old ghost stories."

"While you're not wrong," she admitted, "all myth is rooted in truth." She licked her lips and continued, despite the way her heart raced in her chest. "What if there was another possibility?"

"Like what?" Avalon asked.

"What if we're not the only ones in the ocean?" Once the idea had taken root, she couldn't let it go. "Think about it." Mer began to pace back and forth. "We can't survive the cold, so when have we ever explored the North Sea? What if there are sea people of the north?"

"Then why would they not have made themselves known to us?" Alanis asked.

"Because of their physical limitations. We cannot handle the depths and the cold. They cannot handle the reefs and the warmth."

Joiakim scoffed. "What proof do you have? Just the words of a bard and the pretty words of a fairytale?"

Her experience with the kraken rose to the forefront of her mind. She had sworn that day she had heard someone else calling—a haunting tune in the water but she'd brushed it off. And then again in the Bay of Laos had she not also heard another song? She'd dismissed it as her mind longing for home.

Tell them.

"I've experienced the call twice," she whispered.

Joiakim bolted upright. "What do you mean the call?"

"Two separate times I heard someone call to me."

Four pairs of Sirenidae eyes stared at her.

"The first time I was trying to soothe a kraken."

Reef spluttered. "You mean it wasn't you who kept it from making our vessel a snack?"

"I tried, but when I stopped singing another tune

swirled through the water. I believe I helped, but the other song definitely called the kraken away."

Joiakim cursed and sprang to his feet. "If what you say is true, then the other entity can control the beasts of the deep." His expression settled into deep worry. "Do you know what this means for us?"

Mer knew exactly where his mind was going. "We'll be blamed."

"Why?" Avalon cried. "We're helping the people here."

"And this newest *outbreak* coincides with our arrival," Alanis surmised. "If a poison from the sea is discovered, they'll take our lives."

"I won't allow that," Mer promised them.

Reef hugged Avalon to his side. "How will you do that? You're just a foreign queen."

Mer crossed her arms. "One way or another I'll discover the truth. I'll protect you myself. I promise."

"Do it quickly," Alanis said. "Because we have little time before everyone in this village is dead. Including you."

Chapter Thirty-Five

RAZIEL

RAZIEL GAZED AT THE FIRE IN THE VILLAGE square, trying to decide if he should return to the cottage.

His wife had been avoiding him all day.

Skye hadn't even shown up today for a visit. His fiilee didn't like the scent of the pyre and Raziel didn't blame him.

He thought they'd reached a truce and maybe had even been building a tentative friendship.

"Have you seen Coven, my king?"

Raz blinked up at Isla, shaking the thoughts from his mind. "What was that?"

"Coven, have you seen her?"

His brows furrowed as he ran over the day. When was the last time he saw the quiet girl? It had been around lunch. "Last I saw Coven she was washing linens. Perhaps she's at her home?"

"She actually lives with my husband and I, my king."

"I think we're close enough to drop the title, Isla." Raziel smiled when she blushed and shook her head. "So Coven is your daughter." That explained why Coven was always hovering around Isla.

The older woman smiled. "She was our miracle. We were not blessed with children so when Coven came into our lives, I was overjoyed."

"She's lovely," he replied. While he hadn't gotten to know Coven very well, she was one of the hardest-working people in the village. "If you don't mind me asking, was she a ward of your family?"

"No, in fact you would hardly believe how she came to be with us." Isla laughed and gestured toward the ocean. "The sea gives, and it takes. It took my father but blessed me with a daughter."

"How did the sea give you Coven?"

"One morning my husband went out to fish and there in the surf sat Coven. She was only two years old." Isla blew a strand of graying black hair from her face. "We tried to find her parents, but there's no village close by. It would have been impossible for a toddler to travel so far."

"Was she hurt?"

"No. Not even a scratch. She didn't speak for five years. It was only with kindness and patience that she began to speak at seven years old."

Raziel was stunned. "How do you think she got on that beach?"

"My best guess is that she fell off a fishing vessel. All the villages along the coast fish. Even at two, she was an extraordinary swimmer. It seems bizarre but I think she swam to our village. The poor thing slept for almost two days once we'd discovered her."

Raziel smiled. "You're fortunate to have such a daughter. She's a hard worker." He slapped his thighs and stood with a groan. "Do you want help looking for her?"

Isla pulled a face and glanced at the sun that had almost completely set. "The girl is always running around. I'm sure she'll show up soon." She wrung her hands and the skin around her eyes was a little too pinched.

A worried mother.

"I need to take a walk and work out the kinks in my back. I'll keep an eye out for her."

"Thank you, my king." A relieved smile touched her lips. "Please let Mer know that I'll drop supper off in a little bit."

Raziel nodded. "You know you don't have to cook for us."

Isla gasped. "And not be hospitable to my king and queen who risk so much each day for our home? I'll not hear of it."

"As you say."

He waved and meandered through the village, hating all the blue slashes of paint along doors. A sign of sickness.

It was the ones without any light glowing from the inside that made his heart ache.

Raziel found himself pulled toward the cottage he shared with a mercurial Sirenidae. It surprised him how much he'd enjoyed the mundaneness of their evenings. Bathing, eating, speaking a little about their days, and then sleeping. Although, he would love a real bed. Sleeping on the hard, cold floor left him aching.

The thunder of waves hitting the sand grew louder as the ground sloped to the beach, the sunset leaving only the tiniest hint of light. Raz turned to the west and strolled down the beach, his boots sinking into the black sand with each step.

Their little home rested at the end of the beach, nestled near the curved outcropping of rocks that stretched into the ocean like a crooked finger. It was odd Mer hadn't met at the village fire tonight. Those who were still strong and not ill started meeting there to boost morale.

The Sirenidae seemed to take great pleasure in joining in. Asking questions about Methian legends, telling stories of her home, or just listening empathetically to the villagers' struggles.

It was a whole different side of his feral wife that he was experiencing.

And he... liked it.

His steps sped up just thinking about Mer. Raziel kicked the sand and physically forced himself to slow down. Too many obstacles were between them for him to start forming any real attachment to her. At least that was what he kept telling himself.

Each day more of her personality began to show and she intrigued him.

It was an unhealthy addiction... wondering what she'd say next.

Raziel scanned the sea and spotted her floating in the distance, her pale skin a beacon in the dark water. A wry smile pulled up his lips. She was probably searching for more herbs, speaking with sharks, or charming the creatures of the sea.

Like she has you.

Raziel huffed at the thought.

Even though he didn't like it, it made it no less true. During their time in the village, he'd softened towards her. It was a problem. A real problem.

As he drew closer to their cottage, he frowned at Mer. She lay face down in the water, not moving a muscle. A tread of alarm tugged in his chest.

She breathes underwater.

His speed picked up anyway, his thighs burning as he jogged through the sand. He couldn't get rid of the real fear that something was wrong.

A wave rolled forward, picking Mer up and his heart stopped.

Long brown hair tangled in the waves.

Brown hair, not silver.

It wasn't Mer.

Coven.

Raziel yelled at the top of his lungs, sprinting for the water. He stopped in the surf and tore his boots from his feet then ran deeper into the water, lifting his knees high to get through the breaking waves. He sucked in a deep breath and dove.

Cool water surrounded him for one breathless moment before he popped up and swam forward. His heart raced in his chest as he cut through the dark water.

Not fast enough.

He gritted his teeth and swam harder, determined to get to the girl. Raziel reached her just as a waved rose and crashed down, shoving them beneath the water. He grimaced as saltwater flooded his mouth. He blindly groped for Coven, catching her hair. Water filled his ears, but a haunting melody reached him. Raziel opened his eyes but there was nothing but darkness.

He surfaced with a choked cough, dropping Coven's hair and grabbed her arm, pulling her to his chest.

"Wake up," he shouted in her ear.

She didn't respond.

Raz wrapped his arm around her bare chest, her back resting against his own as he towed them toward the shore. Another wave shoved them beneath the water but he managed to hold on to Coven.

He kicked hard, bringing them to the surface again, glimpsing the cottage in the distance.

"Help!" he bellowed, praying the Sirenidae heard him.

Mer stepped out of the cottage and spotted him almost immediately.

She bolted toward the water.

As his toes met sand, a warm pair of hands touched him. "Let me help."

He shifted and Mer practically tore Coven from his grip, swimming back to the shore quickly. Raziel struggled to catch up, dropping to his knees beside the pair. Mer had placed the girl on her back and was blowing air into Coven's mouth. She then proceeded to lace her fingers and press on her chest.

Coven's bare chest.

Sourness churned in his gut and Raziel yanked his shirt over his head and covered the girl's torso.

His hands began to shake as Raz took a good look at Coven's body.

Blue lips. Vacant eyes. Gray skin.

"Will she be alright?" he rasped, his throat raw from all the seawater he'd inhaled. In his heart, he knew she was not okay. Raz took her limp hand in his own, running soothing touches across the back of her palm.

Mer didn't answer him but continued the compressions.

"Come on," the Sirenidae growled, never stopping her ministrations.

He watched in silence, his heart sinking with each second.

Get yourself together.

Raziel swallowed the lump in his throat and switched off his grief. Someone had hurt the girl. Her clothes had been torn off. He stared at her bare leg, his mind finally noticing that something wasn't right. Leaning closer, he examined the striped pattern that ran up and down her legs. It wasn't a tattoo. Had she painted it herself?

He moved to the hand he was holding, looking at her nails. All were torn and broken. Like she'd been clawing to get away from her attacker.

I'm sorry.

"Raziel."

He lifted his head and met Mer's solemn gaze as she continued to work.

"What?"

"Look at this." She nodded to Coven. "Her ears."

Raziel lifted a strand of Coven's hair away from her face, where her ears should have been. She had little siphons like an octopus instead of ears. They were covered with the orange goop that still clung to the wound on his chest.

"What am I looking at?" he rasped.

"Later. I can hear people. Isla is bound to be with them."

Raziel gently laid Coven's hand on his shirt that dwarfed the girl. "I'm sorry," he whispered before standing.

Reef, the tallest Sirenidae, rounded the house first, followed by his sister Avalon.

Then came Isla. She caught sight of her daughter and released a guttural wail.

The older woman sprinted toward them, her hair tumbling from her bun. Raziel caught her up in a hug. Isla wailed again, bending over his arm, tears streaming down her face, straining toward her daughter.

"It can't be possible."

Reef and Avalon took over for Mer, murmuring in their lyrical language to each other as they checked over the girl. His wife sat back on her haunches, watching them with her lips pressed thin. The two Sirenidae siblings locked gazes and Avalon finally turned to Raziel and shook her head no.

Isla screamed and he released her. She scrambled to her daughter and fell to her knees, pulling Coven's head into her lap. She cried harder, rocking back and forth.

"No, no, no, no, no," Isla chanted, soul-wracking sobs shaking her frame.

Avalon moved to the older woman's side and sat beside her, combing her fingers through Isla's loose curls, a soft hum falling from her lips.

Mer slowly stood, swaying on her feet and stumbled back a step. Raziel broke from his stupor, tapping on Reef's shoulder. "Bring Isla's husband and a few men. We'll need to move her," he whispered.

The Sirenidae jerked his head up and down once, then climbed to his feet and ran toward the village.

Raz reached his wife and stood beside her. He lifted his arm and Mer pressed into his side. Raziel found himself wrapping his arm around her shoulders as she leaned into him.

"This isn't right," she said, her voice wooden.

"No. It isn't."

They waited.

Mer sang with Avalon.

Isla's grizzled husband arrived and the devastation on the older man's face just about brought Raziel to his knees. He held Isla and his daughter, crying until snot and tears mingled on his face.

More men arrived with Reef.

They all waited until Isla cried herself out. Her husband helped her to stand. Reef made to pick up Coven but her father held out his hand.

"No. I will carry my daughter home."

Raziel watched as the older man lifted Coven into his arms. Avalon adjusted the shirt laying on top of the girl to cover her.

One by one the people left.

Reef eyed Mer. "We need to speak."

Mer nodded. "Tomorrow."

The tall healer strode away, the darkness swallowing him up.

Raziel and Mer just stood there in silence.

Bioluminescent plants glowed softly around the cove, but it wasn't as charming as he'd found it before. Today it felt insidious.

She shivered and he forced his legs to move toward their cottage. She let him lead her into the house. Raz released her by the fire and moved back to the door, shifting the large chunk of driftwood in place.

"Did you see her eyes?" Mer whispered.

Vacant eyes.

Raziel shuddered and leaned his forehead onto their makeshift door. "I did."

"Did you know those markings around her eyes only happens when someone drowns?"

He pushed away from the door and moved to the fire, staring into the flames. "Are we not going to talk about her... *siphons*?"

Coven was Sirenidae.

"I've never seen anything like that in my life," Mer murmured.

He flinched, staring hard at his wife. "She is one of your people, is she not?"

Mer met his gaze, her magenta eyes burning. "No. I don't know what she is."

Chapter Thirty-Six

RAZIEL

HE WOULD BE A LIAR IF HE SAID THAT HE WASN'T attracted to his wife.

After the adrenaline wore off, he caught whiffs of the Lure teasing the air. Raziel backed away from his wife and sat at the small kitchen table, the rickety old grain groaning beneath his weight.

Raziel dropped his head into his hands and closed his eyes. He was so tired.

Soul weary.

The rustling of clothes captured his attention and he lifted his head, watching his wife pulling the wet, sandy dress from her body and tossing it in front of the hearth. She caught his eye but he didn't look away and neither did she. The moment stretched, filling with tension until it broke as she turned her back to him.

He mapped scars along her back as she walked around the bed, yanking her nightdress from a cord strung above the bathtub. Raziel stifled a groan. The nightdress had been given to her as a well-meant gift, but it was so thread-bare that it was nearly translucent.

While Mer had no problem walking around the house in all sorts of undress, there was something about the shabby little nightdress that made him want to ravish his wife.

You're a fool.

It was true. He could scarcely keep his eyes from her odd yet pleasing figure. She was so pale compared to his burnished skin. Her little scales glimmering softly in the light along with the gills that rested nearly invisible along the sides of her neck.

While he'd been out of his mind with the Lure the first time they met, part of him recognized what was going on. He remembered the silky soft texture of her gills between his fingers, and he had not imagined the way she had shuddered before she pushed his hand away.

Despite their best efforts, there was attraction blooming between them.

This was just supposed to be a political marriage.

Yet, each time a man looked at her with appreciation, he wanted to punch them in the face. It was ridiculous. Didn't that make him a selfish blighter?

Raziel forced himself to look away when she began oiling her skin.

If he wasn't careful, he'd end up kneeling at her feet, begging for her to let him have just one taste.

His body stirred and he shoved himself up from the chair, pacing to the fire. He leaned a hand on the mantle and prayed his body would behave.

This is not the time.

Scrubbing a hand over his face, he pulled himself together. Tonight had been traumatic. They were both vulnerable and when you mixed in the Lure, everything became more convoluted.

"Are you alright?" Mer asked.

His gaze flickered to her once more.

It didn't help that his wife pranced through the house in a scrap of a nightdress. Even now he could clearly see her breasts right through the dress. He cursed and snatched a blanket off the nearest chair and slung it over her shoulders.

"Here," he said gruffly. "You looked cold."

A grateful smile lifted her lips.

It struck him.

"Beautiful," he breathed.

Her smile froze and Raz cursed himself for being so stupid but he was transfixed by her lips. They were the color of the inside of the softest pink shell. He found himself leaning toward her before he jerked upright.

No.

Raziel backed away before flopping down into the old armchair with a heavy sigh.

This would not do. All he was feeling was loss and was desperately seeking comfort. Nothing more, nothing less.

Mer padded over to the bed and pulled back the covers. She stared at the mattress for a long time.

What was she doing?

"You can sleep in it," she said.

He flinched. "Excuse me?"

She slowly faced him, playing with the hem of her nightdress before finally meeting his eyes. "You can sleep in the bed. If you want."

He'd been making his bed in front of the fireplace and his back hurt something fierce.

His eyes narrowed. Was there a trap here?

"And where will you sleep?" he asked.

She arched a pale eyebrow at him and climbed into bed. "With you, of course."

He crossed his arms. Just what sort of mischief was this? They'd finally found an uneasy truce and now she was inviting him into her bed. His gaze turned to the door. She'd thrown him outside the last time he'd walked in on her bathing.

"Why the sudden change of heart?"

Mer shrugged, the nightdress slipping off her pale shoulder, revealing so much creamy skin that his mouth actually watered.

The bloody traitor.

Was that intentional or was she just naturally seductive? Either way it bothered him.

"You've been working as hard as I have," she said softly. "Today was rough for both of us. You deserve to have a good night's rest." She gave him a crooked smile that made his heart race. "Plus with all your tossing and turning on these creaky floorboards, you're keeping me awake."

All plausible, but did he trust it?

"Also, I'm freezing." She shivered and pulled the blankets higher.

"If you wore more clothes, you wouldn't be so cold."

Her smile turned impish. "They're itchy and I don't like the way they feel against my scales."

"Will your blade be sleeping with us as well?" he asked.

Mer bit her bottom lip and pulled the blade from beneath the pillow. She held it out on the flat of her palm. "You can keep it safe for the night."

If he had been standing, he would have staggered.

She was showing trust. Perhaps he could as well.

Raziel slowly stood and ate up the distance between them. He stared down at her and curled her fingers around the pommel of the shell dagger. "Keep it. I want you to feel safe."

Tears filled her eyes, and she held the dagger to her chest. Mer blinked them away and scooted back onto the left side of the bed. He walked around the bed to the bathtub and changed into a new pair of pants, keenly feeling his wife's gaze.

Did she find him as appealing as he found her? He wiped the sand from his feet, adjusted their makeshift door, and fed the fire one more time. His nerves racked up a notch as he approached the bed. Mer watched him.

"Are you sure?"

"Get in the bloody bed."

Raziel huffed and slid into the bed, facing Mer.

She squirmed until she got comfortable and then stared back.

"Are we going to talk about Coven?" he managed to ask, his grief rising.

"No. I can't tonight."

Some of the tension in his shoulders loosened. He didn't think he could either. "I don't know if I can sleep." He feared the nightmares that would surely come.

Mer nodded in understanding. Her hand crept out from beneath her pillow and she laid it between them.

An offering.

Raziel slowly took her small hand in his own and she squeezed his fingers. "You're not alone. Just match your breaths to mine and close your eyes."

Raz didn't want to look away from the stunning picture she made, but he did as he was told. Mer began to hum, a sound so soothing it seemed to fill all the cracks inside his soul.

And Raz discovered that holding the hand of the

woman you're falling for was the perfect cure for insomnia.

Right before he fell asleep, he heard her whisper. "You once asked me what my trident meant. It's a brand for those who betray the crown. Your tattoos mark you as a king, and mine as a traitor. What a pair we are." He barely registered a kiss on his cheek, his eyelids too heavy to open. "Never trust me."

Chapter Thirty-Seven

MER

Mer blinked hard, trying to get Coven's face out of her mind. She brushed the hair from her cheeks, trying not to wretch. Her body trembled when she noticed a large arm slung over her waist. Mer froze, her gaze flicking up to the man whose legs were currently tangled with hers.

Raziel, the Methian king.

Bile burned the back of her throat. And she slithered away from him, her breath sawing in and out of her lungs. She invited him into bed so they both could find some peace, not so she could curl into his arms like she belonged there. The only person she'd ever belonged to was Ream.

What are you doing?

Her panic rose and she found herself creeping from

the bed. The room felt too small, her skin too tight. She needed to get out now.

Mer slipped to the driftwood door and lifted the side. She paused in the doorway, looking back at Raziel. He muttered in his sleep and reached for her, stilling.

Several times through the night he'd cried out, waking her. Mer had hummed and soothed him back to sleep. It seemed she wasn't the only one with demons. The realization hurt her heart.

He was getting too close.

She fled the small home, feeling like she couldn't get enough air. Mer ran to the sea, the cold water rolling over her feet, causing the scales along her arms to rise. Her chest heaved as she gasped, tears streaming down her face. The full moon glimmered over the water, lighting up the cresting waves.

How could everything turn upside down so quickly?

Mer couldn't handle any feelings for the king. She hadn't even properly mourned Ream. Nor could she let her guard down when men like Keventin roamed about unchecked.

Coven's face flashed through her mind.

She hadn't missed the broken fingernails, the missing clothes, or the scratches on the girl's shoulder. Nor the fact that someone had drowned the girl.

A haunting tone teased the air and Mer's head snapped up. She scanned the waters, looking for the source of the sound. This was not in her imagination. The song seemed to vibrate through the water.

Her gut clenched. She had a feeling the culprits for Coven's death weren't far. And now they were taunting Mer.

She swiped the tears from her face and waded into the water, the icy feeling creeping up over her toes, then to her knees and chest.

"Mer!"

She turned as Raziel sped out the cottage, his silver eyes wide, powerful strides eating up the sand.

"Get out now."

She took another step toward the open sea. He really was beautiful. "I'll be back soon."

"Don't you—"

She plunged into the water, icy needles biting her body. The change took over, forcing the air out of her lungs and water through her gills. Her eyes burned as she pushed forward as fast as she possibly could, diving deeper and deeper, following the call. She yanked a sharp shell from the crevasse of a nearby rock and palmed it. It would do in a pinch.

Mer shut away her pain and fed the rage that seemed to always be brewing beneath the surface.

She reached the open ocean, just hovering over the sandy bottom, shafts of moonlight dancing far above. The song stopped.

"You've called me, and I've answered. Show yourself."

Nothing but silence echoed back.

Mer slowly spun in a circle, searching for any movement. She didn't know what kind of creature she was dealing with. One like Coven? Or something more insidious?

"You've been following me since I arrived in Methi. I felt your presence the very first time I experienced the cold waters of the North. I heard you sing for the kraken."

The silence seemed to be listening now.

She kept rotating, to keep her limbs moving. It was only a matter of time before she needed to return to the cottage. The water was too cold.

Mer drifted down until her toes touched the sand and she walked on the ocean floor.

"I heard you again in the bay. Let's not pretend you don't exist. What do you want?"

"What everyone wants," a voice whispered behind her.

She swiveled but there was nothing. So they wanted to play games. She worked her fingers as they slowly turned numb. Not a good sign.

"All I want is a good night of sleep."

A deep chuckle sounded from her right, but still, she could see nothing.

"Lies. You and I both know you crave blood."

Mer stiffened. While she was a fantastic fighter in the water, there was no telling what she was up against. Clearly the voice was dangerous. She pushed away from the disembodied voice to the south, but her limbs shook, not wanting to cooperate.

Time to go. This had been a stupid idea. She should have never left that cottage. When would she stop making such stupid decisions?

"Was your craving for blood sated when you took Coven?" she demanded on a hunch.

"Her heart was full of betrayal," the voice whispered directly in her left ear. "She earned her death."

Mer gasped, flinging her hand out with the shell. "She was just a child!"

A dark gray clawed hand wrapped around her wrist and squeezed until she felt her bones break. She screamed, dropping the shell. Tears filled her eyes and drifted away immediately, revealing the abomination before her.

A massive Sirenidae stood before her, but he was deformed. He was bulky like the king, with dark gray skin covered with pulsing ribbons of blue light. His waist melded into tentacles that writhed against the ocean floor. He held a black bone trident with wickedly sharp prongs.

His fingers were webbed, and she jerked as he reached for her face. Mer snapped her teeth at him as he caught her chin in his grasp. She punched him in the ribs, but he didn't even flinch.

She screamed as tentacles slithered up each of her legs and her uninjured arm, rendering her immobile. He tipped her chin up, forcing her to look into his face.

"Such fire," he murmured, black eyes pinned to hers.

His blue lights pulsed. "You're just what I have been waiting for, Mer Thalassan."

"I am at a disadvantage here. It seems you know me but I don't know you." Her words slurred slightly and the world began to waver the tiniest bit. He was going to kill her. She no longer struggled in his grasp, barely feeling anything.

Her heart beat in her ears, slowing.

He smiled, his teeth all pointed. "That's a shock since you've been looking for me." The monster leaned into her space and brushed his nose against her own. "Welcome to my domain, Mer. I am Ceto."

His words echoed in her ears.

Mer summoned one last burst of energy and tore herself from his grip. There was no way she was outrunning the creature, but she could put him in a watery grave.

She lunged for his trident, grabbing it with her uninjured hand.

A tentacle wrapped around her ankle and yanked, pulling the trident from her grasp as if she were a mere child. She spun, slashing at the appendage with her nails, drawing blood.

Silver blood. Sirenidae blood.

Ceto roared, releasing her.

Mer managed to stumble to her feet and flee, but each movement was sluggish.

She tipped her head back and pushed off the ocean

floor, determined to get to the surface, get to warmer water. The hair rose along the back of her neck.

Two tentacles wrapped around her feet and towed her backward.

She screamed and fought off another tentacle as it tried to steal her shell.

"It's futile. You are mine."

"I belong to no one."

"Wrong."

She found herself facing the huge male that somehow seemed to tower over her and surround her from all sides. Mer shook, her breath coming shorter and shorter.

"Let me go!"

"Don't you know? There is no escape." He grinned. "Try not to die."

He slammed his head into hers. The world went fuzzy and turned black. Before Mer lost consciousness, she heard him whisper, "The Warlord promised me a beautiful bride. Let's just hope you learn your place quickly."

To be continued with:
Empress of the Skies
Pre-order now!

Empress of the Skies

About the Author

Thank you for reading
TRAITOR OF THE TIDES.
I hope you enjoyed it!

Please leave a review on Amazon or Goodreads.

FROST KAY is a USA Today bestselling author and a certified book dragon with an excessive TBR.

She adores telling stories of strong women, diverse cultures, and epic fantasy worlds filled with relatable characters and true love. She lives in the United States and when not immersed in her newest book, you can find her free diving in her mermaid tail, rock climbing, camping, or soaking up the sun with her cat.

If you'd like to know more about Frost, her books, or to connect with Frost online, you can visit her webpage https://www.frostkay.net/ or join her facebook group FROST FIENDS!

Afterword

I can't believe I've made it here.

Not only has this been really hard so far, but I've been working on Traitor of the Tides for over seven years. I knew when I wrote Siren's Lure that Mer would become a main character in the future.

Over the years, I've jotted down and sketched scenes from Traitor of the Tides. Then when I reached the final two books in the Aermian Feuds and she kept showing up as this strong fierce woman, Traitor of the Tides really took shape.

Raziel on the other hand, was a bit harder to pin down. The kingdom of Methi was cloaked so much in shadow. I knew he had a good heart by how he treated Mira. Her choice not to marry him showed his good heart, but his experiences made him a little jaded.

He was so patient with Mer. Something she absolutely

did not deserve at times. I think that's what makes their connection so special. This definitely is a romantic fantasy – leaning hard on the fantasy. I knew with both of their pasts that a reconciliation would not come easily or swiftly.

I can't wait to share Empress of the Skies with you all! I've been waiting FOREVER to get these two on the same side and to become the power couple they can be.

The Aermian Feuds world have always dealt with darker themes that don't get talked about enough. Special thanks to my sensitivity readers, Beta readers, and ARC team. You really helped round out this story so that it became the best it could be.

To my dear author friends, you know who you are. Thank you for your insight and willingness to hear me grouch. You're precious.

To my editors... this book was ROUGH to finish. I can't tell you how much I appreciate the fact that you were willing to be flexible with your schedule when my life went sideways. I'm looking at you, Kate. You're irreplaceable.

To my lovely readers, some of you have been with me since the very beginning. You all created a cult following for the Aermian Feuds. I'm so excited to give you more in this world. And yes, there will be crossovers in the next book.

Xo,
Frost

The Heir

The Beast

The Hood

The Wolf

DRAGON ISLE WARS

(Epic Fantasy)

Court of Dragons

Queen of Legends

Throne of Serpents

ENTANGLED WITH TRICKERY

(Romantic Fantasy/ Monster Romance)

Frost Bound

Scorched Wings